SWORN TO SHADOWS

LISA BLACKWOOD

SWORN TO SHADOWS

Legacy of Shadows / Book 1

Lisa Blackwood

Sworn to Shadows

Legacy of Shadows Book 1

Paperback ISBN: 978-1-990608-57-5

Hardcover ISBN: 978-1-990608-56-8

Edition: 07/10/22

❀ Created with Vellum

BOOKS BY LISA BLACKWOOD

Gargoyle & Sorceress

Dawn of the Sorceress

Sorceress Awakening

Sorceress Rising

Sorceress Hunting

Sorceress at War

Sorceress Enraged

Legacy of the Sorceress

Sorcery & Firedrakes

Scion of the Sorceress

Sorceress Eternal

In Deception's Shadow Series (Epic Fantasy Romance)

Betrayal's Price

Herd Mistress

Maiden's Wolf

Death's Queen

The Prince's Gryphon (forthcoming)

Ishtar's Legacy Series (Epic Fantasy Romance)

Ishtar's Blade

The Blade's Beginning (short story)

Blade's Honor

Blade's Destiny

The Blade's Shadow

First Queen of the Gryphons

The King of the Anunnaki (forthcoming)

The Anunnaki's Blade (forthcoming)

Huntress vs Huntsman (Epic Fantasy Romance)

Master of the Hunt

Night Huntress

Dragon Archer

Soul Mage (forthcoming)

Gargoyles and gods clash against evil. Can one weary soldier wield a celestial force to save the world?

Earth, modern day. Corporal Anna Mackenzie has had it up to here with fate. Irritated to be woken early from a two-year healing nap after inheriting a demigod's immense power, she's already battling the fractious magic that can't wait to draw blood. But she's seriously pissed to discover the military outpost she was sent to protect has been totally annihilated without any signs of survivors...

Being temporarily outclassed is one thing, but now her reckless action has awakened her dangerous gargoyle protector and he's bigger and scarier than ever. Except he's lost his memory, and Anna's got to do some major hand-holding if they're to hunt down a powerful creature unseen since ancient times. Oh yeah, and save the planet from doom... again.

Can the damaged pair unleash their formidable skills in time to stop Armageddon?

Sworn to Shadows is the fearsome first tale in the Legacy of Shadows contemporary fantasy series, a spin-off of the bestselling Gargoyle & Sorceress Tales. If you like snarky fighters, unbreakable bonds, and epic battles of good vs evil, then you'll love Lisa Blackwood's breakneck adventure.

FREE BOOKS

GET TWO FREE STORIES FROM MY
BESTSELLING SERIES WHEN YOU SIGN UP
FOR MY NEWSLETTER.

I send regular monthly newsletters with details about
new releases,
special offers, freebies, and other bookish news.
If that's something you'd be interested in, just follow the
link below.

http://lisablackwood.com/join-the-newsletter-here/

SWORN TO SHADOWS

*M*ind groggy, her body sluggish, Anna didn't want to move. Yet some overly zealous instinct was urging her to wake, shouting that she needed to be somewhere else to complete an important task. Nothing about what she was currently feeling was normal or a good sign.

First, she was a light sleeper, her mind alert even before her body.

Second, her instincts were never wrong. And third...

Fuck third all to hell.

Third, if her never-fucking-wrong instincts were urging her to face some danger. It could only mean Fate had some new plan for her.

With a groan, she rolled to a defensive position even as she blinked open strangely blurry eyes. Her hands groped the ground as she searched for something to use as a weapon. All her fingers could find was a cold, hard surface. Polished stone, if she were to guess.

At last, her blurry vision cleared.

A snarling visage full of sharp teeth filled her view. Jerking back, her field of vision expanded to take in the sight of a large grey muzzle, lips pulled back in a snarl, exposing teeth a shark would envy. Yelping in surprise, she fell back on her ass. Then she scrambled back farther, adrenalin and survival instincts ruling her.

Two seconds later, her brain caught up with the adrenaline-fueled instincts currently running the show, and it registered upon her how foolish she would have looked if anyone had been watching.

"The fuck, Obsidian? You scared a year off my life, you big dork!" She growled at the stone gargoyle, then added in a softer voice, "But glad you're here."

She glanced around to be sure they were alone, that no other dangers lurked nearby. A quick scan revealed a windowless room, devoid of danger, with what looked like impenetrable stone walls, ceiling, and floor. The only light came from three mage globes. She huffed out a tense breath when no apparent threats presented themselves. All was quiet here. Wherever 'here' was. Though judging by the three glowing mage lights floating in the air, she was likely still somewhere in the Magic Realm. Her gaze returned to her gargoyle partner.

Calming more, she gave him a shaky laugh. "Glad you weren't awake to witness that graceless sprawl."

Gathering her dignity around her, she stood and then went to him, resting a hand on the hard, cold stone of his right shoulder. "Hey, you can wake up anytime now."

Strangely, she felt nothing at the touch of skin to stone, their mental link a silent void. Her breath froze in her lungs. Fighting back a growing unease, she leaned forward and placed her other hand on his opposite shoulder. "Come on, big fellow. Fate is telling me our naptime is over. That *Bitch* has plans for us. Time to wake up."

Once again, she willed her mind to touch his.

And felt nothing.

No stir of magic. No brush of his sleeping mind against hers. No sense of a mind dreaming away the time while he healed.

She felt no more than she would have if she'd touched a lifeless boulder.

Frowning, she tried a second time with the same result. Only one other time, in all the years since he'd first forged their mental link by converting her into a gargoyle, had he vanished so thoroughly beyond the ability of their soul link to find him. That time he'd still been a child; she'd been undergoing the slow metamorphosis into a gargoyle, their mental link in its infancy, and he'd been captured by the enemy and transported from Earth to the Magic Realm.

She pushed away the rising panic and assessed the situation. Maybe this was normal? Obsidian had never been in such a deep, healing stone sleep in her presence before. Hell, after they'd been reunited, she'd only had a short time to complete her training and get to know the adult version of the gargoyle she'd thought of as a little brother. Despite all the knowledge she'd gained these last few months, she still knew too little about magic.

Walking around him, trailing her fingers along every line and curve, she checked for any signs of injury on his big, bulky body. Even crouched as he was, his hulking form dwarfed hers. His spiraling horns swept back from the ridge of bone high on his forehead, no damage marring them. And while his large, deer-like ears were pinned against his stone mane in a way that hinted at pain, that was expected considering the battle damage they'd sustained.

She eyed his massive wings next. They were mantled around him, but she saw no imperfections there either. Circling behind him, she patted his tail where he'd wrapped it around his legs.

So concerned for her partner after the last battle, Anna couldn't even remember how he'd positioned his body as he'd turned to stone. Was it different now than it had been then? Had he awakened at some point like she was now and then surrendered to the stone sleep again to finish healing? Her memories of the battle, and its immediate aftermath, were as blurry as her vision had been upon first waking. All she remembered was that they'd won, barely.

Which also raised the question about why she was presently in her human body when she'd been a gargoyle when the stone sleep had claimed her. A gargoyle, or in her case, a gargoyle hybrid, couldn't just shift forms while in stone.

Something didn't add up.

But her questions would wait. She needed to reassure herself that her gargoyle teammate was still on the road to recovery. She checked over every inch of his massive form. Not finding any external damage, she pressed a hand upon his brow and closed her eyes, again seeking the mental link that bound them in the hope she'd be able to ascertain if he'd suffered any internal injuries from the stresses upon his body, mind, or soul from becoming the vessel for Lord Death's power.

This try yielded no better results than her first attempt to touch his thoughts, but she breathed out a ragged breath in relief when she finally sensed the spark of life deep within the stone. He lived. Another breathy sob hissed between her lips in relief. Her partner might not be near waking, but he was alive, and she had every confidence that he would one day return to her.

"Yeah, you better hurry and heal. I'm going to miss you, you big goof."

Now that she'd reassured herself that nothing was wrong with her gargoyle partner, she turned her attention back to her surroundings. The dimly lit stone-walled room she found herself in wasn't even remotely familiar, which, going by the last thing she remembered, wasn't a surprise.

She and her big Rasoren had turned to stone on the battlefield; her wings spread to shelter her gargoyle partner after they had helped the Avatars defeat the Lady of Battles.

Yeah. So, finding herself in a dimly lit room wasn't unreasonable. It wasn't like her allies would just leave her and Obsidian sitting on the battlefield like glorified garden ornaments. It made sense that she and Obsidian would be moved to a protected, secure location.

So, dimly lit stone room. Check.

That made sense.

Glancing down at herself, she noted something else that made her uneasy.

She was human and didn't remember shapeshifting back, but she'd just assumed she'd shifted back after becoming flesh and blood again before waking. But now that she wasn't fretting over Obsidian's wellbeing, she realized she was attired differently than she'd been on the battlefield. Gone was her armor. In its place was a long, pale blue tunic top and matching drawstring pants. The last time she'd worn something similar, she'd been under the care of the Gargoyle Legion healers, in their version of a medical wing.

That she couldn't remember how she'd gotten from her gargoyle form to her human form, and now was wearing clothing typically provided by menders, sat uneasily with her.

Then another realization hit.

Something else was absent.

"Oh fuck. No. No. No, fuck no." But when she reached for her shadow magic, nothing answered her mental call. Going deeper, she realized she couldn't sense her gargoyle nature at all. Usually, it was waiting just below the surface of her skin, like a predator eager to hunt. But now, she felt nothing like that.

But there was something else that answered her call—that foreign restlessness that had first dragged her out of sleep. She could feel it rising within her again.

She knew what it was now that the cobwebs of sleep had released her mind. It could only be one thing.

The Battle Goddess's power.

And Anna was damned sure it was that power that had roused her from her stone sleep. But was the reason because it had sensed danger, or was it trying to control her? She hoped it was the first. Better to fight an external enemy than an internal one, she reasoned.

"Why'd I agree to become the new vessel for a demigoddess's power?" she muttered as she glanced around, her gaze landing on Obsidian. "Yeah, yeah. I know. It was the right thing to do."

Her gaze shifted away from her gargoyle partner to search the room again. The only thing to greet her eyes were six equally spaced alcoves. Each one was dark. An empty room would not offer any answers. She'd just have to go hunting them herself.

Moving to the closest alcove, a quick search confirmed it was empty, and the deep shadows were not concealing either a source of danger or escape.

"Or answers," she mumbled.

Systematically searching each alcove and finding nothing in the next three, her blood pressure and concern crept higher. She needed to get out of this damned room and find out what had been happening while she and her Rasoren had been trapped in the stone sleep.

As she moved toward the next alcove, a breeze brushed against her legs. She followed the air current to its source, coming to the last alcove. Go figure. It would be the last freaking one she'd searched.

This time, when she stepped into the alcove, she found a tunnel. She walked into the darkness, cursing that she wasn't presently a gargoyle. Night vision would surely have come in handy about now.

Thankfully, she only had to walk less than twenty feet, and she could see the outline of the end of the tunnel where it dead-ended in another dimly lit corridor. Upon reaching her new destination, she discovered it wasn't a tunnel, but another sizeable circular chamber with a vaulted ceiling. Eight corridors converged, giving Anna the opportunity to make seven wrong choices before finding the way that led out of this catacomb.

"Fuck," she muttered and picked the one to her immediate right. Had she been in gargoyle form, her heightened senses would have led her to the nearest exit or even the nearest living soul. But her human senses were dull in comparison, and she was left to guess blindly. There wasn't even dust or cobwebs to help her rule out the least used tunnels.

"Overachieving gargoyles," Anna muttered to the dimly lit corridor she'd picked, "excelling at all things, even mundane household chores."

Her long-legged strides swiftly carried her to the end of the tunnel. Shoving open a door with well-oiled hinges, she discovered a storage room full of baskets of fruits and tubers. With a curse, she marched back to where she'd started.

The second and third tunnels were much shorter, but both ended in more storage chambers filled with a harvest. Everything looked fresh, but she knew gargoyles had a broad array of magic at their command and used preservation spells on food to store it long-term. So, nothing in any of the chambers hinted at how long she'd been asleep.

The fourth and fifth tunnels were equally short, ending in chambers full of weapons.

She hit the jackpot at the end of tunnel six, finding her and Obsidian's armor and weapons displayed on racks. Next to the racks were shelves full of his belongings and the few things she'd accumulated during the short time she'd lived with him in the city of Haven. It was the contents of his life he'd lived there. Anna had been aware everything from that city had been evacuated before the final battle against the Lady of Battles, but she hadn't had time to concern herself with what became of their belongings.

Now she was glad to stumble upon it.

Proper clothing and weapons always made a girl feel better about her situation.

Swiftly rooting through the supplies, she whooped with delight to find a military rucksack full of all her gear. Tucked on top was a letter. Unfolding it and glancing at its contents, she immediately recognized Major Resnick's handwriting.

Glad you're awake to read this. Thought you'd like a clean uniform. Get your ass back here as soon as possible. That's an order.

The note was as concise as she would expect from her CO and made her grin.

"Yes, sir!" she barked out to the empty room and laughed.

A quick search inside the pack revealed more than just clothing. She tried the radio, but it was dead, likely fried by staying too long in the Magic Realm. Magic was not kind to technology, guns, or anything explosive, which was likely why she didn't find any earth weapons. The radio was probably just overlooked. She also found rations. Not feeling hungry, she tucked them back into the pack.

She saw no point in wasting further time, so she traded her tunic and drawstring pants for the neatly folded uniform and familiar boots. She gave her booted feet a stomp, finding the boots strangely confining after traipsing around as a barefoot gargoyle for so long. But she'd adjust. She always did.

Briefly, she eyed her swords and assorted daggers with longing, but she was returning to the human world as Corporal Anna Mackenzie, not Kyrsu Anna Mackenzie of the Gargoyle Legions. With that in mind, she left behind most of the legion weapons, taking only a small knife and matching sheath that would fit in her boot. Then she continued her hunt for an exit or another living being.

The seventh tunnel was much longer than the others, and she felt hope flare within her as the light grew brighter. Soon, the tunnel ended in another chamber. She hung back in the shadows at the tunnel's threshold, scanning the room beyond, but two things became immediately apparent.

First, it was occupied.

And second, the two gargoyles standing guard beside a dormant portal spell spotted her and came forward three steps before dipping into swift bows.

"Kyrsu," they mumbled in unison before straightening and returning to their original positions on either side of the portal, standing ramrod straight, their wings nearly rippling with their tension.

"At ease," she said, without even thinking about it. They both seemed nervous to see her.

Hmmm. She didn't recognize them, but she thought they may have been younglings. They were of a slimmer build than the average gargoyle, though they had the height. That suggested they may have recently emerged from their mothers' hamadryad trees. There had been much chaos in the days leading up to the final battle. And while she was second in command of the gargoyle legions, she certainly hadn't met them all, not with the newly awakening sleepers joining the force.

"Hello," she began, giving them both kind smiles. "You seem to have a disadvantage over me. I'm afraid I don't know your names. Are you recently emerged?"

"Yes, Kyrsu!" They echoed each other, dropping into bows once more.

Well, that would be more than beneficial.

"Your names?" She asked them gently.

Like all gargoyles, they were similar in appearance, but she'd been a gargoyle long enough she could now quickly recognize the subtle differences among her winged brethren. The older of the two, judging by his marginally broader shoulders, sharper horn tips, and slightly darker skin tone, took another step closer and said, "I am Novice Hunts in Moonlight." He paused. "My friends just call me Moon. We beat all our peers in this year's trials and won the honor of guarding the outbound portal for the day."

So, they weren't the regulars, which made sense since unless a lot had changed, the Legion didn't put their youngest members on guard duty. And he'd mentioned it was an outbound portal. If someone or something wanted to travel through this portal, they'd have to infiltrate all the layers of this compound. No enemy was stupid enough to attack a gargoyle stronghold. From a defensive standpoint, the portal was safe, simply because of its location. Hence the young ones weren't really being given a dangerous task. Just one that would make them feel honored.

And that makes my unannounced return to Earth much less complicated, Anna mused.

"It's nice to meet you, Moon. And your friend?" She turned her gaze to the other gargoyle where he was hanging back a step.

At her attention, the other gargoyle bowed again but kept his head ducked when he straightened. She'd never met a bashful gargoyle before, but she was pretty sure she'd just met her first. After a few seconds stretched into a long awkward pause, he murmured a soft, "In the human tongue, its rough translation is Shattered Ice Upon a Winter Lake. My friends call me Novice Winter."

And it was at that moment that Anna realized she'd lost more than her magic. She'd lost the language of the gargoyles. She'd been speaking English, and they'd answered in kind.

What else had she lost and didn't yet know about?

But that didn't change the fact that she was still military and duty-bound to report to her commanding officer as soon as possible. Hoping she wasn't projecting her thoughts, she gave them both reassuring grins and willed confidence into her bearing, expression, and voice.

"I require you to open the portal to Earth." She wasn't at all sure that this portal went to her home world, but it was a reasonable guess, since they were already in the Magic Realm. The only reason for a permanent portal was if the destination was very far away and challenging to get to—some place like Earth in the Mortal Realm.

"Of course, Kyrsu," Moon said with a respectful nod to her. "It will be as you wish." He paused then, exchanging a glance with Winter. "You have been brought up to date by the elders?"

Damn. He was suspicious, and gargoyles could all sense a lie.

"Major Resnick left a letter outlining a couple of things," she said and then added silently in her head. *'A letter that told me absolutely nothing, but that doesn't change the fact I need to get my butt back to base.'*

"Ah," Moon said with another nod and a glance at Winter. "The elders—"

Anna cut him off before he could finish that line of thought and then, feeling more than a little guilty for what she was about to do, straightened and gave both gargoyles a sterner look. "Are you questioning your Kyrsu?"

"No, Kyrsu!" They echoed each other and dropped into synchronized bows once more.

Anna grinned and mouthed the words 'sorry' over their bowed heads. "Good. Because the sooner I leave, the sooner I can return and rejoin my Rasoren."

Which was the absolute truth.

CHAPTER TWO

The edges of the portal that would take Anna home calmed, settling into a more serene shimmer as the turbulent silvery-blue power required to breach the Veil Between the Realms at last mellowed. The outer edges of the magic faded and left behind a window to another world. Only that same faint shimmering hinted that she was standing in front of a magic portal, not a regular window.

Looking through the threshold, she gazed upon a scene of a heavily forested landscape shrouded in the shadows of night. The forest could have been anywhere, but the land had the familiar look of home, even in the darkness.

And she trusted Moon and Winter to know what planet the portal had opened onto.

Still feeling mildly guilty for cowing the two youths

into obeying, she promised she'd send back a message to their mentors not to punish them. After all, they were obeying a superior officer. Clearly, no one had left instructions to detain her.

"By the way, I didn't think to ask earlier, but where on Earth does this portal arrive?"

"Just outside the human military base, Kyrsu," Moon answered. "The Avatar said the inbound and outbound portals can't exist in the same spot. This one will deposit you just a quick run from the primary base."

"But there is an outpost there," Winter injected into the conversation for the first time, "The human soldiers there will arrange transport for you." He glanced up and back down at her human form, no doubt realizing it would be more than a 'quick run' in her current form.

"Thank you, Winter." Then she nodded at the other gargoyle. "And Moon."

A gargoyle's strict code of honor did not allow them to lie or practice deceit. If they said the portal opened just outside a base back in the Mortal Realm, she could trust that's exactly where the portal would take her. She was lucky they weren't questioning her more. But then again, it wasn't like they would openly question their Kyrsu.

There *were* a few benefits to having inherited the role of second in command of the Gargoyle Legions. And since their Rasoren was still deep in the healing stone sleep, Anna was technically the highest-ranking gargoyle.

But that wouldn't stop one of the elders, or worse, a council member, from questioning her. And if one of the councilors caught wind of her awakening before she escaped through the portal...

She could already hear their lectures about the foolishness of running from her Rasoren and her responsibilities. They'd have her feeling like a petulant child in no time. It had happened before.

And since her guilt was already kicking in, it wouldn't take much persuasion to keep her here.

Yeah. No. Better to slip away unnoticed.

And that was why she needed to leave now. She'd already spent too much time dicking around wrestling with her conscience, worrying about leaving Obsidian while the two young gargoyles had begun the process of awakening the portal.

Still eyeing the portal, she adjusted the clean new uniform once more. It still felt slightly unfamiliar to wear one after all this time.

Swallowing hard, she did her best to ignore the aching hollowness where the Rasoren-Kyrsu bond once resided. She swallowed hard a second time while pretending that the tightness in her throat was because of the dryness of the air.

On the other side of the portal was a normal life. Or as close to normal as Anna was likely ever to have again.

She needed normal.

It had been too long since she'd seen her family. She needed to know what was happening back on Earth, to leave all things magic behind for a time. Unfortunately, that also meant leaving *him* behind.

Anna's mind shied away from the hurt that thought induced.

It was probably a blessing that Obsidian wasn't awake. As the Rasoren of the Legion, he could order her to stay until they were both recovered fully. And that right there was a battle she never wanted to fight. Leaving Obsidian was hard enough, and he was still sleeping.

"He won't even know I'm gone," she silently reassured herself. *"And I absolutely plan on returning long before he wakes."*

But if he'd been awake, that would be a different matter altogether.

To go against his wishes?

Their purposes had gone hand in hand since he'd been a cub. Hell, she couldn't remember when they weren't unified in their goals. Well, that wasn't entirely accurate, Anna mused, a smile curving her lips briefly. Their first meeting had been a little rocky. That time she'd woken healed after she'd thought she was dying to discover an eight-year-old gargoyle had saved her, and he felt a human would make a good pet. Once she'd gotten over her shock about learning magic was real, and other intelligent creatures walked the Earth hidden from the humans, she'd seen how lonely the young gargoyle was and had forgiven him for trying to keep her as a pet.

They'd become friends, and he'd naturally filled the role of the 'little brother' she'd always wanted.

The memory faded, and reality returned in all its harshness.

The gargoyle cub was nothing more than a memory now, and while she'd come to care for and respect the adult he'd grown into while she'd slumbered, unaware in the healing stone sleep for thirteen years, this new situation was rather too much like losing the cub all over again. Her gargoyle partner might sleep for years yet. She hadn't had the balls to ask Moon and Winter if they knew how long Obsidian might sleep, too afraid she'd break down into a blubbering mess in front of them if they said it would be years.

And having their Kyrsu sob in front of them was likely to result in them summoning one of their mentors.

So, yeah. No crying. She also reminded herself that as much as it hurt to know she would be leaving her friend for an unknown length of time, there was nothing here she could do for him.

Obsidian was beyond all outside aid. Only time, his inherent stubborn gargoyle nature, and his steel will would see him restored to lead the gargoyle legion once more.

In the meantime, it was time to see to other duties.

She drew herself up to her full height and tugged at her uniform once more, shouldered her pack, and then with a determined set to her jaw, she stepped toward the portal.

"Anna Mackenzie!" A voice boomed from a muzzle two inches from her ear, equal parts humor and threat lacing the words. "You were *NOT* about to leave without so much as a goodbye, now, were you?"

Anna nearly swallowed her tongue. She sputtered and gasped, but only an undignified squeak escaped her lips.

Fuck. She hadn't even heard the gargoyle approach.

Fisting her fingers and forcing her body back under her control, she kept any other reactions from showing that she'd nearly freaking jumped out of her skin.

Her mind churned, instinctively hunting for suitable curses. But she swallowed them back at the last moment. She recognized that voice. This gargoyle wasn't one she needed to annoy.

Bloody fucking infuriating gargoyles. It wasn't fair that anything that big could also be stealthy.

Attempting to restore dignity, she took a moment to smooth a hand down her slightly wrinkled uniform before slowly turning to face the hulking eight-foot-tall reason her stomach was up in her throat and her heart was slamming against her ribs.

"Thanks," she grumbled as she tilted her head back and then back some more to study the hulking form of one of the largest of the gargoyles. Master Banrook, or Rook to his friends, was stockier than the average gargoyle. Only Obsidian had more muscle. But the Lady of Battles had augmented her Rasoren when he'd still been developing in his mother's hamadryad tree, so the comparison wasn't valid. Obsidian was in a class of his own. But Rook had to be the second scariest gargoyle in existence until you got to know him. "I think I'm now deaf in that ear."

One of his long, deer-like ears flicked in humor before tucking tight against his mane again.

"It's true," she grumbled. "Everything is still ringing."

Master Banrook snorted in that classic version of a gargoyle's eye roll and tossed his head back. The light glinted off the silver metal tipping both horns, the movement causing the two tiny blue crystals dangling from them to clink against the bone. While she mulled over what to tell him to explain why she was leaving, her gaze dropped to his throat, where a hammered silver collar with matching blue crystals circled his throat. Gaze dropping farther, she noted that even his long beaded-loincloth and wrist, arm, and ankle bracelets all had embedded delicate blue crystals.

"Stylin' there, Rook." She grinned suddenly. "You trying to impress someone with all that bling?"

"What?" he asked, his expression one of honest confusion, and then he snorted and rolled his eyes in understanding. "No, you uppity youngling."

She'd had her fair share of disdainful snorts bestowed upon her during her time among the gargoyles. Her mentors had all had fun at her expense more than once. Master Banrook had taken particular pleasure in drilling and teasing her and Obsidian during the months of their training. Only Adept Thayn outperformed Rook in that regard.

Perhaps she was lucky it was Rook and not Thayn she was facing now. The oldest of the gargoyles outshone all others when it came to being a pain in the ass. Fate must have taken a day off or was giving her a break.

If Thayn were standing before her now, she probably wouldn't be returning to Earth soon. Or alone. He'd want her to stand with her new gargoyle family.

But she no longer belonged to this world of magic. She could feel it in her bones. Or feel the lack. Her gargoyle magic, so newly mastered, was dormant or burned away. She wasn't even sure if she was still a gargoyle. Could the Battle Goddess's magic have destroyed her gargoyle nature?

Master Banrook may have been able to answer that question for her, but she wasn't sure if she could handle his answer.

Either way, she was just regular old Corporal Anna Mackenzie once again and belonged back on Earth.

"I did not know our young Kyrsu was a coward," Rook grumbled, perhaps picking up on her emotions and not understanding the reason. "I never pegged you as someone who would run away from something you feared."

She turned to face him and bared her teeth. "I'm not running away. Nor am I afraid of anything. I'm fulfilling an obligation. I'm duty bound to return to my superiors."

"And what about your duty to your Rasoren?"

The wave of grief she'd been battling welled up inside her at hearing Obsidian's title spoken aloud, as if it held more power over her that way. She whirled back around to face the portal. "Our Rasoren is still a stone statue, as well you know. There is nothing I can do to speed up his healing. I can't even touch my magic." Her lips twisted into a bitter grimace. "I think our bond is severed."

A large hand with talon-tipped fingers landed heavily on her shoulder. "Young one, have faith. Do not grieve your Rasoren or your sacred bond. Both he and your link will return to you one day."

Anna nodded and swallowed hard.

"He's a fighter." Rook squeezed her shoulder.

"He is." And so much more. In all the Universe, she wasn't sure if there was a scarier fucker on the battlefield and a bigger dork off of it.

"He's too stubborn for there to be any other outcome," Rook said, again trying to comfort her with his words.

Anna swallowed hard, emotions rising within her,

wanting to pour out and share the hollow grief that threatened to eat her up. "I will miss him."

Rook snorted out a gruff laugh. "Of course you will miss him. He's your other half. But he survived you sleeping in stone for thirteen years while you healed. And he was a child. You're an adult. You'll survive a few months on your own while he heals."

"Fuck, man. Your bedside manner needs work." But she laughed, feeling hope again because Rook had revealed with his words that Obsidian would only sleep for a few more months.

"Bedside manner?" He asked, his muzzle pulling up at one corner and his opposite ear drooping in confusion. "Human phrases are strange, but usually I can hash them out. But what does a bedside have to do with anything?"

"Never mind." Anna grinned and thumped him on the shoulder, walking by him on her way to the portal. "We'll chalk it up to something lost in translation."

"You're still going to run away and leave your Rasoren behind?" he asked, a hint of challenge in his voice.

Anna snorted. "Trying to guilt me into staying will not work. I have an obligation to my people back home —a duty to them. Honor demands I return, if only for a short while. Obsidian would understand."

"That he would." A rumbling huff issued from the big gargoyle's muzzle. "And yes, I was trying to guilt you into staying. It's hard for mentors to step back and watch the younglings venture forth on their own."

Anna glanced over her shoulder and made a face. "I'm not that young."

He tossed back his head and roared with laughter, great belly-shaking chuckles. "Whatever you say, Cub."

She flipped him the bird, and he only laughed harder. Of course, he knew what that was. Turning her gaze back forward again, she marched for the portal spell.

"Wait," he got out between chuckles. "At least let me divulge a few bits of information first."

Anna halted and then glanced over her shoulder again. "You should have led with that. I thought you were just being stubborn, and I wasn't about to feed your penchant for mischief, not after calling me a kid."

"You've been asleep for over two of your Earth years."

Two years. It could have been worse. Anna arched a brow, urging him to continue.

"The healers say you won't be able to shift forms for several months yet. Your body is still adjusting to the Battle Goddess's power. Once it has healed and adjusted to the strain, your gargoyle nature will reassert itself."

"Thank God," Anna muttered. "It'd be difficult to carry out my duties as the Kyrsu of the Gargoyle Legion if I wasn't actually a gargoyle anymore."

"Fear not. Obsidian's gift to you is very permanent." Rook's expression turned serious once more. "And speaking of permanent things. You will be the vessel of the Battle Goddess's power for a long time, even as a gargoyle judges time. And while the Avatars have said you are a strong and worthy soul to house that power, they also mentioned in passing that you cannot wield that power without risk for many years. They will be the ones to train you and Obsidian in using your new gifts."

"Gifts, my ass," Anna muttered, too low for even a gargoyle's ears to pick out the words.

"What was that, Cub?" He smacked her hip with his tail.

"Sorry. Nothing. Just muttering to myself." Anna wasn't surprised by his words about getting trained by the Avatars. A person couldn't ask for better mentors than the Divine Ones' right hand. "Anyway, in the meantime, I'll be careful not to call on that power."

"A good idea," he agreed dryly. "I hardly think the homeworld of the humans needs more war."

Anna snapped her mouth closed when she realized she'd left it hanging open when words failed her.

'Yeah, Anna,' she muttered in her head. *'No starting World War 3 when you're PMS-ing.'*

Out loud, she asked, "Any other hazards I should know about?"

Rook just shook his head. "Nothing that will concern you. While you may be up and around, you will not participate in any missions until you and Obsidian are fully healed and well into your apprenticeship with the Avatars."

Anna nodded again, agreeing with him for another reason. She'd likely be buried under reports for years. And when not reading or completing reports, she was pretty sure the scientists would have their way with her.

Unaware of Anna's thoughts, Rook continued, "Once you cross the portal, I'll send word to Adept Thayn that you have awakened. He's busy off somewhere in the human lands discussing," Rook waved his hand dismissively, "whatever he spends hours and hours and hours discussing with the leaders of the human world. Better him than me." He shuddered, even his wings quivering delicately with his evident disgust. "As for the soldiers on the other side, they will notify your human commanding officer of your return." A dark chuckle escaped him. "If your human *superiors*," he dragged the word out a touch disdainfully, "give you trouble, remind them you are still Kyrsu to both Gargoyle Legions. And family to the Avatars."

"I don't know about the family part...."

"You are family to Obsidian, and his biological sister houses the soul of the female half of the Avatar pair. I don't know what humans consider a family unit, but I, for one—"

"You're correct, of course," she said, cutting him off before he could launch into a long lecture about family dynamics among the legion and the other fae races. She was sure he was just trying to stall her until the council members could arrive. "I should probably go. Duty calls."

"Fine. We'll continue our reunion at a later date. If you need anything, three gargoyles are stationed at the human base. They will be more than willing to aid their Kyrsu should she require their assistance." Her gargoyle mentor gave her a shove toward the portal with a rumbling huff. "Until we meet again, Anna Mackenzie."

After recovering her balance, she laughed and flipped him the bird without slowing. When she was a few feet from the portal that would carry her back to Earth, she whispered, "Goodbye, Obsidian, but I promise I'll return just as soon as I can."

It was silly. He was sleeping and couldn't hear her even if she still had the magic to touch his thoughts, but she'd needed to whisper that promise to her dear friend for her own peace of mind. And it was a promise she fully intended to keep.

But then she was crossing the portal, its energy snapping around her, and she had other things to focus on.

CHAPTER THREE

With a stomach-dropping sensation—like vertigo on steroids—she stepped through the portal, and the powerful spell carried her from one realm to the next. The feeling was familiar, but still as unpleasant as always. She'd probably never get used to it.

Actually, she never wanted to get used to it.

Familiarity would mean way too many stomach and brain-twisting trips between the realms. And Fate already had too much fun at Anna's expense.

But one blessing was that it was over quickly, and between one step and the next, she'd left the Magic Realm behind for the mortal one. At least she better be currently standing on Earth. From her vantage point, it was hard to tell. She gazed around in mild alarm, hoping her eyes would adjust to the darkness.

"It's as black as the inside of an elephant's ass. What the hell, Rook?"

She wouldn't put it past him to play a trick on her. He hadn't been happy she was leaving the Legion, but he hadn't seemed that butt hurt either. She didn't think the lack of lights was his doing.

Slowly, her eyes grew adjusted to the darkness. She stood in a clearing surrounded by a forest. Several low, squat buildings dotted the area. No lights shone from within them. The only light source came from the soft illumination of distant stars in the moonless sky.

If she'd still been able to call upon her gargoyle nature, she'd easily be able to pierce the darkness and gather more details about the location. Her eyes narrowed, straining to see even as her other senses sharpened, attempting to compensate for her sight's lack.

Even if the lack of lights wasn't enough to tell her something was amiss, the absolute silence was. No human or animal sounds reached her ears. Something was very much not right.

Rook had said there should be a unit of guards stationed here.

Eventually, her eyes picked out more details. She crouched down and noticed she was standing in the middle of what looked like a helipad, but this wasn't designed for any mundane vehicle.

Her eyes picked out the softly glowing symbols, their

silvery color continuing to fade away to almost nothing as she watched, but when she brushed a boot toe across one symbol, she could feel where the spell had slowly eaten its way into the tarmac over many uses. She could only conclude that the portal hadn't misfired and sent her to a secondary emergency site. She was exactly where she was supposed to be. But where the hell was everyone else? It wasn't like a portal spell was subtle and easy to miss.

"Why couldn't it have been a misfire?" she muttered. "And why didn't I bring a bloody sword with me?"

Not that a sword would be helpful against a rifle or sidearm. Even so, it was better than being weaponless.

Worse, the absence of light and the lack of any sound that would suggest a living presence were enough to tell her something untoward had happened here recently.

To her immediate right were several military vehicles sitting idle. She made her way toward them. They were better cover than nothing.

Just because the darkness hampered her vision didn't mean there wasn't something out there capable of seeing through the gloom.

The roadway angled off to the left. She could just make out another smaller building—likely a gatehouse or checkpoint before entering the small compound. Crouching next to the nearest vehicle, a newer model pickup truck, she glanced around again, and seeing no movement, she tried the door handle. Unlocked. Casting a second furtive glance around for danger, she cracked the door open a hair. None of the interior lights came on. Easing the door open enough to squeeze in, she felt around for the keys and found them but didn't attempt to start the truck. Its battery was probably dead. She reached deeper into the darkness and snatched up the radio.

It, too, was dead. No surprise there. Powerful magic tended to destroy technology, and she was now sure that whatever had happened here involved powerful spells.

Slipping out of the disabled truck, she stalked forward, low to the ground, using the vehicles as shelter. Before approaching the other buildings, she made her way to the gate first, wanting a better idea of what she had walked into. If things went south in a hurry, she could bolt for the forest and lose any pursuers among the undergrowth.

Crouching down beside the last vehicle in line, she studied her surroundings, but there was still no sign of movement.

The hell with it.

She lunged up and darted toward the small building beside the gate, noting as she ran that the gate was open, which was handy if she needed to beat a hasty retreat. Crouching down outside the booth, she waited and listened.

Nothing.

Moving low to the ground, she went for the door and pushed it open just enough to peer inside.

Bodies.

Two.

A blond man and a dark-haired woman.

For some reason, they'd been stripped of their clothing. She didn't dwell too long on that but noticed their clothing and weapons were nowhere in evidence. Frowning, Anna's mind jumped to the possibility that whoever had killed these two had done so silently and then assumed their identities to infiltrate the compound.

The how was a mystery for later.

She scanned the dark interior but didn't see so much as a glint of casings, which reinforced her theory that these two victims were the first to fall with none of the soldiers on duty being the wiser. Another quick examination of the bodies found no apparent wounds to suggest a cause of death. It hadn't been the work of a sniper. She examined the man's neck and was surprised to find it hadn't been broken. The bodies lacked any kind of wound that she could find. If there were bruising, she couldn't see it in the darkness.

Anna was dead certain she wouldn't find bruising even in the full light of day. Instincts whispered that magic was involved in their untimely demise.

"Balls," she hissed low. "Why does it have to be magic?"

She had learned something else. The bodies were still warm, maybe dead a half an hour.

With renewed caution, she eased back out of the building and made her way to the next nearest structure. She needed to check for survivors and hunt for clues as to what the hostiles were after and where they were headed next.

She also needed to get her hands on some weapons and a radio to call this in.

The second building was empty, containing no bodies like the first. It was also devoid of anything she could use as a weapon. No radios either. It had been thoroughly cleaned out of any useful supplies.

With another mental curse, she headed off to the next building. She didn't like searching the buildings with no weapons and no backup, but the longer she searched, the more certain what she sought wasn't here.

Which was a strange thought, she mused as she narrowed her eyes. She didn't yet have a clue what she was looking for.

Before she could pinpoint what she was feeling, a power rose within her, stealing her breath and making her heart pound with surprise.

This power wasn't the welcome—if somewhat chilled—magic of the gargoyles. No shadows vibrated to her call.

No.

This was foreign. Alien.

Harsher.

Deeper. Older. A sense of danger oozing from it.

This wasn't her gargoyle nature wakening to aid her search for the enemies. She would bet her favorite rifle this was magic that, until very recently, had belonged to an evil demigoddess.

"Sweet baby Jesus. Not now," she muttered and pressed a hand against her chest as if that would somehow hold back the power rising like a tidal wave within her.

She stood frozen, her breath coming in pants and her heart doing its best to crawl out of her chest.

"This is bad. Really freaking bad. Stupid idiot. Why didn't you stay behind as Rook suggested?" She hissed, the words too low to be heard. "Oh yes, because I'm a stubborn fool."

But some merciful god must have been looking down upon her and took pity because the foreign power that had been pressing outward against her skin, as if looking to burst her like an overfilled balloon, eased off a touch, the tremendous pressure growing less with each breath. She continued to take several deep breaths to calm herself; eventually, her heart got with the program and slowed to a reasonable rate.

"Okay, that's better. Shut that shit down. Good magic. Nice magic."

However, she still didn't know what had first caused it to stir awake, what had triggered its retreat, or what the actual fuck she was supposed to do to stop it next time. And there was always a next time. But she wasn't going to find any answers here, and she still had to find out what had happened to the rest of the unit stationed here. Her life might depend on it.

There would have been more than two guards. Rook had said as much.

There might be hostages.

Regardless, she needed to secure the rest of the compound and find a working radio to call this in. She started for the last building but only made it three steps in that direction when that foreign magic stirred again.

Anna halted, crouching low to the ground as she attempted to remain calm even as nervous sweat trickled down her back. She frowned at the building she'd intended to scout next and pressed her lips in thought.

Was the power trying to warn her of some danger, or —and her second thought was more likely—was the power of the defeated Battle Goddess trying to stop Anna from finding something?

For fuck's sake, no one had said anything about the power being sentient and manipulative when she'd agreed to be a temporary vessel for it.

Locking her jaw against the unpleasant sensation of the foreign power rising within her a second time, she did her best to ignore it and stubbornly stalked toward the building.

She remained alert for danger, but this building was as empty as the last one.

There was no discernable danger and nothing else of use here either.

Scowling at the surrounding forest, she once again ignored the power rising within her and continued with her search.

After another ten minutes, she was sure nothing living still resided here. But her searching had uncovered where a section of the security fence had been removed.

Upon a closer look, it appeared to have been melted away or vaporized.

"Lovely. Remind me not to get into hand-to-hand combat with this bunch," she muttered.

Her new unwelcome power was still simmering below the surface of her skin, but at least now, it seemed happier with the direction of her search.

That realization didn't particularly reassure Anna. But she'd found the trail the enemy had taken, and it cut through the forest in a westerly direction. Toward the primary base? Hell if she knew? She didn't know where she was and didn't know what freaking direction the base was in. But she could follow the road and hope the main base was close. But the service road could easily join another artery, and she'd waste hours wandering blindly, or she could follow the tracks the enemy had left.

Better to follow the enemy, Anna decided.

CHAPTER FOUR

The trail wasn't that difficult to follow through the forest; the enemy wasn't trying to hide it, which suggested they didn't expect anyone on their back trail, or they had somewhere to be in a hurry and time constraints prevented them from taking the time to hide the trail. The second would suggest an imminent attack. Possibly on the main base. If so, they were on a tight timeline. If the inbound portal base missed a radio check-in or shift change, the main base would know something was wrong.

Anna kept to a swift jog. She was already an unknown number of minutes behind the group, anywhere from twenty minutes to an hour. She needed to close the distance, but she had to be cautious not to give herself away or to overtake them.

It wouldn't do her people any good if she tipped off the enemy or got herself killed.

But she'd spent months training with the best hunters and trackers the Magic Realm—or likely any realm—had to offer. She'd polished her skills during her time among the gargoyle legion, and even in human form, the enemies were no match for her tracking and stealth hunting skills. Of course, if she'd still been able to call upon her gargoyle form, the task would be much easier. Four-legged transportation was much swifter than two.

Less than an hour later, Anna had covered enough ground that she now had the group in her sights. She would have loved to know what the group was discussing as they stood in a little huddle with only three sentries monitoring the forest, but without her gargoyle magic to boost her senses, her human ears just weren't up to the task of deciphering the words over the distance.

She didn't dare close the distance more. She'd crossed enough of the Battle Goddess's minions to know just how refined their senses were. At least the breeze was on her side, carrying her scent away from them.

Anna waited, hidden by the thick clump of underbrush, to see what the group would do next. After a few minutes, the group broke into two parties. The larger bunch moved north while two others remained behind, hunting through packs at their feet.

Anna was debating which group she should trail when one of the two remaining enemies, the taller of the two—a male with spikes on his shoulders and elbows—shook out what was clearly a military uniform.

Well then, she'd just discovered why the two bodies she'd found had been stripped. Anna carefully moved closer, attempting to hear what these two might say now that there were fewer of them and the risk of discovery was marginally less. The breeze aided her a second time, carrying snippets of their words to her. Unfortunately, whatever part of her magic nature let her understand other languages wasn't working at the moment.

Hell, she hadn't realized how much she'd grown accustomed to magic and all its benefits. She also hardily wished for the ability to touch another gargoyle's mind with only a thought. So much better than a radio. And it would have been so very beneficial in this instance, calling for backup as easy as reaching out to the nearest gargoyle mind.

With nothing else she could do, she watched her two targets.

The second warrior's build made Anna think it was a female. Maybe. Though the rest of the second being's features were rough in appearance. The skin appeared more like petrified tree bark than flesh.

During the time she had been held captive by the

enemy, she'd come to know several of the species in service to the Battle Goddess, but she'd only ever come to know a small portion. She couldn't guess what species these two were or what kind of elemental power they might command. Not knowing their natural and magical weapons was a disadvantage.

The tinge of rising magic across her exposed skin had her mind sharpening back on the two enemies where they were calling upon their power, weaving the flows of energy into intricate patterns in the surrounding air.

Shit. Were those defensive spells?

Anna tensed. Had they somehow detected her hiding place? She readied herself to haul ass if it looked like the spell was about to roll over her location.

The power bleeding off the two hostiles continued to build, brightening around them. The intensity continued to expand around them for a few seconds more, then it shuddered and contracted around them so suddenly, Anna momentarily thought something had gone wrong. But they didn't react as the power sank below their skin.

The male moved then, using his thumb to open a vial Anna hadn't seen before. He downed his vial's dark contents and then licked his lips. The woman did the same.

All right. That wasn't a tracking spell or any kind of defensive magic she'd seem used before. Perhaps it was a spell to strengthen them for a coming battle?

The bigger of the two loosed a hissing groan and doubled over. His hissing took on the tone of words. A second spell? Or perhaps those were merely curse words in his native tongue? He dropped to a crouch with one fist braced against the ground to aid his balance. His companion was soon on the ground next to him.

Both were clearly in pain, but Anna highly doubted they were attempting suicide. This had to be something else.

They confirmed her suspicions in the next few moments as the two enemy combatants shifted forms, their otherworldly features—the spikes and fangs and scales and bark-like skin—absorbed back into their bodies to be replaced by smooth skin and human features.

It was difficult to be certain, but from what she recalled of the two dead soldiers back at the compound, the enemy warriors' new bodies matched the gender and physical characteristics of the two fallen human soldiers. She'd bet they were now mirror images, copied down to the genetic code. The dark liquid in the vials had probably been the soldiers' blood. Though she hadn't seen wounds on the bodies, she'd seen magic perform every imaginable nastiness. There wasn't much magic couldn't do if the wielder was powerful enough and well enough trained in using that power. Magicking a little blood into a vial for later use wouldn't have been that difficult.

The male attempted to stand, drawing Anna's attention back to him. He managed a couple of stumbling steps before sinking back to his knees and resting with his head in his hands.

Having experienced how hard it was to weave powerful, complex spells here on Earth with its lack of magic, she had a good idea of what he was feeling.

"Welcome to Earth, Jackass," she thought and grinned savagely.

But the two enemy soldiers soon mastered themselves, shaking off their weakness, which told her they were both powerful.

After they'd dressed in their stolen uniforms and gear, they packed up the rest of their clothing and armor and stowed it in a pocket of space beneath a fallen tree.

Then they were striding off in a direction that Anna would bet was toward the main base.

Judging by the work they'd gone to in order to gain human bodies and military uniforms, they were clearly planning on infiltrating a military compound for some dark purpose.

Anna followed on silent feet, planning to do her level best to ruin their plans.

nna tracked her two targets to their destination, which was, in fact, a military base. One she didn't recognize, but from her hiding spot at the edge of the forest, the buildings and pavement all looked brand spanking new. This had to be where Master Rook had said the Earthside permanent portal was housed. And if this was the portal's location, then she could only assume the enemy combatants were trying to reach that portal to escape Earth and return to some other place in the Magic Realm.

But that didn't quite make sense either. Where had the larger group gone? Maybe the two she followed were instructed to get to the portal and escape to the Magic Realm to gather reinforcements? But how many reinforcements could still be alive? The allied forces had won the battle, and the Gargoyle Legion wouldn't have just been sitting on their asses these last two years. They would have been hunting down the surviving enemies.

"So many fucking questions and no answers," Anna murmured.

With no other option currently open, she could only continue to shadow the two enemies as they boldly walked out of the forest and along the gravel strip between the forest and the perimeter fencing.

They didn't hide, marching along like they belonged there.

Ahead, Anna noticed an oddity. Maybe a hundred meters distant, a section of the pristine new fence was no longer pristine. The supports, chain-link, and barbed wire bowed and twisted out. One sizeable area of the fence was completely missing. But a repair crew was on site, using blowtorches to cut away the most badly mangled fence sections. New materials were stacked off to one side, waiting to be used.

In no way did the base look like it was on high alert, as if it had just come under attack, and she noticed that the two enemy combatants she was following had slowed to take in the damage, surprise clear on their borrowed human features. If there had been an attack, it was news to them.

Ahead, the female slowed to point out something to her male companion, gesturing at the ground. The male followed the direction of the female's pointing and then jerked his shoulders up in the universal 'hell if I know' shrug. Then the two continued to march toward this base's main gate.

When Anna reached the section of fence being repaired, she peered between tree trunks and her leafy cover to study what had caught the attention of the two enemies. Tracks were torn into the grass on the other side of the fence, tracks that continued right through the fence line and the gravel strip beyond.

They didn't end until they reached a tree. By the torn-up bark, underbrush, and a few stray pieces of debris that looked like they belonged to the headlights of a vehicle, this was clearly the site of a crash. But had it been an accident? Unlikely. The tracks were long. The driver would have had lots of time to stop. Or, more likely, it almost looked like someone had rammed the fence to escape.

One of the soldiers by the truck shouted something, and Anna jumped, thinking she'd been spotted. Her two targets also halted to glance over their shoulders, but a moment later, Anna realized the soldier was carrying a cooler. Apparently, it was break time.

With a shake of her head, Anna left the site of the damage and moved on to keep pace with her two targets but stayed well back in the forest, not wanting to be spotted by the enemy and give them any kind of warning. She thought about approaching the work crew, but a glance confirmed they were all strangers to her. They may or may not believe her if she went to them with what she'd seen. But even if they knew her name and believed her story, they'd still take her to their superiors, and it would take precious time to sort everything out.

Time the enemy could use to infiltrate the base and carry out whatever they had planned.

As much as she wanted backup, it would be better to follow the two enemy combatants and hope she ran across a familiar face on the base. Rook had said there were gargoyles stationed with the humans. She hoped one of them was on base, and they weren't all out on missions. A gargoyle would recognize her and believe her word without question.

The next best option would be if she could find any familiar faces and get them to alert the base to the intruders while Anna continued to follow the enemy to whatever their target within the base was.

When her targets were nearly at the main gate, they slowed to adjust their IDs and gave their uniforms a once over. Anna swore softly. Of course, they had IDs stolen from the two humans they were impersonating. And she didn't, which put a wrinkle in her plan to follow them.

While Anna mulled over the best way to reveal herself, her two targets had reached the gate. There was a slight hold-up when there was some pointing behind them toward the inbound portal compound.

A couple of seconds later, she deciphered what the hand motions were about.

The guards on duty had to be questioning why the two soldiers were on foot. Anna figured the 'on foot part' might have something to do with the powerful spells used to overwhelm the other compound's defenses swiftly and silently, which had also taken out the vehicles.

"Not so smart now, are you, eh?"

But whatever excuse the two enemy soldiers came up with satisfied the base guards on duty, and Anna's two targets were waved through the first checkpoint.

Her only choice was to approach the gate and reveal herself and what she'd seen and hoped they believed her and could raise the alarm without warning the enemy. Because after what Anna had seen in the first compound, she knew this enemy possessed fearsome magic.

There would be a bloodbath if they couldn't take these enemies by surprise.

Then, in a flash of insight, a solution presented itself. The broken fence. The work crew taking a break.

The Divine Ones might as well have put out a signpost with flashing lights saying: 'idiot female, here's your way in.'

Anna swore again and then darted back the way she'd come. When she reached the section of fence, sure enough, the four workers were all taking a break, sitting in the shade of one of the trucks, food in hand.

Murmuring a heartfelt thanks to the Divine Ones,

Anna continued to weave her way through the underbrush until she could approach the broken fence with the truck between her and the four men.

"I need another drink," one man said. "Anyone want something while I'm up?"

Anna crouched, dropping down out of the soldier's line of sight. But he was walking toward the back of the truck, and if he came too close to this side, he'd see her damned shadow. She went to her belly and eased under the truck as silently as a ghost.

Momentarily safe from discovery, Anna scanned the immediate area, watching for anyone approaching from around one of the nearby buildings. The work crew might not be able to see her, but she'd be in the line of sight for anyone coming around the buildings to either side.

She silently willed the soldier at the back of the truck to get his drink and sit his ass back down so she could make her way deeper into the base and relocate her targets. But that didn't happen. He parked his ass on the tailgate instead.

Anna didn't have time to formulate a new plan. Heck, she didn't even have time for a mental curse before that foreign power arose within her again, feeling mightily impatient.

Not now. Terrible timing. Not now, please. No, no, no...

But the power wouldn't be denied and continued to

flow up out of her flesh and bones, her body unable to contain it.

"What did you call my sister?" The soldier by the tailgate growled out, anger rising in his tone as he jumped down and advanced upon one of the other soldiers. A scuffle ensued, and the other two soldiers were soon dragged into the fight. At first, their hesitation suggested they were as surprised as Anna by the violent outburst from their buddy. Still, soon the power of a demigoddess was rolling over them too, and they swiftly descended into a rage, the fight turning vicious.

Anna cursed as she rolled out from under the truck and darted away, running all out toward one of the buildings, putting as much space between her new power and the four men as quickly as possible. Pelting full tilt toward the nearest building, she swiftly covered the distance. She darted around the corner, hoping having a physical structure between her magic and its hapless victims would be enough to dilute its influence.

Unfortunately, she couldn't wait around to confirm her theory because a security patrol was rolling toward her. She leaped behind some evergreens near the building's entrance. The last thing she needed was for her magic to attack another group. She waited for the truck to pass her location before easing out of her hiding place. She brushed bits of grass and other detritus from her uniform and then calmly walked to the roadway and headed back toward the gate, moving as fast as she could without drawing attention to herself. Her top priority was locating the enemy combatants and reporting them to someone she could trust.

Now, if only her new cursed magic would cooperate.

There was no one near her location. Scanning further afield, she spotted a few more personnel on foot and in vehicles going about their business. She was nearly back at the gate when she spotted her two targets coming up the walkway toward her in the distance. It was too late to dip out of sight, so she moved to one side and crouched down, pretending to tighten her boot laces.

Anna kept her head down and strained to hear their footfalls while also pretending that the wait to see if they sensed her power wasn't harrowing. But she figured they would have already detected her if they could feel the Battle Goddess's power. She'd been on their asses most of the way while the power hunted them, and they had sensed nothing.

As if in agreement with her thoughts, the power burrowed deeper inside, like a predator waiting for its prey.

Ah.

There.

She could just hear their brisk march, which, if anyone had been paying attention, would have given them away.

No soldiers were that perky after coming off duty.

Anna waited for them to pass and then waited

longer until a vehicle came down the road. When the vehicle was almost to her position, she used the noise of the motor to hide her footfalls. No one raised the alarm.

And her targets showed no outward signs that they were aware they were being followed. It likely helped that a meeting or debriefing had just ended, and several other service members walked from the building, offering a little protection from her targets spotting her should they glance back.

So far, so good.

Now she just had to keep them in her sights while waving down a friendly face without giving away her presence to the two enemy soldiers.

The last part was proving more difficult than she'd thought. So far, a good twenty personnel had exited the building, and she recognized no one. But just then, she glimpsed a tall, solidly built figure with reddish hair. The hair was a little longer, but that face with its strong features was familiar.

Perhaps the Divine Ones were looking kindly down upon Anna because that was Private Erika Emerson stomping down the walkway, her brows furrowed and a scowl on her face, making her somewhat severe features downright mean-looking.

Still, Anna could have crowed with delight. There wasn't any human she would rather have at her side in battle.

Not that Erika was a regular human, strictly speaking.

As a powerful Null, the other woman had the delightful ability to devour all magic in her immediate vicinity. Anna had watched the private knock even the most powerful magic users on their asses. And a pissed-off Null could likely eat those two enemy combatants for lunch with room for dessert.

Private Emerson didn't notice Anna, her expression morphing into surprise and then battle readiness, her gaze scanning the surrounding crowd, hunting for the source of the foreign magic she'd be feeling, either Anna's new power or that of the enemy combatants.

Emerson didn't head in Anna's direction, instead going toward the enemies, homing in on their foreign power like a bloodhound on a scent trail. Anna hurried to catch up to the other woman before she intercepted the two foreign fighters. Before she'd even reached the other woman's side, Erika spun around, her eyes widening in recognition.

Anna swiftly jerked her chin toward the two enemy soldiers. Erika squinted and then nodded subtly in understanding; no words were needed. Danger close.

Together Anna and Erika followed their two targets, maintaining a position far enough behind so as not to draw attention. Erika even started up a conversation to help them seem harmless.

"Glad to see you're here in time for the party," Erika

said, her Texan drawl as thick as Anna remembered. "Looking forward to it?"

"Always," Anna agreed with a chuckle. "Love crashing parties. It's my specialty."

"Don't I know it?" Erika nodded toward a long line of vehicles parked beside a building ahead. A door banged open, and a soldier carrying combat gear started toward the vehicles, readying to leave on a mission. Anna eyed the weapon cases already stowed in the vehicle for transport. There were two other soldiers bent over, arranging gear in the back. Erika grabbed Anna's arm and steered her toward the group.

Anna tensed, fearing that Erika didn't trust her sudden appearance and was going to turn her over to this group. That was until Erika called out to them. One man stowing gear turned, and Anna recognized Sergeant Maribel, the Mohawk sniper from her old unit. And then a second figure popped up from where he'd been leaning inside the vehicle, stowing his gear. She instantly recognized his shit-eating grin.

Spotting Anna, Jason's grin grew larger, and he was about to broadcast to the entire area about Anna's arrival. Maribel was quicker and slammed a hand down on Jason's shoulder hard enough to startle the younger man into silence. Maribel then nodded in greeting to Anna but kept silent.

Erika pitched her voice to carry, "Just the boys I wanted to talk to about the party we're planning. We need some dates. Want to join the fun? It's guaranteed to be wild."

Erika signaled to them that danger was close and then indicated the two targets. Jason and Maribel had seen enough weird shit that they didn't even bat an eye at Erika's unusual comments.

Maribel gave Anna a once over and then, without hesitation, turned to dig into the gear already stowed for transport. Straightening, he handed her his rifle, a sidearm, and enough ammo to make the enemies sorry they ever crossed Anna's path. Then he spun on his heels and peeled away, vanishing into the building to call for backup out of the hearing range of the two infiltrators.

Moments later, four more soldiers, already sporting combat gear and weapons, emerged from inside the building and joined Anna, Erika, and Jason. Without a word, Erika led them all on the hunt.

CHAPTER SIX

In less than ten minutes, Anna and her new team weren't the only soldiers on the hunt. Out of the corner of her eye, she spotted other teams ghosting between buildings, moving into position. Somewhere ahead, she knew more units out of her direct line of sight were moving into position.

"Down, down, down!" Erika bellowed, shattering the otherwise quiet morning.

Trained to obey, Anna and the rest of the team hit the pavement. On the heels of Erika's warning, a wave of destructive power rolled toward them, displacing currents of air before it and tossing anything in its path around like paper in a hurricane.

It roared down upon them, blasting everything it touched outward like the shock wave from a bomb. Moments before it slammed into them, Erika raised her arms out wide. The air screamed, and the ground bucked as the wave of power shivered, seeming to whirl around Erika's body before the magic was sucked violently inside.

Anna arched an eyebrow. Well, then. Someone had leveled up over the last couple of years. Anna didn't have time to worry about what else she'd missed while taking a two-year stone nap.

"That was a nice snack," Erika shouted insolently back at the two hostiles, distracting them while the rest of the team recovered and moved into position. "I'm ready for the main course now!"

As if her words were the command to unleash hell, Anna and the other soldiers did precisely that. But their rain of bullets lodged into a shield shimmering in the air surrounding the pair of hostiles. The two enemies didn't fall under the heavy fire. Anna hadn't expected them to. But she also knew a shield was only as strong as its creator. And every drop of magic a wielder was using to shore up their protective shields was magical energy diverted from offensive spells.

Anna and the others continued their barrage, knowing it was only a matter of time before these two fell. They were far too outnumbered to win this fight.

But the female hostile changed tactics just then, sending the magic lashing at objects near the Null's position, ripping light poles, trees, and even part of a retaining wall out of the ground and launching them at the human soldiers.

"Fuck." Anna dodged to the left. A tree narrowly missed flattening her as it sailed past. One of its outermost branches pummeled her, knocking her feet out from under her before it crashed to the ground, its trunk a few feet from where she'd been standing.

Grimacing at the close call, she admitted she was lucky it was a small ornamental tree. Otherwise, she'd be pinned under the large branches, either dead or helplessly waiting to be killed by the enemy.

Other soldiers weren't as lucky. Three were down, pinned under debris or unconscious. Near at hand, Jason crawled out from under what looked to have been part of a streetlight. An engine's roar told Anna that reinforcements with heavier artillery were coming up on her six. She grabbed one of the unconscious soldiers and dragged him off the road and behind a cement planter. Not the best of cover, but it was all she had time for.

Instincts and that foreign power waking in her blood had Anna looking back at the enemies. A lance of raw destructive energy leaped forward, arcing through the air like lightning, closing in on one of the light armored vehicles. The driver attempted to swerve, but the magic twisted in mid-air, slammed into the side of the vehicle, and flipped it over like it weighed no more than a golf cart.

Time slowed, or something strange happened

because Anna was suddenly next to Jason, shoving him hard out of the way of the vehicle as it skidded past in a shower of sparks and the screech of abused metal. More vehicles and personnel rolled up to the fight, giving Anna a moment to regroup and figure out what had just happened. She grabbed a stunned Jason and shoved him none too gently in the direction she'd last seen Erika.

Rounding two more hunks of twisted metal, Anna found the Null. The other woman was bleeding from several shallow cuts along one arm but seemed otherwise unharmed.

"You get hit?" Anna asked.

"No. Tripped over my own damned feet while trying to avoid a flying tree. You?"

"I'm good." Which may or may not have been a lie, but currently, the Battle Goddess's power wasn't moving her body around like a pawn on a chessboard. "Let's move."

Anna surveyed the battle, noting a clear line that would get them and Jason out of the hot zone. The male witch was still looking stunned. "As much as I'm ready to put down a couple of rabid evil henchmen, Jason needs a time out."

Erika glanced away from the two enemies long enough to take in Jason's stunned expression. "What happened to him?"

Half his face was covered in blood from a nasty cut on the side of his head. There may have been other injuries that were less apparent.

"Tried to headbutt a streetlight," he muttered. "I think."

"Nice one." Grinning, Erika slapped him on the shoulder. "That was stupidly male of you."

"I made sure to take it on the side of the head. Didn't want to mess up this face." He attempted to brush one hand along his face in an elegant motion, but the tremor ruined the effect. Jason's snort of humor turned into a pained groan as he touched the side of his head. "Remind me to duck faster next time."

Anna and Erika rolled their eyes nearly in unison before guiding their injured teammate to a safer location.

They wove their way through the brutalized vehicles and other debris until they reached a dumpster in the shadow of a building. It was good enough cover for now. They sat him up with his back against a wall.

"You're done fighting for today, cowboy," Erika muttered.

"Hey, I'm not the cowboy, but if you think I'd look hot in a cowboy hat...." He started to rise, only to collapse back down to the ground. "You know what? Think you're both right. I'm going to sit and rest for a minute."

"You do that," Erika agreed, and patted his shoulder. While they tended to Jason, several of their team arrived, carrying more of the injured, led by Sergeant Maribel.

"Our forces have the two hostiles pinned down," he said, then gestured at Jason and the other injured soldiers. "Thought you could help patch this bunch up."

Anna moved to help with the other injured but kept half her attention on their surroundings because the magic was rising within her again. It wasn't over.

"Is it just me," Jason muttered as Erika removed his helmet and examined his head, "or are these two nastier than the usual run-of-the-mill evil henchmen type?"

"You'll live," Erika announced a moment later. "And, yeah, it's not just you. Those two have an axe to grind and the strength and stamina to do it all day long."

"Why would they be here?" Anna questioned. "Why attack this base? The portal?"

And what, Anna mused silently, did her new power want?

Erika shook her head. "The portal will only open for a gargoyle. And last I looked, the only gargoyles to be guests of the Battle Goddess were you, Obsidian, and big O's dad. Unless something was missing in the reports."

Anna shook her head. If it wasn't the portal, it had to be something else. "What other high-value assets are kept here?"

"You know that's top secret, but my bet's on the

recent crop of prisoners we caught. Maybe these two were looking to rescue their buddies."

"Maybe," Anna muttered, "but why only send in two? There's still a larger group somewhere outside the base. They'd have had a better chance of success if they all attacked at once."

As if in answer to Anna's comment, a great explosion rocked the ground. A giant fireball rose into the air south of their position.

"Fuck. Sorry, I said anything. I think I know where their main force is." She grabbed Erika's shoulder. "These two were likely supposed to create a distraction. Where are the prisoners kept?"

"In the basement of the Portal Complex," Erika answered. "It's the most secure building on base."

Erika bolted off, leaving Anna and the rest of the team to hustle double time to catch up. Either Erika had grown reckless over the last two years, or she knew more about the prisoners than she was letting on. Anna had a sneaking suspicion it was the second.

The path to the portal complex was relatively clear, and they made good time. She noticed other reinforcements also converging upon the same building. Someone must have called it in. Sergeant Maribel or one of his men. Or brass had already come to the same conclusion that the hostiles were trying to free the prisoners.

Just ahead, Erika was hunched down next to one of the armored vehicles parked in a semicircle in front of the building that housed the portal. But her gaze was drawn to the front of the building where a molten ruin of twisted metal and melted stone had replaced what would have been the entrance. Fuckers had power that could melt goddamn rock.

Turning her gaze away from the destruction, Anna recognized the big, bearded man with the Null.

Erika and Major Resnick were hunched down low, their heads close together, while the other woman relayed something to the major.

Anna dropped down next to them. Resnick nodded, his teeth bright again his dark beard as he talked, but any warm welcome would have to wait. She was just relieved to see someone as competent as her commanding officer already here and drawing up a battle plan.

"An unknown number of hostiles are inside the building," Resnick informed the group gathered around him. "The few scattered reports we got before the communications went dark suggested the enemy is working their way down, level by level."

"There's at least fourteen of them," Anna interjected. "Or at least I only saw fourteen others on my way here. They hit the inbound portal compound just shortly before I arrived. They were already on their way here. Otherwise, I would have landed in the middle of it."

Resnick cursed. "There were three units on duty there."

His jaw flexed, but he turned his attention to the building in front of them. Aside from the molten ruin that had once been the building's main entrance, the facility had taken minor damage otherwise.

"This was a precision strike," Resnick growled. "They knew exactly where to infiltrate, where to hit to cause the maximum amount of chaos."

"Doesn't surprise me," Anna mused. "The two I followed onto base seemed to know their way around. Though I think they were supposed to confirm the location of their targets and then create a diversion to allow the rest of their team to come in and liberate the prisoners."

Resnick arched an eyebrow. "You seem rather well informed for having just woken up from a two-year nap."

Anna just shrugged. "Wrong place. Wrong time. The usual."

Resnick snorted, but he kept his focus on the building. Anna noted that more teams were moving toward the site, firming up the perimeter. While she studied the structure, that strange foreign magic stirred within her again.

After a moment, she knew why.

She'd stopped hunting.

The magic wanted her to hunt.

'Dammit all to hell,' she directed the mental curse at the magic. *'Now is not the time.'*

The magic didn't listen to her complaints.

While she silently battled the power rising within her, Resnick used his radio, updating his superiors on the fluid situation.

Once he was finished, she asked, "What do you have in there? The prisoners. What species are they?"

While she wasn't in the mood for a conversation, it helped her focus on something else other than the foreign magic trying to force her on the hunt once more.

"We don't know," Resnick muttered darkly. "But the three captives killed forty-seven of our men, three fae, five coven members, and one gargoyle before we could get Erika close enough to neutralize the enemy. After today, that tally will far exceed what I'd thought this bunch would cost us."

A chill raced down Anna's spine. So many. And even a gargoyle? So many casualties for just three enemies? "Are they some of the Battle Goddess's surviving captains?"

"We're not sure what they are, but I don't think so," Erika said. "They're like nothing I've ever encountered. I'm unsure if Gryton or his elemental dragon knows exactly what we've captured."

One of Anna's eyebrows arched in surprise. So, Commander Gryton—the Battle Goddess's top soldier-turned-traitor to ally himself with his Avatar parents—had survived the battle. The last time she'd seen him, he'd been in dragon form, on the cusp of losing control and vaporizing everything on the planet. To save everyone, or perhaps just the Null, the elemental dragon had streaked off into space—to die, Anna had thought.

Apparently, he'd survived.

Too bad. He'd been a major jackass and the reason she and Obsidian had been captured by the Battle Goddess.

"Where's Tin-Man?" Anna asked because as much as the armor-clad asshole had been a thorn in her side, and no matter how much she disliked him, he was wicked powerful and handy to have in a fight. And they could sorely use some heavy firepower.

And if her own new and unwanted powers were on the rise, it would be a comfort to have something equally big, bad, and scary on their side. And he might know how she could put a lid on her new magic.

"It's complicated." Erika's reply was distracted sounding.

Something else occurred to Anna. "Hey. Are we one hundred percent sure Gryton isn't a part of this? He's not exactly the most solid of allies, given his history."

Erika shook her head. "No. Gryton isn't a part of this. He and his elemental dragon self still haven't recovered, and he's currently back in the Magic Realm, doing time as a sun."

The words rolled off the other woman's tongue as if she was commenting on the weather. Anna was silently mouthing the words 'doing time as a sun' while she stared the other woman down.

Alrighty then. She supposed Erika would know since the Avatars had sliced off a piece of Gryton's tarnished little soul and grafted it onto Erika's so the Null could better control the elemental dragon and ensure Gryton's loyalty.

"I don't like that Hot Stuff doesn't know what the three prisoners are," Erika said. "He's old as the hills and hasn't ever crossed anything like them."

Resnick cleared his throat. "That's why we were shipping them back to the Magic Realm as swiftly as possible. Unfortunately, the outbound portal takes four days to power up when Gregory isn't here to fuel it. The prisoners just arrived for transport this morning. We were hit before we could send them to the gargoyle legion. No one is even supposed to know the location of the two portals. The male half of the Avatars did the two spells' cloaking himself."

"What? Wait. They were just captured? There's no way the others could organize this in so short of time. They know the base's routines. Where to hit. Where to find the captives. Fuckers been planning this hit for some time."

"I concur." Resnick's expression turned darker. "This was planned. It only reasons that the three prisoners must have planned their capture as well."

"Are you sending me in?" Erika asked, clearly itching to get in on the action.

Anna couldn't blame her. Sitting back while others died was never a good feeling.

"No," Resnick said. "Before we lost all communication from inside, we instructed anyone still alive to fall back and evacuate. A few made it out. By their accounts and what our coven allies have confirmed using magic, everyone else is dead. We're waiting for a strike package. They've killed enough of our people. We're not risking more to attempt to go in and extract them."

That's why the perimeter was as far back from the building as it was. Anna frowned as her magic stirred again. "What if they're going for the portal?"

"Then I wish them well. The Avatar wasn't stupid. He told me he placed protections on the portal. So even if the enemy activates it, the gargoyle legion on the other side will be waiting for—"

For the second time that morning, the world exploded in ear-shattering chaos. Blinding white light blazed across the sky. The ground shook worse than before. Anna and the others were tossed off their feet. White noise roared in her ears. Vision sparking with patches of white interspaced with dark spots, Anna blinked until her sight blurred back into focus. With a pained groan, she rolled over. She could only watch from her new position on the ground as another giant fireball erupted into the sky.

With a sinking realization, she knew it was the airfield.

Cursing with every breath, Anna struggled to her feet and made her way over to Resnick and Erika. The major grimaced and spat blood, snarling something Anna couldn't make out. Or maybe that was because her ears were ringing. Resnick was already barking orders into the radio.

After a moment, Anna realized the Null wasn't moving.

"Erika!" Anna shouted as she stumbled toward the other woman. "Erika, can you hear me?"

She checked for a pulse, breathing a sigh of relief when she found one. After checking her over for possible injuries, she gently rolled her onto her side. Blood seeped from a cut at her temple, where her head must have hit the ground when she fell.

"Bless me," came the words in a groggy Texan drawl. "What the hell hit me?"

Resnick was crouching next to Erika now, checking her over even as Anna had done. "That was two surgical hits. They got both the armory and the airfield. The strike package didn't make it off the ground. More reinforcements aren't—"

"Contact! Contact! Contact!" Sergeant Maribel's voice bellowed over the distant explosions and roar of fire.

Anna and Erika both scrambled for their fallen weapons. The other soldiers conscious and capable of standing, did the same. For all the good it did them.

A wall of power, churning and wild and howling with an unholy noise, rushed outward from the ravaged maw of the building. Behind the ever-expanding force, Anna caught glimpses of a cluster of enemies.

But then the power was upon them, a savage wave that battered against the vehicles and barriers they were using for shelter. The power pushed against the vehicle Anna was sheltering behind, slowly moving it a few feet, forcing her, Erika, and Resnick to do some fancy foot-work to stay ahead of it. Still, it didn't go flying like how the other two hostiles had launched trucks and armored vehicles around like toys.

"I think someone's batteries are running low," Erika muttered as she studied the vehicles.

Anna could only agree, but not everyone had been as lucky. The soldiers closer to the building had been tossed fifty feet away. Other men had been crushed against stationary objects by the force of the blast.

Even on 'power saver mode' this bunch was lethal as fuck.

"I need to get closer," Erika shouted above the roar of magic crackling in the air, "and attempt to feed on them directly, give our side a chance at killing them. As it is now, by the amount of power that group is tossing around, I will hit the upper limit of what I can absorb before I can neutralize them all."

Anna nodded in understanding. The Null could only absorb so much magic before she tapped out.

"Understood. We'll concentrate on them one at a time," Anna agreed.

"Yep," Erika said with a savage grin. "We're going to work those evil henchmen like a pack of wolves after a herd of fat sheep."

Just then, Major Resnick dropped down next to them. "Hold up. Just heard we're about to get some backup. Gargoyles inbound from the direction of the other portal."

At the news, Anna's heart did a little flip, but then she reminded herself it wouldn't be Obsidian. But at this point, Anna would give a big ole kiss to whatever gargoyles showed up. Hell, she'd even give Reaver a smack.

But just then, her new power rose in her blood, warning Anna a moment before the enemy launched their next attack.

"We're about to get incoming!" Anna shouted the warning to the others even as her own magic was selecting targets for her. It was the first time Anna was certain her new power wasn't actually in league with this unknown enemy. The battle magic flooded her, transforming her vision into something else entirely. She could still see clearly—clearer actually—but colors now swirled strangely around every living thing.

It was almost like she could see auras. Or, at least, something similar. But it was so much more than that. She could see a differentiation between the enemies, from the strongest in power to the weakest. But it was more detailed than that. The weakest points in their shields were apparent to her enhanced sight, showing as a fading or blurring in the intensity of the colored auras.

She tested her theory, targeting the weakest among them and aiming for the most frayed-looking part of his shield. Her target looked and felt male, though there was little to see that wasn't covered in armor. A large helm with wings on the side, the visor coming to a point like a bird's beak, effectively hid the enemy's features. Behind the eye slit in the visor, there was only darkness. But she didn't need to see him clearly when she could easily see his weaknesses. She raised her rifle and took out her target with short bursts of rapid fire at his chest.

The distant figure crumpled, out of the fight, if not actually dead.

Her power surged again, showing her even more. No, her target wasn't dead. Not yet, but she could rectify that issue.

Her power grew. She could feel them now, read their emotions and intentions, felt what type of spells they were conjuring, instinctively knew how the battlefield would shift, what direction the fighting would flow into next.

So, when the cluster of hostiles scattered suddenly, she was ready.

Five members of the group broke off, heading east.

No amount of firepower slowed them, and they smashed their way through the perimeter like it was paper.

They were advancing, clearing a path straight through the kill box. They were strong, but not the strongest.

Nine others were heading toward Anna's location. Three remained only a short distance from where they'd exited the building, watching the battle, she realized. Waiting. They wanted something.

And Anna became confident that one of the three enemies standing aloof was the leader and her new magic was certain the leader would be the strongest.

Her magic just needed to get them to drift apart a little, to determine the leader and cut the head off this beast. Focused on the hunt for the leader, her power ignored the nine enemies heading directly at them.

Bloody hell. Anna aimed her borrowed rifle at the closest enemy. Her magic-enhanced sight told her this one was powerful, too powerful for bullets to be effective. But that was the best defense she had just now.

As expected, the bullets didn't penetrate his shields. She changed tactics and aimed for the ground in front of him. The bullets bit into the asphalt, breaking it up and causing bits of it to fly up and hit the warrior.

It confirmed the type of shield. "Resnick!" She bellowed at her commanding officer. "Their shields are designed to stop high-velocity impacts. Incendiaries might be effective."

Resnick nodded and then shouted orders into his radio. "Everyone, go for grenades and any other incendiaries we've still got left."

But then they were out of time, and the first of the enemy combatants was leaping over the armored vehicle. Anna bolted into motion, bringing her rifle up under the invader's shield.

He hadn't seen Anna until it was too late. Now he was practically on top of her. She smiled as she shot up at him, catching him in the underside of his jaw. The bullet ripped through the soft tissue and up into his brain. He howled in rage and stumbled away.

Anna's eyes widened in surprise. Some magic wielders were more challenging to kill than others, but a shot to the head usually put them out of commission for a while, at least.

Not this bastard.

She dived and rolled, narrowly missing having her head taken off by a sword bleeding magic into the air as he lashed out blindly in her direction.

Anna darted out of his way, disappearing around a burnt-out vehicle. The fighting raged around her, but her battle magic swiftly spotted where five of the enemy combatants were trying to corner Erika between a parked vehicle and the wall of a building. A glance around showed other groups of soldiers fighting off their own opponents. But none had so many enemies to face as the Null.

Her dagger clutched in her hand; Anna ran toward Erika. She picked out her target—the closest enemy—an enormous beast of a woman. She held a sword in one hand, which she used to herd the Null farther into a corner. In the other hand, she held a length of chain and what looked like a collar and cuffs.

And there wasn't a hint of magic about them.

Shit. The Null's abilities wouldn't be able to fight such an item. There was no magic for her to absorb, no spell to unmake.

That's when the truth hit Anna like a cement truck. This wasn't a random attack, not if they'd brought such an item.

They had not explicitly come to attack the base.

They'd come for the Null.

Well, Anna had something to say about that. She ran at the enemy and collided with the woman. Her momentum and the element of surprise combine to send the armor-clad woman stumbling away. She didn't go down or drop the sword, unfortunately. But it gave Erika an opening to bolt to freedom.

Anna provided cover fire. It did little damage, but it slowed the enemy somewhat.

"I'm out of ammo," Erika said between panting breaths. "And there are too many in close proximity for my power to drain anyone of them to a lethal level."

"Time to retreat and regroup," Anna said, grabbing the other woman by the shoulder. But when they turned to dart for freedom, they found the path blocked by two more of the enemy. One was the first one she'd taken out.

"Fuck me!" Anna growled. "Don't these bastards ever die?"

CHAPTER SEVEN

*J*ust when Anna was sure they were both about to get their asses handed to them, clan and coven members arrived, heading toward their location. Accompanying the witches, she spotted several fae—sidhe and dire wolves. And then a club-wielding troll-like creature came charging up from behind the newcomers.

The leshii, Greenborrow, charged forward in his large, troll battle form, wielding his club and leading a pack of dire wolf shifters and the elf-like sidhe warriors. Anna whooped in delight at seeing the local fae wading into the fight. A little behind, Anna spotted Major Resnick, his team, and several coven members.

Greenborrow wasn't in a friendly mood and stormed right through every defensive weaving the hostile soldiers tossed up in front of them. He swung his massive metal spiked club like it was a baseball bat.

It connected with one of the enemy combatants and sent the armor-clad male flying backward. He hit the cement base of a streetlight, shattering it on impact, leaving a big dent in his armor. The figure slumped motionless on the ground, and Anna breathed out a sigh of relief. One fucker was finally down for the count.

Just sixteen more to go.

She was picking out her next target, hunting for the weakest of the remaining enemies, when movement by the downed pole drew her gaze.

Was he...?

The figure rolled over and forced himself up to his knees. Then, with a mighty push against the ground, he straightened, his sword lifting back into position. Though he was moving slower than before.

"You've got to be kidding me," Erika muttered the words Anna was thinking.

"How did that blow not stop him?" Anna growled. "His fucking chest is caved in!"

"Can they be killed?" Erika looked concerned for the first time. Even the ancient leshii was eyeing the male in disbelief.

"Everything can die," Anna muttered and pointed out the next weakest of the enemy, another armor-clad female. She was currently advancing on a group of soldiers. The priority was disabling as many enemies as possible before they could do more damage.

"Greenborrow," Anna called to him, "That one!"

The leshii nodded and then grinned savagely. Aiming higher this time, he swung with even more power, the mighty club slicing through the air so quickly that it was nothing more than a blur. A meaty wet crunch echoed over the other sounds of battle, and his opponent's head tumbled away.

Greenborrow nodded to Anna, and she picked out the next weakest target. Before either of them could engage their target, a black streak blurred past. Anna only had a moment to hear the ring of hooves on the pavement before she glimpsed a silky black body, mane, and tail flying behind him as the pooka joined the battle.

A loud neigh was the only warning the pooka's target got as the small black pony, with glowing yellow eyes, spun and kicked up his heels, driving them into the enemy's chest. Three soldiers joined the pooka.

Battles continued all around her. There was no lack of targets, but the power rising in Anna's blood wasn't interested in any of them. She glanced around for Erika, the only person presently able to help Anna contain the power of a demigoddess. But Anna didn't see her. She scanned the battle zone again before her magic forced the issue, but she still didn't see Erika anywhere.

Alarm growing, she looked again but there was no sign of the other woman. Then, against her will and anything that looked even remotely like common sense, the Battle Goddess's power grabbed the reins, and once again, Anna found herself a puppet to that magic.

Hating every moment, she stalked away from the battle, striding down a sideroad and then turning left down another.

Hunting again.

Less than thirty feet later, she rounded the corner of a building and discovered what had riled up her magic. She put on a burst of speed, giving chase to one of the enemy combatants directly ahead. Like all his brethren, he was clad head to toe in armor, his species a mystery, but the unconscious form slung over his shoulder as he ran was familiar.

Anna broke into a run, knowing only that she needed to save the Null. For once, she and her new magic agreed. Three more of the enemy materialized from around a corner, coming between her and the retreating figure carrying Erika.

Fuck.

For good or ill, the power of a demigoddess was guiding her, and it said these three enemies were minor obstacles in her way to something far more deadly that needed to be destroyed. Something that must not be allowed to possess a null.

But all they saw was a human, unarmed and without magic. The one in the lead grinned at her and advanced, magic rising to swirl around his armor until even a glint of magic could be seen inside the darkness of his lowered visor.

She knew how to kill them. That information hadn't come as words, but thoughts, knowledge, almost like memories. She didn't question it. There was no more time to question—only act.

Time slowed, and in the moments between heartbeats, the nearest enemy launched his attack, magic swirling around his armor, coalescing into three spears of hardened energy. Nothing good could come from being impacted by those six-foot-long harpoons, Anna mused, feeling strangely calm as her arms instinctively shot out from her sides in what would have been an instinctive move to deflect something tossed at her. Still, there was nothing ordinary about today, and her new power became visible for the first time as threads of smoky blue and radiant silver magic shimmered in the air between them, forming a thick mist.

When the enemy's magic met Anna's new power, the three harpoons halted so suddenly they vibrated in the air, like an arrow newly embedded in a target. Anna wasn't sure who was more surprised. Her or the enemies.

The pause in the fighting lasted only a moment. Then her silvery smoke magic launched the three harpoons back at their creator. They smashed into him with a force at least three times what he'd used, and the impact pierced his armor and tossed him back into the other two enemies.

Huh. Interesting. His shields couldn't defend against his own magic.

She followed them out the other side of the narrow alleyway and onto a stretch of green lawn running along a practice course. Intent on finishing off the three closest threats, Anna didn't see the new danger until it was too late.

A torrent of power slammed into her so hard it pushed her backward. Luckily, her new magic had sensed the hostile power in time to shield her, but it didn't stop or slow the onslaught. Anna braced against the opposing force, trying to stop her skid across the morning dew-dampened grass. She dug her boot toes in hard. It helped slow her backward momentum, though it hadn't stopped the relentless force of the power pushing against her shields.

She squinted through the bright flare of the two opposing powers and glimpsed the source of the opposing energy. It was one of the three prisoners who had stood aloof from the rest of their henchmen. She'd known one of them was the leader, the power or brains behind the attack.

These three lacked the armor of their rescuers, and she could see it more clearly now that she was closer to their location. Two were definitely once members of the Battle Goddess's army. An incubus and a succubus. Not captains, Anna didn't think, though she hadn't met all the captains during her time there. Yet these hostiles were undoubtedly upper echelon.

But the third.

He was new, a species she'd never seen before, his magic wholly foreign. She'd bet he was also the leader, since he was the one the Battle Goddess's power wanted to destroy.

Anna could understand why. Nothing about the beast made her want to go near it. Tall, nearly as tall as a gargoyle's lofty eight feet, but thin, as if its body had been unnaturally elongated. Its eyelash-less sunken eyes, so dark they seemed to eat the light, dominated a narrow angler face, the chin so sharp it was almost a point. Mobile ears—that had to be a good ten inches long—were decorated with delicate chains and bits of bone. It also possessed skin so lacking in color that she wondered if the feel of the sun upon its skin was a new experience. This beast looked a little like a sidhe had gotten knocked up by a fox, then the resulting offspring had spawned with a naked mole rat.

Whatever species it hailed from, it was an entirely unwholesome sort.

It raised one of its spindly arms, impossibly long fingers spreading at least ten inches wide. Its power slammed into her shield a moment later, joining its two brethren in their attempts to destroy her. Its magic was like orange flame-laced lightning. It hit her like a train, buckling her shield inward until more power poured from her body and reinforced her defenses.

The longer the leader bombarded her, the dirtier she felt, his power seeming to sink past her defenses and infiltrate her mind even though she saw no evidence that his magic had breached her shields.

This was what despair tasted like, she thought suddenly.

She was doomed. Nothing could fight such a creature.

Wait one fucking minute!

She shook her head as if to clear it, then narrowed her eyes in rage.

Those were not her thoughts. That was an alien thought in her head if ever she felt one.

"You. Yes, you. The Ugly Fucker. Get out of my goddamn head!" Her new magic seemed to agree, and another wave of power built within her, rising so swiftly it was a physical pain ripping through her bones. That power severed the other creature's mind connection, burning back along the link, where it plowed into the enemy. He staggered back a step and wiped blood from under his nose.

He glanced at it in seeming confusion for a moment, then what she could only call glee overtook his features.

"War," he purred as if drunk on sex. "Lovely, beautiful war. So young and untrained. Join me. I can teach you how to harness your power. We could rule this world and any other we so choose."

Another massive surge of magic welled up from within her bones, spreading outward, her skin unable to contain it. It howled for his destruction, the skinny, pale-skinned creature's utter and absolute destruction. Nothing else would do.

"Never, Ugly Fucker!" she screamed at the top of her lungs. "If you could feel half of what I'm feeling right now, you'd be turning tail and bolting as far from me as you can."

He didn't react in anger to her words, just tilted his head to one side, studying her as if she'd performed some exciting trick. "How regrettable. We could have reshaped worlds together."

The power ramped up twice as high at his words until a soundless howling filled her ears and threatened to shatter every bone in her body as that power fought to break free.

"Fuck. Me." She gasped out as she tried to wrangle the pain and battle on. Even her skin and muscle burned with its strength.

At that moment, she realized her new power was just as much a threat as the external enemy attacking her. The power of a demigoddess was not something a mortal body was meant to contain. That was the reason for the two-year stone nap. Her body needed that time to heal and strengthen. Anna started to fear her body hadn't yet adapted enough to contain this level of magic.

But the power did not seem to care if it burned her mortal body to ash in its pursuit of this new enemy—whatever he was.

Even as the Battle Goddess's magic was weaving some new spell, the leader of the hostile force was summoning more and more magic to toss at her. And as Anna's new magic reacted to counter the enemy, her body grew hotter. Sweat poured off her like she was burning up with a fever in the Florida Everglades. But she held her ground against the three enemies attacking her.

She may even have outlasted the strength of these three creatures had the air not just rippled with power and spat out six more from a temporary portal. By the dents and dings and blood on their armor, the six newcomers had already been in a battle but must have been summoned to aid their leader.

Fuck and double fuck. A three-on-one fight she might win. But six-on-one?

Power rippled and snapped through the air. Then, with the subtlety of a tectonic shift, the air currents changed, and the temperature plummeted. Ice crystals formed, drifting down from the sky. Fog rose off the warm grass even as snow fell.

Now, what was happening? Anna wondered, even as her power ramped up its assault on the pasty-skinned leader, seeming unconcerned about the sudden changes in the surrounding environment.

It grew dark suddenly. Anna glanced up to see vast black wings blotting out the sun. Shadows bled from those massive ebony wings. Spreading wider, the darkness expanded, exploding across half the sky. A roar echoed above the other sounds of battle, and then in an angry blur of wings, talons, fangs, and lethal shadow magic, the winged being streaked past her position and slammed into the closest enemy line.

The world shook as his magic impacted the ground.

Then that being of shadows and menace was amid the enemies. Before the first hostile knew what hit him, he was hoisted high in the air.

Then, with talons digging deep and massive muscular shoulders flexing, the being of shadows ripped the body down the middle. The sickening, wet, fleshy sound of a living creature being torn in two filled the air for long moments. Then the newcomer tossed the two pieces aside with a spray of blood and gore.

The sight should have horrified even a battle-hardened soul. Instead, with a feral joy flowing through her body, Anna and her magic leaped forward to join him in slaying their enemies.

Impossible as it should be, considering he was supposed to sleep for another few months at least, that ball of muscle, rage, and breathtaking power was her partner, Obsidian, Rasoren of the Gargoyle Legion.

Her most trusted friend and teammate had come to save Anna's ass.

And fuck, had he ever leveled up in the power department while he'd slept.

Not having time to ponder that new development, Anna ran, closing the distance between them in seconds, and then she was in the thick of battle again, but this time she was back-to-back with her towering partner, her soul nearly singing to have him near once more. She lashed out at the nearest enemy, noting it was one of the fellows who'd been with the harpoon guy.

He came at her with a sword, and that ancient magic riding Anna thrust her left arm forward and formed a shield longer than she was tall. The enemy's sword shattered at the contact, but Anna barely felt the impact.

Well, wasn't that handy?

'I wonder?'

She'd barely formed the thought, and then the magic was summoning a sword made of solid power in her right hand. It might be made of magic, but it moved and cut through the air like a real sword. While she was relatively new to swordsmanship, she was proficient, thanks to her gargoyle mentors.

Her opponent drew his second sword, and then they were slashing and thrusting, circling each other in a deadly dance. Her opponent kept stepping back, just out of reach, attempting to draw her away from Obsidian's back.

"Not borne yesterday, dickhead," she muttered.

Even if her instincts hadn't been telling her to stay glued to her Rasoren's back, her training had drilled in the fact that you did not leave your partner exposed. She stayed close, forcing the enemies to come to her. And come the fools did. The Battle Goddess's magic was only too happy to end them.

When there was a sudden lull in the fighting, she glanced over her shoulder to find Obsidian casting aside another defeated enemy. Her eyes widened as she took in the blood and gore coating him and then glanced at the carnage spread in a twenty-foot radius around them. Perhaps 'annihilate' was a more accurate word than 'defeat' to describe what he'd done to his enemies.

Shredded. Their bodies were nothing more than bits of tissue, like a wickedly violent explosion had minced them to a pulp.

"The hell?" she muttered as she glanced at him. She'd never seen shadow magic do that to a body before. And now that she looked closer at the magic vortex still swirling around him, she spotted tiny flashes and swirls of icy blue magic floating among the normal shadowy power of a gargoyle.

Obsidian stood unmoving, his fierce yet familiar features twisted into a snarl of rage the like she'd never seen upon his face before. His burly muzzle was scrunched in a snarl, his gleaming fangs impossibly white against his midnight skin and the dark threads of chilled shadow magic. More of the strange blue sparks were laced with the shadows that bled from him, sweeping around her in a little caress as it flowed out and away from them. It reminded her of stars in the night sky.

With his wings mantled around him, he lashed his tail slowly but otherwise did not move.

His stillness was unnatural. He didn't blink. She wasn't even sure if he was breathing.

She reached out and touched his chest. His pectoral muscles felt like stone beneath her hand. And his skin was cold, so cold it burned.

And while shadow magic held a hint of frost to it, the power rising off Obsidian felt more like what she'd expect from the frigidness of deep space. The only time she'd felt such a cold power had been when Gregory called upon magic directly from the Spirit Realm. But he was the male half of the Avatar—a being possessing godlike power.

Obsidian was just a gargoyle—a powerful and very well-trained gargoyle. But still a gargoyle with limits to how much power he could summon. Then she realized that was a lie. He wasn't just a gargoyle. He was more. Like her, he'd agreed to become a vessel for a demigod's power. And while Lord Draydrak was by far the much nicer of the two demigod siblings, he was also Death incarnate. And Obsidian was now host to Lord Draydrak's power.

It stood to reason that the power her gargoyle

partner was wielding was pure death, and if she was to guess by his vacant stare, his power was riding him hard, even as hers had been only moments before.

"Obsidian?" She called softly. He didn't respond to his name.

She reached out, wrapped both hands around his muzzle, and jerked down as hard as she could until his gaze was upon her. Now she had his attention, but not in a good way to judge by the rolling growl he issued.

"Obsidian, it's me." His eyes, typically two solid black reflective pools, now shimmered with an icy blue light deep in their depths. All right then. This was apparently Obsidian 2.0, but her gargoyle partner was still in there somewhere. She just needed to reach him.

After another moment's study, she realized it felt like he was still not fully awake.

She could feel his mind now, unlike when he'd been asleep, but his thoughts weren't calm or organized. They were more like a raging river, the current too swift and deep to allow her to catch and hold any of his thoughts. But their essence tasted of dark turmoil, of unending nightmares.

Sliding her fingers along his muzzle, she cupped his cheeks, stretched up on her toes, and then closed her eyes. Again, she tried to touch his mind, to gain purchase on one of his thoughts. Anything that would allow her to find her Rasoren and bring him back from wherever he was trapped.

His rolling growl halted so suddenly it was as if someone had punched him in the throat. After a moment, his muzzle dipped down as he inhaled her scent.

"Come on. Wake up, big fellow. We don't have time for this shit. I think the leader of this bunch might be getting away unless he's some of the blood and gore covering the grass. Either way, one of the enemies has the Null. I need your help."

He blinked. At last, the cold shimmering blue power in his gaze ebbed. "Anna?"

"Yep. That's right. Stay with me." She released his face and grabbed his hand, realizing his starry death magic, which was still crawling over his skin, hadn't harmed her.

'Great time to think of that, Anna,' she muttered to herself as she guided him away from the scene of the slaughter. That his power didn't harm her didn't come as a surprise. Lord Death's magic couldn't hurt his twin sister either, and vice versa. So, it stood to reason that Anna and Obsidian couldn't harm each other. Small blessings.

"You need to keep a rein on Lord Draydrak's magic. I think it's trying to roll you under its control," she explained as swiftly as she could. "My new powers have been riding my ass since I arrived here. Maybe even before. Probably the reason I woke up early."

He squinted at her and then shook his head, but it

wasn't a denial, more as if he was trying to make sense of her words.

"Obsidian, do you understand?"

"I—I think so. But where am I? How did I get here?"

"You don't remember?"

"Would I ask if I did?"

Good point.

A shiver rolled down his body. Closing his eyes, he pressed his muzzle against her shoulder.

There was something very wrong with her gargoyle partner.

"Maybe you should sit this one out?" Anna gave him a gentle pat, concerned for him now. "Rook had told me you wouldn't be waking up for several months yet. I think that means you took more damage than me when you became a vessel. How about a change of plans? You use your gargoyle senses to help me hunt down the one who has Erika, and I'll do the extraction."

"No." He lifted his head as if to look her in the eyes but swayed instead, losing his balance and bumping into her before he could right himself. With a groan, he pressed his muzzle back into her shoulder.

"No?" She questioned him gently, even as she started looking around for other dangers and a safe place to stash her Rasoren. Standing in the open with no cover, they might as well be carrying flashing neon signs. "You're in no shape to fight again so soon. I think it might be better for everyone if I round up a team and go after Erika without you. We've put a dent in their numbers, and the remaining hostiles have to be running on fumes."

"No, we are stronger together than apart by design," he growled against her neck. "I go wherever you go. We're a team."

Just her luck. He gets his brain scrambled by magic but still retains his stubbornness and protective instincts. Fucking perfect.

Anna had a powerful urge to shake her fist at him. It wasn't like she could physically shake sense into him. He was too damned big for that. Might as well attempt to shake a small mountain.

"Fine. Prove to me you can walk in a straight line."

He lifted his head, stepped away from her, and this time walked a mostly straight line.

Shit. He could walk well enough that the stubborn ass would follow her. She wouldn't be able to leave him tucked somewhere safe until the battle was over. "Just stay on my six. We'll get through this. Come on, let's go break some more bad guys."

She turned in the direction her new magic urged, then stopped.

"Can you pick up Erika's scent?" Anna asked. She wasn't one hundred percent sure which enemy currently had Erika, and she didn't trust her magic to prioritize Erika over the leader of this group if the two weren't together. If they'd planned to abduct Erika from the beginning, there was no way Anna was letting them get away with the Null.

And Anna's magic might be more interested in stopping the evil leader, but that didn't mean one of his lieutenants wouldn't continue with the plan. So, Erika was the priority.

"I will try," Obsidian said. Turning in a circle, he inhaled several times before dropping to all fours and trotting off in an easterly direction.

"You found something?"

"Yes," he called back to Anna. "Her scent is strongest this way."

Anna followed closely on his heels, weaving in and around the other battles. It was clear the enemy warriors were trying to retreat. She wouldn't normally leave her fellow soldiers to fight their opponents alone, but just now the sky was darkening once more. Gargoyles descended from above in the hundreds, their wings blotting out the light. Obsidian had just been the fastest.

She put on a burst of speed, pulling ahead of Obsidian now that she knew which direction to run. They needed to make up ground if they hoped to rescue Erika, but Anna used some of her precious breath to ask, "Jeez. Did you bring half the legion with you?"

"No. They followed me." Obsidian overtook her, running on all fours, his strides lengthening as she watched.

Fuck.

She was about to shout at him to wait for her when she felt his tail coiling around her waist. Then her stomach was left behind as she was jerked forward and up, then roughly deposited on his back. She'd ridden gargoyle back enough times that it came naturally to her. Leaning forward, she wrapped her arms around his neck and gripped his waist with her thighs. It was undoubtedly more secure with a saddle, but he wasn't taking flight. This was going to be a ground race. She'd make do.

"Careful," Anna shouted as he was about to round the corner of the portal complex. "We're going in the direction my battle magic wants, and I think we're getting close. So be careful. Their leader—whatever the hell he is—packs a motherfucking punch."

"So do I," Obsidian rumbled.

"Yeah, about that. I think we need to try rescuing Erika using our new powers as little as possible. The more rein I allow mine, the stronger its hold on me grows. And yours seemed to have a pretty good hold on you when you first arrived."

"Understood," Obsidian said and then paused. "And I think your caution is wise. I wasn't even aware mine had a hold on me until I found myself looking down into your face and having no memory of how I got to that spot."

"Yeah. Thought as much," Anna muttered. "Welcome to the shitshow."

"They're just ahead," Obsidian whispered. "I can scent Erika and something else. It..."

"I know. It's not like anything we've ever encountered before. And I don't like it. At all. So, let's not blunder upon them like I've been doing all morning."

Obsidian nodded and shortened his strides, seeking cover to hide their approach. It didn't take long to find their targets. The one Anna had pegged as the leader was standing a little apart from three of his underlings. Erika was with them. Unconscious by the look of it. However, her ability must still be working to drain the magic wielders because the tall, lean armored figure currently holding her passed her off to his neighbor with obvious relief.

When Obsidian halted—having come as close as they could without giving their location away to the enemy—Anna slid from his back and eyed their surroundings. She eased away from him to glance around the building's corner. The terrain wasn't in their favor. Too open. Nothing beyond this point to hide their approach.

"Remember how I said we shouldn't use our new powers? Yeah, about that. I don't see a way to extract Erika without some magical aid. My gargoyle nature is dormant. It would just be your shadow magic. Fearsome though it is, I'm not sure you're up for a four-on-one fight against them. We should keep tracking them and wait for backup."

"Other gargoyles will track us. They won't be far behind. However, I don't think the enemy will give us the luxury of time." Obsidian pointed out the spell work already glowing on the ground.

They were still too far away for her to see the spell's runes clearly over the distance, but she thought she knew what it was by its size and circular shape. "It's a freaking portal spell, isn't it?"

"Yes."

"Bloody fucking hell!"

"Hmm. Indeed." Obsidian returned to all fours and bumped his muzzle under her hand. "Get on."

"Planning to do something foolish?" she asked, fatalistic humor twisting her lips.

"Depends how this turns out for us."

"Waiting for reinforcements is overrated, anyway." Anna placed one hand on his lower back, the other on his rump, and then vaulted up. After dropping down smoothly, she shifted forward until her legs gripped his sides and her knees were tucked against his wing joints.

"Now unleash your power and merge it with mine," he ordered.

"Fuck me! I thought you said foolish, not suicidal. Merging our power is bound to be reactive, and by 'reactive,' I mean explosive."

He shrugged, jarring her insides with the motion. "Together, we've always been stronger than apart. I think that will still hold true for our new powers. The

Twins were always supposed to work together, their separate magics complementing each other."

She hesitated a moment, flashing back to what she'd seen in his gaze earlier, when his power had held him in its grip. There'd been nothing but power and rage. "I don't think—"

He cut her off. "This is what we were created for, the roles the Divine Ones ordained we would fulfill."

Words were good and all. But what if Lord Death's magic rolled Obsidian back under its control? What if she couldn't draw him back from that seductive power a second time?

As if sensing her thoughts—and maybe he could with them touching—he rumbled out words she'd said to him when he'd been a cub, and they'd been prisoners of the Battle Goddess. "We've got this. We're a team."

She'd never put much thought into things beyond this mortal life, but she'd seen enough to trust his words. And what other choice did they have? Allowing this enemy to steal the Null wouldn't be good for anyone.

"Yeah," she agreed softly. "Let's do this."

All it took was for her to relax her grip on the mental reins holding the power in check, and it eagerly rushed out to continue its hunt. His magic did the same. Then, without even needing any urging from her, the Battle Goddess's immense power merged with its twin.

The two powers completed each other, opposite and yet the same.

Anna gasped.

She felt complete for the first time since she woke back in the Magic Realm, as if their Rasoren-Kyrsu bond was still intact. It wasn't, she knew. This new feeling wasn't the result of that bond, but it was close.

It was...

It...

Fuck. The feeling was damned near orgasmic.

"Perfect," Obsidian rumbled softly, and then he gave himself a full body shake and leaped into motion.

They raced across the expanse of the parking lot, one soul in two bodies, the magic of the Twins rushing out ahead of them. Her smoky silver magic blended with his icy blue power, swiftly merging to form a shield to wrap around them. But their powers didn't stop there. More spears of magic formed. With barely a thought from her, they launched themselves at the enemy currently holding Erika captive.

CHAPTER EIGHT

Anna's magic took control and strengthened their protective shield as Obsidian's icy blue power sparked against the velvety darkness of his shadow magic, readying another assault. She'd already witnessed what those starry filaments could do to a hostile when they coiled around the enemy's shields. The layers of death magic crushed an opponent's defenses while a second wave of magic obliterated the target in gory spectacle. But it took the death magic long moments to crush a shield, allowing the enemy to bombard her and her gargoyle mount. Their own defenses were taking a beating.

They couldn't keep this up and needed to change tactics.

"I wonder what combining a battle magic spear with your death magic will do?" Anna mused as she launched one of her spears at the nearest enemy. It smashed against his shield, weakening it, but it didn't collapse.

"Let's find out," Obsidian said, a dark tone rumbling through his words.

Anna nodded, already putting her idea into action as Obsidian dodged bolts of enemy magic. The fiery orange lances of power came at them thick and fast, but her nimble mount twisted and leaped, evading most of the attacks. Only a few strikes landed on their shields.

At her silent command, the newest spear forming in her hand sucked in the nearest filaments of his death magic. Her weapon's color shifted from a steely blue-gray tone to a more vivid shade marbled with the icy-blue power. Then with an arm given greater strength and accuracy by her new power, she launched the spear. It flew true, piercing an enemy's shield. It didn't collapse the defensive dome as she'd expected, instead passing through it, encountering no more resistance than if she'd sent it through a bank of fog.

The spear lodged deep in the gut of her target. Before he'd even dropped to his knees, a bright flash blinded her to what was happening inside his shield. Seconds later a red spray exploded out from where the hostile had been and viscera and less identifiable bits coated the inside of the dome.

A moment later, the shield popped like an overly large bubble. The sound of gore hitting the ground turned her stomach.

"Fuck, that's nasty," Anna muttered even as she selected her next target, "but effective."

"Indeed," Obsidian huffed out between ragged breaths as he leaped to the left so suddenly only his right wing kept her seated on his back.

But there was a cost for such heavy use of her magic.

Pain as bright and fiery as the filaments built in her bones. She felt like she might combust at any moment.

But then Obsidian was inside the enemy's perimeter, lashing out with claws, fangs, and blade-tipped tale. Even new to the use of Lord Death's magic, he conducted himself with a lethal beauty, his new power rushing out of him, looking like a delicate blue fog shot through with glimmering lights.

What that fog did was anything but pretty or delicate.

The first body it touched...

Words failed her.

The body ruptured? Exploded? It was almost too fast to see and adequately comprehend, and then the body disintegrated into bloody bits.

They plowed through the enemy—her power destroying as many as Obsidian's. Two more enemies fell. They were closing in on Erika's position when Anna felt another powerful spell flaring to life. It had to be the portal. Nothing else would put out enough power to register over all the other energies bombarding them from all sides.

"The portal!" Anna shouted. "We're running out of time."

Obsidian leaped over what remained of the enemy line, landing a stride away from Erika. In a blink, Obsidian latched onto Erika with his hind talons, gripping the woman with his powerful feet even as his wings beat the air, driving them up into the sky.

But having the Null so close weakened them both farther. Anna channeled all her remaining energy into shielding them from an attack from below.

And even with all her remaining power feeding their shield, a new spell flew straight through their combined defenses, slicing into Obsidian first, and then Anna. It wasn't like the other spells. This one was different. And yet its oily tainted-essence was horrifyingly familiar. She'd nearly been destroyed when a blood witch had tried to enslave her soul with a spell of this type.

Only Lord Draydrak had been able to save her.

This time, Obsidian took the brunt of the attack, and there was no Lord Draydrak to save them.

CHAPTER NINE

The ground raced toward them. Obsidian spread his wings wide, slowing their descent and breaking the uncontrolled downward spiral. But the grassy stretch of lawn beside the parking lot still came at them too fast. A crash landing turned into a skid. Anna lost her grip on Obsidian. Instinctively, she tucked into a roll.

Coming to a halt, Anna sprawled on the ground, dazed. Pain radiated from all parts of her body. Blood coated her tongue and ran hot down her face.

'Alive,' she thought, *'I'm alive. Death wouldn't hurt this much.'*

She blinked up at the sky, the sun bright overhead. Groaning, she rolled over and began crawling to Obsidian and Erika. She noted that other members of the base's personnel were engaging the enemy.

The portal? What's happening with the portal?

And what about Obsidian? He still wasn't moving.

Fuck the portal. She crawled the last of the distance to Obsidian.

He'd taken the greatest assault by the spell.

Was he...? Her breath froze in her lungs even as a denial fought to break free.

She touched his shoulder and rolled him over. He moaned in pain. A sound she'd never thought would fill her with joy.

"You're alive, thank fuck!" She hugged him and then glanced over at Erika. As Anna watched, the other woman flopped over and struggled to sit up.

"What happened?" she asked. "How'd I get here?"

"We rescued you."

"T-thanks," Erika slurred as she tried to gain her feet. She failed and landed back on her ass and grabbed her head. She moaned and then looked up, glancing around. "Looks like the enemy is on the run, anyway. Think I'll sit the rest of this battle out."

Taking in the enemy's movements, Anna realized Erika wasn't wrong. The enemy was on the run and retreated through the now open portal spell.

"Why are they running? We just got our asses handed to us." Even as she spoke, Anna marveled as an injured hostile limped to the portal spell and half staggered, half fell through it. They were running scared.

Why?

"Me. They run because of me," came a gruff, growly voice, the tone suggesting the speaker had lost all patience with her and maybe the universe in general.

Anna and Erika both jerked to attention and swiftly looked behind them.

A gargoyle strode toward them. His expression was as thunderous as his earlier words had been. Vast quantities of magic flowed from him, swirling little currents of air as a breeze from the Magic Realm interacted with one in the Mortal Realm. The gargoyle's wings flared out as if in threat, and he sniffed the air, his muzzle scrunching as his lips pulled away from his fangs.

He huffed and shook his head, and the gargoyle, who wasn't a gargoyle at all, stomped the last few paces to Anna's side.

Halting, he towered over them and glowered. "I always forget how much the air of this world stinks, and the scent of warlock does not improve it. Blah."

The demigod—the male half of the Avatar soul— paced around them in a circle. His eyes widened when he took in Obsidian's slumped form, then he swore in what sounded like four different languages. "He called upon Draydrak's magic?"

Anna nodded.

More cursing followed.

"Gregory, please tell me Obsidian is going to be fine." Anna couldn't keep the worry from her voice.

The Avatar huffed in answer and then scooped up

the still stunned Erika. "Sorry, Null, this will not be subtle."

"Wait one min—" Erika's words ended in a squeak as Gregory dragged her over Obsidian's still form like she was a blanket.

"Hurry. Drain the warlock's spell of its magic," the Avatar urged. "It'll be faster than me digging out and eradicating the spell."

"You could have just said as much," Erika muttered as she braced her hands on Obsidian's shoulders and her knees on his thighs, but Anna could already feel as the Null went to work.

Gregory ignored the Null's comment and knelt next to the injured gargoyle, placing one hand on his forehead and the other on the center of Obsidian's chest. "I'll protect his mind and soul from further damage."

"Yep." Erika agreed.

Even though every cell in her body was screaming to help Obsidian somehow, Anna forced her feet to step back, away from the Null. Erika had to be close to her upper limit, and she'd need everything she had left to drain the spell currently chewing into Obsidian's soul.

"I see I'll need to shore up the vessel containing Lord Draydrak's power." Gregory grimaced, his sharp teeth glinting bright against the darkness of his skin. "And reinforce that you two shouldn't—"

Obsidian burst into motion, roaring loud enough

that Anna's eardrums throbbed with a sickening pressure.

"Sleeping beauty is awake!" Erika yelled over Obsidian's roars. "A little help here?"

Anna rushed forward, but Obsidian was faster, and in the next moment, Gregory and Erika were airborne. A powerful force washed around Anna's shields but didn't repel her, as it had her two allies.

"Calm him!" Gregory shouted even as he raced back to Obsidian's side, trying to hold down the struggling gargoyle.

Anna leaped into motion and slammed into Obsidian, using her body weight to help Gregory hold him down.

"Do what you can to calm him," Gregory instructed. "I'll shore up the vessel."

"On it!" She scooted up Obsidian's broad chest, straddling him as she reached for either side of his face. Then she forced him to look directly into her eyes. Hell, it had worked last time. She prayed it worked a second time. "It's me! Calm, my Rasoren. I know you're in pain, but you're not under attack! You must be calm."

He bucked and fought, blinded by pain, but a spark of recognition flashed in his gaze.

"Yes. That's it. Stop resisting!" Anna eased her death grip on his head. "Look at me. Listen to my voice. You're going to be okay. I've got you."

"Anna?" He gritted out her name and then stiffened

and hissed in pain as another wave of power rolled out from him. It wasn't enough to displace her. "It hurts. What's wrong with me?"

"The leader of the hostiles hit us with a spell. You took the brunt. It felt like one of those soul enslaving ones, like the blood witch once used on me."

He nodded but said nothing more as his jaws locked to muffle a scream.

"I'm here. You'll get through this." She dropped one hand from his face to grab his hand. Anna hated feeling useless. "Everything is going to be fine."

'Please don't let me be lying,' Anna whispered silently to God, the Divine Ones, or whatever creator existed and might be listening.

"There!" Erika hissed. "Think I got the little bastard."

Obsidian's head lulled to one side, the terrible tension in his body easing. His eyes drifted until they were half-lidded, as if keeping them open was too much effort.

Gregory leaned closer, sniffing even as he poured another surge of power into Obsidian. Her Rasoren didn't respond to the fresh energy flowing into his body. The Avatar grunted and then nodded and answered Erika's question. "Yes, you were successful."

"Thank God," Erika muttered and rolled onto her back, panting and wiping gore from her hands onto her fatigues. "I'm just going to rest here a bit. Good? Good."

While knowing Erika was likely as exhausted as the rest, Anna knew the Null would live to fight another day. She turned her full attention back to her Rasoren. Physically, under all the blood and gore, he looked fine. But what he'd suffered spiritually...

"Will he be okay?" Anna asked, half-dreading the answer.

"Yes, he will recover. Although you're both insolent cubs for running off to the Mortal Realm after I left explicit instructions..."

"Hey!" Anna gestured wildly around. "All this—I had nothing to do with this! We both just woke up. None of this is our fault. And I'm not a cub!" Anna knew she was rambling, but fuck it. Her head throbbed as if she'd been drinking for hours and had jumped straight to a hangover.

"It was a compulsion," Obsidian wheezed out, sounding nothing like his usual self. "Couldn't fight it...."

Anna scooted closer and patted his shoulder, her hand growing even more smeared with bright red blood. Whatever the fuck they were fighting, at least the blood was from a 'fresh' body. Better than being covered in the rot of the Riven or any of the hundred horrors she'd seen in the blood witch's workshop back in the Battle Goddess's kingdom.

Gregory growled. "Running off like that, you both behaved like cubs, so I shall treat you as such until you can once again prove you are adults," he said, barking the words at them. Then he snorted in frustration. "Cubs! You behaved like little ones waking from a nap, then finding their parents distracted, bolted from your nest to see what trouble you could get into."

"Fine. I'm sorry," Anna rushed out. "It was stupid to leave, but in my defense, I wasn't aware I was about to walk into the middle of a shitstorm." She gestured at Obsidian. "Please, fix this now and lecture me later... Obsidian shouldn't be the one to suffer for my mistake."

'Did I just flippantly order around the Divine Ones' first creation, a being older than the freaking universe? Yes, yes, I did.' It might be stupid and stubborn and foolish of her to challenge him, but this being was also one of her mentors, and she had thought of him as her friend.

"You should see your faces." Gregory laughed and then quieted, his piercing gaze going distant. "Lillian also sends greetings." Another long pause, and then the older gargoyle grinned. "She also sent an image of two bare-assed toddlers running away from their parents."

"Tell her 'Hi' for me," Anna said, her full attention already back on her Rasoren. He was unmoving, out cold. "How bad is it?"

Gregory continued his examination of Obsidian in silence for so long that Anna began fidgeting. Then, realizing what she was doing, she methodically began wiping her hands free of as much of the gore coating them as possible. The action kept her from grabbing and shaking a demigod until he either answered her questions or swatted her like a fly.

At last, he straightened and pushed himself upright. "Physically, he'll recover in a couple of days. But spiritually? That will take longer. The spell was designed to attack and enslave a soul. He bears many wounds of that nature. Under normal circumstances, he'd be stubborn and robust enough to shrug them off. But these are not normal circumstances. He woke up months earlier than he should have, as did you. Your bodies are still undergoing changes needed to host the magic of a demigod long-term. But after seeing what just tried to abduct Erika, I think I know why you woke early. The Battle Goddess's magic must have sensed the warlocks and began to hunt them. Sound about like what happened?"

"Yes," Anna agreed, her gaze still locked worriedly on her Rasoren.

"I thought as much. However, that doesn't mean you had to go along with your new power's demands. You should have told someone of your unease." Gregory held out his hand. "Now, let's fix this mess caused by a youthful error in judgment, shall we?"

Anna looked at his outstretched hand and then gestured at the unconscious Obsidian. "You can fix this fuckup?"

"Yes, Corporal Anna Mackenzie, I can fix this 'fuckup' with a little help from my Sorceress. You are lucky to be hosts to Lord Death's and the Lady of

Battles' magic. Their powers make you and Obsidian harder to kill. Get into all kinds of predicaments? Yes. But die yourself? Not easily. But this world will not like what will happen if you do. So, listen to your mentors next time. And by the Divine Ones! Tell someone if you sense something wrong!"

She drew a breath to bite back that this was all so new. She hadn't even known what she was sensing when she'd first woken. If it was danger or just her new magic messing with her? She certainly didn't have any kind of benchmark to judge what 'normal' was anymore. But venting any of those things would just make her seem like more of a petulant child. She sealed that shit down. Instead, going for humble and apologetic.

"I'm sorry. It won't happen again."

"Sleep now, younglings," he crooned to them both, and Anna found herself drifting, her mind losing its hold on the waking world.

"What...? Wait..." But her thoughts were too difficult to herd into order.

"When you wake," a pleasant and comforting voice rumbled over her head as she felt herself gently lowered to the ground, "you will begin the journey of healing."

"Will we turn to stone again?" Anna asked before sleep claimed her.

"No. But I *should* force that upon you simply for being such a pain in my ass. I was having a very nice vacation with my mate. The first vacation in my existence. Sex. I'm finally allowed to have sex with my beloved whenever we want...."

"Hmm? Sorry?" Anna offered in the way of a sleepy reply.

The demigod, with the eccentric name of Gregory Livingstone given to him by his human-raised soulmate, merely laughed.

"Sleep and fear not. You will wake again all too soon. And considering what the Divine Ones may have planned for you this time, you'd likely prefer to sleep for a hundred years instead. But we don't have the time."

"Fate is being," Anna started, but broke it off to yawn hugely. "... a bitch."

"Fate?" The Avatar clicked his tongue at her. "Strangely, I haven't met such a being. And I know them all."

CHAPTER TEN

"What asshole in a tank ran me down and then reversed back over me for good measure?" Anna muttered, her words coming out as more of a drunken slur than actual words, which kind of destroyed the tough bitch persona she was going for.

Anna blinked open her eyes and peered around. Instincts had her searching for her Rasoren, but it was Private Erika Emerson she spotted first. The Null was standing with her back braced against a wall. Closer at hand were the broad back and massive wings of a gargoyle. Though she knew this one wasn't Obsidian. The shoulders were slightly narrower and his hips, while muscular, weren't as beefy as her Rasoren's.

No gargoyle was quite as big as her gargoyle partner, not even Gregory, Anna mused as she sat up and nearly fell headfirst off the table she was lying on.

"Easy," Erika called, hurrying over to support Anna.

With the Null's help, Anna was able to sit up. The room still spun for a bit, but soon, even that settled. Even if she wasn't a hundred percent, she had bigger concerns. "How's Obsidian?"

"You're barely conscious, and the first question out of your mouth is 'how is Obsidian?' Why doesn't that surprise me?" Erika chuckled and squeezed Anna's arm. "He's as hardheaded as you. He'll be fine. Gregory is still working on him."

"How long have I been out?" Anna noticed she was in a hospital gown and blinked in surprise.

"A little over two days. You were in and out of it for a while. Ate and drank. You even showered once. But you didn't know where you were or what was going on. Gregory said that's normal after the trauma you and Obsidian suffered."

Anna rubbed her temples.

'Yeah. Okay. More weird shit that I'm going to pretend didn't happen,' Anna mused to herself.

Onward and forward. "Obsidian will be okay? That's great news. But what do we know about the purpose of the attack or that Ugly Fucker leader of theirs?"

"They were something called warlocks. Gregory hasn't had time to explain much else. Too busy putting you two back together. We know little else. No idea why they tried to grab me or why they're here or where they came from." Erika shrugged. Her easy-going expression failed to cover her concern completely. "Gregory promises to tell us more once he finishes working on Obsidian. His top priority has been making sure you and your Rasoren didn't go critical mass and destroy the Earth."

"What the hell? Gregory hadn't made it sound anywhere near that bad earlier!"

"Yeah. I think a demigod who has been around since the beginning of time has a different set of benchmarks for disasters than the rest of us. Our fearless political leaders weren't as calm about it as an avatar. Brass got orders from higher up, ordering you and Obsidian to be sent through to the Magic Realm. Gregory nixed that plan, saying it's relatively easy going from a place with a high concentration of magic to one with a lower concentration. Going the other way, say from the mortal to the Magic Realm, is far less pleasant and would likely have killed you both, unleashing the full force of Death and War upon the three realms."

"The fuck you say?"

"Yep. Glad he mentioned that. No more portal travel for you or Obsidian. You're now permanent residents of Earth. At least until you heal fully."

Anna tested her legs, swinging them while she sat on the side of the hospital bed. When she was sure they would support her, she jumped down. There was only a slight weakness, but she soon worked that out. When she was sure she could walk without landing on her face, she moved toward Obsidian, only to stop and glance over her shoulder at Erika before turning her attention back to Gregory, where he was still standing with his head bent, magic flowing from his body as he continued to work on Obsidian.

"Is it safe for me to go over there, or will I be interfering with whatever spell he's working on?"

"Should be fine," Erika said. "I've been here on and off for the past couple of days, sharing some of my stored-up magic from the battle. That didn't cause any issues. I don't think your presence will mess anything up."

With those words of reassurance, Anna made her way over to Obsidian and Gregory.

The Avatar paused in his spell work to nod to Anna. "It's good to see you up and around. Obsidian's healing is a little more involved, but he'll return to his old self in a few days. Maybe a week in this realm."

"A week?"

"Hmm. Yes. His physical injuries weren't the problem," Gregory mused as he continued to lean over Obsidian's still form. "It's the stress on his soul having to cohabitate with Lord Death's power and repair the damage from that warlock's spell. As part of his body's adaption process, this life's memories are now merged with his soul, not just stored in his physical brain. Yours are the same."

"Pardon?"

"I told you your bodies would change as they adapt to hosting this power." Gregory continued like he was explaining something familiar that she should know. "As you grow in power, there will be a point where your physical bodies may transform into a state that is more spiritual than flesh and blood as you prepare to transit to the Spirit Realm at the end of this life. To be ready for that day, your thoughts and memories—your essence—will fuse permanently into your soul so that at the end of this life, when you and Obsidian become one being in the Spirit Realm, that being will have access to both souls' experiences."

"Stop." Anna held out her hand as if that would somehow block his words. "Too much information."

Gregory laughed. "Youngling, fear not. You need not worry about that for thousands of years. You and he will live a long life in these flesh and blood bodies before you journey to the Spirit Realm to achieve the Divine Ones' greatest gift—their reward for your service."

"Still talking. Way too much information before coffee." Anna just shook her head and circled Gregory to get a better view of Obsidian.

Gregory made a face. "I will never understand why you humans love that black, tar-like-tasting substance so much...." He paused his spell work to glance up at Anna. "What *would* you like to talk about?"

"Obsidian and what you meant about his healing

taking a week because of something to do with his memories and soul."

"Ah, yes. His soul took some damage from calling upon Lord Draydrak's power. That was compounded by the warlock's last spell."

"He's lost his memories?"

"No. It's more like a disorganized jumble. I've been putting them back in proper order, but it's time-consuming, delicate work. And my time here is finite. I must return to the Magic Realm soon. Lillian is with child—a djinn child that needs vast amounts of magic to grow and thrive. But before I return home, I need to learn how a group of warlocks came here and what created them...." He paused again, his muzzle scrunching with some unhappy thought. "I would have suspected the blood witch as their creator, but my son killed her, and we found no evidence that she was training an apprentice. But the blood witch *had* been foolish enough to summon a djinn, so there's no guessing what else she might have had dealings with."

"What the fuck is a warlock?"

"Something like a male version of a blood witch. They tend to be much, much less powerful than a blood witch, but they can turn other species into their kind like a vampire. A single warlock can spawn an entire infection of them."

"Less powerful?" Anna couldn't keep the incredulous

tone out of her voice. "Those fuckers were pretty damn powerful."

Gregory's expression darkened further. "I know. That's why after I wake Obsidian, I shall seek clues that may help solve that mystery."

"How can I help?"

Gregory laughed. "Staying out of trouble for the next few years until your bodies have adapted would be a good place to start."

"Hey! Not fair. I had no idea I was walking into a shitstorm!"

Gregory nodded. "My apologies. That *was* a low blow. Whatever happened in this realm under my nose has nothing to do with you and Obsidian. But you can help by staying with your Rasoren and guiding him through the next few days. He's bound to find," the older gargoyle paused and gestured around him before continuing, "current events confusing since he won't remember everything leading up to today."

With a sinking feeling, Anna fully absorbed what Gregory was saying. "How bad is it going to be?"

But even as she asked, she knew it didn't matter. Obsidian, her beloved best friend, was alive, and he'd recover in time.

"I've only organized a little better than three-quarters of his memories, starting with the oldest and working my way forward. I've cordoned off the rest so as not to confuse him unduly. As his mind and soul finish healing over the next few days, the rest of his memories will restore themselves. There will be no long-term damage or memory loss."

"He was twenty-one when we ended up taking the stone nap," Anna muttered to herself, doing the math. "He'll be missing about four years of memories."

"A little less than three years, actually. I'm not counting the eight years he grew in his mother's hamadryad before birth."

"Three years," Anna said, mulling over his words. "Then he'll remember events up until he was eighteen or so. Could be worse."

Anna rested one hand on Obsidian's chest, over his heart, reassured by its steady beat and the solid warmth under her hand.

"We've got this," she whispered to him in her mind, even if he could no longer hear her thoughts.

"Indeed, it could be worse." Gregory snorted humorously, then added, "Considering it's you two, but it will only be for a few days, and then we'll have the Rasoren of the Gargoyle Legion back."

How hard could it be to keep their butts out of trouble for a few days?

Anna felt herself relaxing, the cold core of dread she'd been carrying in her middle since first waking, easing at last.

"There," Gregory said, straightening from where he'd been bent over Obsidian. "He will wake soon. Stay with him. And whatever you do, don't touch your magic."

"I won't leave him again. Promise. But what if our magic isn't interested in listening?"

He placed his large hands on her shoulders. "Your will is strong. I do not doubt that you will adapt and overcome this new weakness. But if it puts your mind at ease, know that several of your and Obsidian's mentors will stay behind to aid you. I have confidence in their ability to help you maintain control. But I must now discover what kind of servant of evil was hiding within the Battle Goddess's domain and has made Earth its new home. Warlocks don't just will themselves into being."

Gregory released her, turned, and made his way toward the door, calling for Private Emerson to join him.

"Is there anything else I should know?" Anna called after them.

"Likely," Gregory tossed over his shoulder and then chuckled. "But the Divine Ones like a soul to learn and grow each lifetime. Even their Avatars. I and your allies will aid you, but ultimately your life and fate are your own."

With that, the male half of the Avatar soul started away but slowed and called over his shoulder, "Under no circumstance are you or he to go anywhere near a portal spell until I say so!"

After that last utterance, he exited the room to begin his hunt.

Anna turned back to Obsidian, where he was still sleeping on the large examination table.

"Guess it's just you and me again." She stepped closer to the table until she could stroke a thumb along his forehead. After a moment, she moved her fingers up into his mane, giving him a good scratch like she'd done when he was a cub seeking reassurance. "Just like old times, eh?"

CHAPTER ELEVEN

*H*ad he been injured? Had the healers dosed him with something beyond the usual herbs to speed his mending? Because Obsidian felt like he'd just emerged from the strangest, most vivid dream of his life, and usually, only the healing herbs had that effect. If it was herbs, he was almost tempted to ask for more so that he could hear Anna's voice again.

It had been almost eleven years since he'd last heard her voice. Now he wanted to go back into that dream, strange though it was, because Anna had been a part of it.

In the dream, he'd concocted a scenario where he was in a future where they had already defeated the Battle Goddess. But that victory was not without cost. They'd been hurt and needed the healing stone sleep.

Waking two years later, they'd encountered a lethal new enemy.

A strange dream indeed.

Yet he'd felt happier than he had in years because he'd convinced himself that Anna was healed and awake in a dream. They were partners once more, a Rasoren and his Kyrsu.

Gods, how he missed that closeness, her friendship, and everything else about her.

He groaned and tossed an arm over his eyes, refusing to wake up. Maybe he could go back to sleep for a time and find Anna in his dreams again. But a warning niggled in the back of his mind, alerting him that something was not as it should be, but at the same time, everything was perfect. Even if it was only a dream.

Anna spoke to him, her voice equal parts firm command and comforting reassurance just like he remembered. Her fingers against his scalp were bliss as they ran soothingly through his mane. He didn't want to move or open his eyes, for this had to be a dream, and if he woke, Anna would be gone, and he missed his best friend too greatly to banish her, even if she was only in his mind.

"I know you're awake," she said, sounding amused. "You can stop pretending to be asleep."

"Dream," he murmured sleepily.

"Nope. Not a dream." Anna's fingers continued to groom his mane.

Not a dream? Hope fluttered in his chest.

"What do you remember?" Dream Anna asked him.

What did he remember? He remembered being in Haven, going to sleep in his home high in a hamadryad after a long day of training. But his senses told him he was no longer in his home.

"How did I get here?" he asked and opened his eyes to find Anna leaning over him. His mind stalled, going blank for several moments, as happiness eclipsed all else. Then at last he formed more words. "Where is here?"

Anna frowned. "You're in the Mortal Realm once again. We have a new enemy that must be defeated, and it has been creating an army of warlocks to serve it. Do you remember none of this?"

"I...," he paused. This time, it was his turn to frown. "You speak of what happened in my dream. But that wasn't real. You can't be real."

"It wasn't a dream," Anna corrected gently.

"You're not a dream?" he asked cautiously, hope blooming in his heart.

"Nope."

He launched upright, clumsily falling off a table. Now on all fours, he glanced around to orient himself, but the room swam. He groaned, fighting past the dizziness to seek out Anna. She was standing next to the table, her expression startled. She halted with one hand reaching for him, as if caught in a moment's indecision. Then her expression shifted to one of concern. She crouched next to him, her gaze full of unquestioning love.

"You must be confused. I'll try to explain." She drew in a deep breath as if to ground herself. "You were injured. Gregory has done what he can to restore your memories, but you're still missing about three years' worth. And the most recent ones may seem disjointed. What do you remember?"

He was only half listening to her words. Other clues were now finally penetrating his befuddled mind.

Inhaling another deep breath, he could taste her essence on his tongue. His breaths came faster. He was in danger of hyperventilating, but he needed more of her scent to prove she was here with him, that she was real. Yes, his senses picked up the soft beat of her heart, the sound of her breaths.

Real.

She was real, not a dream.

"Obsidian," she said his name softly, "are you okay?"

"Yes." The single word was hard to squeeze out. However, he wasn't sure if that was because he was choked with emotion and that single word was all he could manage, or if he'd said the single word to prevent himself from unleashing a torrent of all the things he'd wanted to tell her over the years but couldn't because she'd been deep in the healing stone sleep.

"You're sure?" There was a note of concern in her tone.

"Yes."

'I am now that you're awake.' he thought.

Joy flowed through his soul. Anna was awake at last! Standing on all fours, he held himself in check, barely. A quiver started in his ears and rolled down his neck and spine, traveling to his tail tip. Even so, he waited, practically vibrating with happiness. But humans did not like to be knocked off their feet, he reminded himself. He was an adult now, not a boisterous cub.

He needed to show her that he had been learning discipline and control while she was healing.

He *needed* to show Anna how much he'd grown and matured.

But he *wanted* a hug!

Anna's expression shifted, her usual calm breaking as tears gathered in her eyes, surprising him. She rarely cried. Then even as tears streamed down her face, she laughed with a joy equal to his own. "I can't tell you how happy I am to see you on your feet. Come here and hug me, you great goof."

Anna opened her arms wide. And that's all the encouragement he needed. He leaped at her and they came together with enough force to knock her off her feet. She grunted at the impact, but he curled around her, his wings and tail snapping out to form a protective shield as they tumbled over and hit the ground.

They slammed into chairs and bumped a table hard enough the strange apparatuses covering it rattled, but he paid that little attention, focusing on nuzzling and licking every bit of Anna's exposed skin. He placed gargoyle kisses on her as fast as he could, knowing she'd order him to stop as soon as she got her breath back.

Most humans didn't like the gargoyle way of showing affection. But then again, humans were quite an odd species. He certainly didn't hold it against Anna. However, he took advantage of every opportunity to shower her in affection.

Certainly, this day of all days warranted the extra showing of affection.

Unable to contain his joy that Anna was awake at last, he leaped and danced around her, looking for new angles of attack when she tried to block his muzzle.

"Okay! Enough, you great overgrown puppy! I surrender! You win!" But she continued to laugh even after he flopped his rump down next to her.

As he huffed and panted and his vision grew dark at the edges, he admitted that he might have overdone it. Soon he was slumping forward on his belly as the room spun. Something besides joy finally made itself known— a wrongness.

His tail slowed its playful flicking as another thought occurred to him. He wasn't where he'd fallen asleep last night. He wasn't in his quarters.

"Are you sure this isn't a dream?"

"It's real. Trust me, I still hurt too much for this to

be a dream, and you didn't see the condition we were in when Gregory saved our butts."

At her words, concern had him coming even more alert. They'd been hurt? Injured enough to require an Avatar's attention? Even as he sought the missing memories that would confirm Anna's words, he tried to heave himself back to his feet, to stand upright, but that made the room spin faster. He slumped against a table as his vision blurred more.

"I think you overdid it a little there." Anna braced an arm around his chest to help hold him upright. "Gregory said it would take you a few days to recover your memories here in this realm."

"What happened?"

"I stumbled on a new enemy, just about got my ass handed to me, and then you came to my rescue. It's complicated." She huffed out a deep breath and then asked, "Obsidian, how much do you remember? How old do you think you are?" Anna's gaze sharpened, growing more piercing than before.

"Eighteen summers..." But something about his answer didn't feel right. He cleared his throat nervously as he rubbed his temples.

"Yeah. Gregory said that would happen..."

Then she explained, giving as detailed an explanation as she could, though it was clear she did not fully understand what was going on herself since she'd only been awake a little longer than him, which annoyed his Kyrsu greatly.

But Obsidian had trouble giving the new danger the focus it deserved; his mind kept circling back to other things.

She was his Kyrsu in truth! They had survived to complete the bond!

"I'm the Rasoren of the Gargoyle Legion? We won the war? We're on Earth?" He glanced around, his vision finally working as it should. "Did we really defeat the Battle Goddess?"

"We did."

He breathed out a sigh of relief. That was good, at least. But now that he forced himself to focus on something other than the strange circumstances, he felt the new power deep inside.

The Lord of the Underworld's power.

If he lost control even for a moment....

"Easy," Anna said, as she gripped one of his hands harder. "It will be all right. We regained control during the battle. We didn't kill any innocent people. We've got this."

Just hearing those words fall from her lips helped him regain his composure. It wasn't a surprise that Anna could still calm him even as an adult. Circumstances had conditioned him to trust his fierce human teammate from a far earlier age.

Reluctantly, he released his hold on Anna's hand. "How may I best serve?"

"Rest. Recover."

Now that he was focused on Anna instead of what he was feeling at seeing her again, he glimpsed a haunted look in her eyes. It was gone as quickly as it had come. But he'd seen it. And it could only mean he'd truly given his Kyrsu a fright.

Trying to lighten the mood, he said, "Now that we're back on Earth, I'm going to raid Gran's kitchen the first chance I get."

"Out of everything that's happened, that's what you fixate on?" Anna laughed and then hugged him fiercely once more. He leaned into her, happy for the support.

"So, you think you're up for a snack? I'll see what I can arrange," Anna said, then glanced down at herself. He noticed she was wearing what humans called a hospital gown. He didn't know why such a simple wrap would be called a gown, but he didn't question it.

"Maybe some clothing for me, and then food." As Anna led him from the room, he heard her mutter. "And let's find out what has been going on here for the last two years."

CHAPTER TWELVE

It was beyond strange to be looking at Obsidian, but not the Obsidian she knew, not precisely. But it could have been so much worse. She was just happy fate hadn't screwed them over more. The first time she'd woke from a long-ass healing stone nap was to find her beloved adopted gargoyle brother had gone and grown up.

Shadowlight had been a cub of eight years old when she'd closed her eyes. When she'd opened them again, it was to discover an imposing gargoyle named Obsidian waiting for her. So much had changed between the cub Shadowlight and the twenty-one-year-old Obsidian. It had been like her little brother had died.

He hadn't, and slowly over time, she'd come to recognize bits of Shadowlight in her new gargoyle partner.

She'd come to terms with the change in their partnership. But that time it had still hurt like nothing she'd ever experienced to know Shadowlight was gone. And now, once again, Fate had tossed another obstacle in her path, and she was presently walking alongside the equivalent of an eighteen-year-old Obsidian.

'Fuck, can my life get any more complicated?'

But her inner battle about this additional complication would have to wait. For when they came to the second set of doors, a team of eight soldiers stopped them. She leveled them each with her most fuck-around-and-find-out expression before settling her gaze upon the highest ranked of the bunch. This was when she'd learn if she and Obsidian were still considered valued allies or prisoners.

"Captain," she acknowledged the tall, solidly built, dark-haired man with a nod, then asked the first burning question on her mind. "Are we prisoners?"

While she knew there was no way she'd be allowed to just wander off base, being confined to the base was a much better alternative to being a prisoner. Behind her, she could feel Obsidian's demeanor changing, going from mellow to menacing in less than ten seconds.

"I assure you, the Rasoren and Kyrsu of the Gargoyle Legions are not prisoners," Obsidian growled.

"Easy," she said and reached back to pat his arm. "Let me handle this."

He relaxed marginally, allowing her to lead. Good.

The captain gave Obsidian a hard stare before

turning his attention back to Anna. "No. You're not prisoners," the soldier clarified. He had a heavy southern accent. American then. But interestingly, his uniform was devoid of a flag or any other markers.

He caught the direction of her scrutiny but said nothing.

"Glad to hear we're not prisoners," she added to break the tension.

"No. Not prisoners. Though you will require an escort until you've been deemed no longer a threat."

"Understood." Anna nodded again. She wouldn't trust herself or Obsidian either after that magic showdown two days ago if she were them. Now to see how much leeway they would be granted. "Obsidian is hungry, and I could also use a bite to eat."

"My men and I will take you to the quarters prepared for you and have food brought. Then I am to take you before Generals Tremblay and Hancock." The soldier paused. "I'm Captain Newman. Follow me."

As she and Obsidian followed the captain, his men took up positions around them. But Anna ignored the other soldiers, dwelling on the captain's earlier words.

Hmm. Two generals?

Twice the fun. She knew Tremblay, but Hancock was new.

"Hancock?" She inquired.

"Four-star General newly assigned to the base. American. Part of the command council."

It sounded like a few things had changed in the two years she'd been napping. Not a surprise, although she hoped the information wouldn't just be going one way. She'd like a better understanding of what had happened here on Earth over the last two years. She'd known that when the Battle Goddess's lines had broken, hundreds of her warriors had escaped through the Earth portal, following the firedrake captain and much of his battalion as they fled from the elemental dragon. Was that when the warlocks had invaded the Mortal Realm? Or had they been created here after?

Lost in her thoughts, she hadn't realized the captain had dropped back a step to walk beside her until Obsidian growled. Her gargoyle partner dropped to all fours and shoved in between her and the captain.

Newman looked startled for a moment, but swiftly put a few feet between them, his gaze narrowing. He'd likely been about to tell her something, but her partner was feeling overly protective or possessive or... something. But whatever the case, it wasn't normal.

The other soldiers bristled, hands bringing weapons up. Obsidian growled again They shouted orders at the gargoyle. The growls escalated.

'Fuck! Me!' Anna cursed in her head.

Blade-tipped tail twitching in threat, Obsidian glowered at the surrounding soldiers, refusing to back down from his battle stance. Still on all fours, he prowled around her, his blade-tipped tail lashing from side to side over his back.

Realizing Obsidian was feeding on her own unease and still out of sorts because of all that had happened, she knew it was up to her to calm him. Placing a hand on his head, between his horns, she attempted to touch his thoughts.

"If you can hear me, don't threaten the soldiers. They are just doing their jobs. The captain wasn't being threatening. He wasn't challenging your authority by taking your place at my side. And after the attack on the base, they are all on edge. Some will be grieving. They sure as shit saw some of their friends die in the attack. We don't need any more trouble."

She wasn't sure if he heard her, but then his thoughts brushed hers, warmth and affection flowing across her mind, followed by embarrassment.

"I can hear you." He paused. *"Barely. It's very weak. I doubt I would if we weren't touching. Please forgive me for my foolish behavior."*

The bit of tension plaguing her since she first woke to learn her gargoyle magic was still dormant, slowly eased. Perhaps it would return sooner rather than later. She had a feeling they were going to need every advantage to defeat this new enemy. *"I'm glad. Now I need to hear your promise not to instigate farther."*

He huffed out a sound that was part sigh and part growl, both tinged with displeasure. *"You have my word."*

Anna had a sinking feeling that as much as this

younger Obsidian looked and sounded like her Obsidian, he wasn't as emotionally mature. He hadn't yet fully developed the deep well of patience she'd come to expect from the Rasoren of the Gargoyle Legion.

But she didn't voice any of her concerns and silently followed as they were led through the complex and up several floors—Anna only then realizing they had been below ground. Not that she was expecting more trouble, but Anna memorized the number of turns, just in case. The last thing she needed was to get lost if she and Obsidian needed an escape route if things went south.

'What am I thinking?' Things absolutely could *not* go south. They had nowhere else to go. Gregory said they couldn't leave Earth until after they'd recovered and learned to master their new powers—something he'd said might take years.

Years.

Fuck.

So, she and Obsidian would have to smooth over any ruffled feathers and make themselves invaluable, which shouldn't be too hard. Even if they weren't allowed to take a direct part in any of the hunts to round up these new warlock enemies, they had experience with the soldiers from the Battle Goddess's kingdom. She and her Rasoren were experienced with how they thought, their training, and their skill levels. With Obsidian's aid, she could help in a supporting role, even if she couldn't currently shift to gargoyle form.

While Anna had been mulling over what their future might look like, the captain used his keycard to access another hallway. This one led to another door, which opened onto a large living area, which was presently unoccupied, though it had a well-lived look to it. Three couches and several chairs arranged in a semicircle around the entertainment center dominated the large room.

Off to the right side of the entertainment area was a homemade bar. Next to it was a small kitchen area with a fridge and stove. Along that same wall was a door marked with the word ladies—a bathroom. Glancing to the opposite wall, she spotted another door marked with the word 'Trolls' in big, bold letters. Anna snorted.

"Let me guess. Jason lives here?"

"The one and only." The captain smirked. "How did you guess?"

"Just a hunch," Anna muttered and turned her attention to the two hallways that flanked the massive television. They were dark, but she could just make out the frame of a door. Living quarters?

"You and your..." the captain sized up Obsidian with a guarded look, "Gargoyle partner will live here with the other clan and coven members." With a jerk of his chin, the captain indicated the nearest hall. "Ladies on the left. Gents on the right. There are a few spare rooms on each side."

He led them down the 'ladies' side first. "Corporal Mackenzie, you can have your pick of the spares."

Anna pushed open the first door he'd indicated. A small, tidy room greeted her gaze. A dresser and desk occupied one side, a bed on the other. At least the room had a window that let in some natural light. No bars or surveillance that she could spot at first glance. It could be worse.

But what held her interest more than the room was the mention of the clan and the coven, but she followed the captain as he continued their tour.

While he led them farther down the hallway until it turned a corner and connected with the men's side, Anna speculated about whom all might live here.

So, Jason, the prankster grandson of the local witch coven's leader, a woman known to many as Gran, lived here. Anna wondered if she'd be rubbing elbows with other coven members as well. Of the local coven, she'd only met Gran, Jason, and Lillian. She rather hoped a bunch of strangers didn't live here. Jason was bad enough.

As for the clan, the term the fae used to encompass all the many fae species, she'd seen the pooka and Greenborrow during the battle. She'd struck up a friendship with the ancient and lethal leshii when Obsidian had been a cub. Anna got on well enough with Greenborrow, even though he was brash and enjoyed a little fun at other people's expense.

As for the yellow-eyed pooka pony, with his little black heart that was at least ten shades darker than his ebony coat, he certainly made a better ally than an enemy, but she couldn't imagine him as a roommate. Especially if it involved living in close quarters with Jason or the leshii. Though all three of them had been united by a common friend, a smart-mouthed unicorn killed on the battlefield. Perhaps that shared grief had forged a peace between them?

Anna realized she and Obsidian might not be welcomed with open arms, being seen as invaders into this small community, especially now that she was a vessel for the Battle Goddess's power and Obsidian could wield the power of death.

Nothing like being host to the powers of an evil demigoddess to set a girl apart.

War and Death certainly wouldn't make for comfortable roommates. Anna wouldn't be surprised if they were greeted by, if not open hostility, then a less than warm welcome home.

With another internal snort, she realized that of all the fae, only the pooka was likely to offer them friendship. His nature always drew him to the darker side of power. But maybe she was making a mountain out of a molehill?

Everyone might be too busy to do anything more than crash here for a few hours after hunting down and eradicating warlocks. Besides, she probably didn't need to worry about the black-hearted fae pony as a room-mate. He preferred to stay in his equine form.

"This will be your gargoyle partner's room," the captain said, drawing Anna back to the tour. He pushed open the door of the room he'd stopped at. Once he flicked on the light, Anna got a look inside.

It was surprisingly spacious, with a good amount of floor space. While it had a dresser like the other room, that was where the similarities ended. The desk was much taller and wider than one a human would use—more the height of a standing desk. Instead of a chair, a padded bench sat tucked under the desk. Not surprising, since gargoyles with their wings and tails didn't fit in chairs. But the room's most noticeable difference was the lack of a traditional bed. Instead, the center of the floor was concave, the depression filled with pillows and blankets, making a perfect nest like gargoyles preferred.

"This shall be my assigned room?" Obsidian asked. His tone was devoid of emotion and any clues as to what he was thinking, but Anna could read him well enough to know he was unhappy about something. But the captain answered before she could get to the bottom of it.

"Yes. Unfortunately, this is the only vacant one of the three gargoyle suites on this level," the captain said with a glance at Obsidian before turning his attention to Anna. "But I was briefed that you aren't currently able to shapeshift and that a regular room would suffice for you, Corporal."

"The other room is fine," Anna agreed. She'd been about to ask about the other gargoyles, but Obsidian beat her to it.

"From your statement, I can assume other gargoyles live here?" His tone was a low, rich rumble. "Their names?"

The captain frowned and hesitated a moment before answering. "I'm not cleared to tell you more until you have the proper security clearances."

Captain Newman looked apologetic, likely because he thought she and Obsidian already knew much higher-level shit than he was privy to.

"Am I not the Rasoren of the Gargoyle Legion?" Beside her, Obsidian stood with his tail tip flicking with agitation as he leaned almost aggressively toward the captain. Her Rasoren was practically vibrating. And not with happiness. His voice nearly a sharp crack, he asked, "How exactly am I *not* cleared for information regarding the gargoyles under my command?"

His sudden outburst was out of character. Neither the cub Shadowlight nor the Rasoren of the Gargoyle Legion had had a temper. Between his earlier outburst and now this one, she knew something definitely wasn't right. As soon as they had a moment alone, she'd start digging to find out if what had him out of sorts was something more than just him having difficulty adjusting to his new powers.

She placed a hand on his arm and silently told him to be calm. She had done this a hundred times when they'd been held captive within the Battle Goddess's kingdom, silently telling the kid not to reveal so much of his emotions to the enemy. And now, she reminded the eighteen-year-old Obsidian in the same manner.

Not that they were among enemies here, but it was hard not to react in the same way when she didn't yet know how well they'd be received with their new and deadly powers.

"It is not that you don't have clearance regarding the legion members," the captain continued. "It's that *I* don't have clearance for those details."

Obsidian rocked back and scrunched his nose in confusion, clearly baffled by human military bureaucracy.

Welcome to the shitshow, Anna mused silently and then decided it was time she grabbed the reins of the conversation and steered it into safer waters.

"I understand," Anna injected before her gargoyle partner started in on the captain again. It wasn't the captain's fault that he couldn't tell them more. He'd likely been more forthcoming than he could have been.

The captain nodded once, never taking his eyes off Obsidian. Nor did he back down, even though the gargoyle was now standing on two legs and towered over him. Anna's admiration of the soldier crept up by another couple of degrees. It took an enormous set of balls to stand toe to toe to the wall of muscle, fangs, and talons that was her Rasoren.

Smirking, she turned from the two males and then tossed over her shoulder, "Rooms look fine. But didn't you lure us here with the promise of food?"

Anna might not be able to shift to gargoyle form, but she seemed to have regained the legendary gargoyle appetite and was more than ready to eat her first square meal in years.

"Food will be here shortly," Captain Newman soothed.

The captain was true to his word and food arrived in record time. Though to the captain it may have felt like an eternity, with Obsidian's unwavering stare focused on him the entire time they waited for the food.

Now Anna sat on one end of an enormous couch with Obsidian occupying the other end, an array of food stretched out between them. They focused on their food and ignored the six soldiers where they stood along the walls.

While they ate in silence, the captain had left to go report to his superiors, but the rest of his men stayed behind. With the onlookers, Anna didn't want to touch on what had upset Obsidian about his new accommodations. They'd slept in worse places. Frowning, she knew she'd have to leave that conversation until later. She hoped the food would pacify him until she could address whatever was bothering him.

Not wanting to waste time, Anna had already polished off two sandwiches, an orange, and was working on an apple while eyeing the wedge of cheesecake.

Cherry cheesecake.

Glorious fucking cherry cheesecake!

Maybe fate didn't hate her as much as she'd thought?

But just then, the captain returned and had a word with one of his men, and she knew Fate had only teased her with the cheesecake before snatching it away.

The captain halted beside them. "You and the gargoyle are required to report for your briefing now."

Yep. Fucking well should have started with the cheesecake, Anna thought darkly. After one last longing look at the decadent dessert, she put on a pleasant expression and nodded to the captain. "Understood."

As they rose to follow the captain, Anna didn't miss how swiftly Obsidian snatched up his piece of cheesecake and shoved it into his mouth whole. She grinned and shook her head at her Rasoren, who looked mildly embarrassed to be caught stuffing his face.

CHAPTER THIRTEEN

The briefing wasn't as long as she'd feared for two big reasons. First, the powers that be were too concerned about the new enemy to focus much of their attention on Anna and Obsidian, now that they knew Gregory had stabilized and strengthened their vessels. And second, a certain Avatar possessing God-like power suggested it would be a bad idea to stress out the new hosts of War and Death.

After only an hour, she and Obsidian found themselves released, their hands full of reading material and new security badges to match their new security clearances. She'd immediately noticed the slight glow of magic around the badges. These were not the run-of-the-mill sort. Which matched what she'd gathered about the base so far.

During the briefing, she'd discovered that her father was halfway around the world, helping to introduce the new Australian prime minister to the existence of magic. With her dad was Journeyman Oath, one of Obsidian's close friends, and Vivian, the witch known to most as Gran, who'd also raised Obsidian's sister, Lillian. They'd also learned that Obsidian's sire, Stalks the Darkness had been injured on a mission and was presently resting as a stone statue in the Magic Realm under Lillian's watchful eye. He was expected to make a full recovery in the coming weeks.

Anna had also discovered that her new home for the foreseeable future was called Special Forces Northern Network Base - 1. Or just SFNNB-1.

Like much of the base, their new keycards had been imbibed with magic as an added layer of protection. For all the good it had done the base during the attack. But then again, most of the base had survived with only moderate damage. All except the armory and the airfield. The armory was now nothing more than a not-so-small crater, but a secondary arsenal was already being planned out and vast quantities of new supplies had already arrived. They were being housed in a repurposed building.

On their drive back to the barracks, she got a look at some of the damage. It had only been two days, but cleanup and repairs were already underway. It was impressive how fast work crews could get things done when there was no choice and all of Earth's very existence was once again in question. And with this being the location of the permanent outgoing portal, they didn't have the luxury of relocating to another base of operations.

As Anna and Obsidian were escorted back to their living quarters, she mulled over that she knew little more than before the meeting. Mind you, she had a shit-ton of classified reports to read that were supposed to get them up to speed on the last two years.

When they reached their quarters, Captain Newman held the door open for them. "Welcome to Not-Normal, Corporal Mackenzie and Rasoren Obsidian."

"The base has been named Not-Normal?" Anna asked with a chuckle.

Captain Newman snorted. "SFNNB-1's full unofficial name is Shit's Fucking Not Normal, but that's a bit of a mouthful, so Not-Normal stuck. If you need anything, don't hesitate to ask. We are all familiar with strange requests here at Not-Normal-One."

As he turned to leave, Anna laughed harder but managed to spit out her question. "Wait? Since there is a NN-1, I assume there are others?"

"There are sixteen spread across the Northern Hemisphere and sixteen in the Southern Hemisphere."

"And just what have the Southern Hemisphere bases been christened?"

Captain Newman's grin spread wider. "SFSNB.

Special Forces Southern Network Bases have been lovingly renamed Shit's Fucking Still Not Normal, which got shortened to just Still-Not-Normal."

CHAPTER FOURTEEN

The urge to pace was growing. Once again, Anna found herself in the clan and coven's communal living quarters. This time she was sitting in front of the big screen television with a cup of tea in her hand and snuggled up in a blanket. While she loved to kick back with a thick blanket, a hot cup of something, and could binge TV shows with the best of them—none of the above was even remotely attractive to her right now when everyone else was out hunting some new variety of enemy, and she was stuck under house arrest.

For his part, Obsidian didn't betray the turmoil he must be feeling. He sat on the sofa, one arm resting on the armrest, the other braced against the back with the largest mug she could find gripped in that hand. The mug was still ridiculously small. So was the sofa even though it was massive by human standards. Its back was short enough, or her Rasoren was just so big, he could sit comfortably with his wings spilling over the back.

In a word—the very picture of relaxed. But she knew it had to be a lie.

While she didn't know where to start, she sensed Obsidian needed time to get to know her.

And since Gregory hadn't had time to stick around and answer questions, Anna would bet her Rasoren had many. Unlike the undisciplined—though loveable—Shadowlight, Obsidian didn't voice his questions or concerns out loud. While she didn't know if that was because he was more disciplined or if he was just uncertain of his footing in this new world he found himself in, she could answer some of his many questions.

After all, if his original memories ended at eighteen or a little older, then as far as he was concerned, it had been over eleven years since he'd last been on Earth. And much of his limited time on Earth had been spent with other of the fae, like Greenborrow and the pooka.

But out of everyone, she was the one best able to understand what he was going through. After all, the first time she'd woken up from a healing stone nap, it was to meet the adult Obsidian. He'd been twenty-one at that point and well into his training as a Rasoren. That time, he'd been the stranger. Now their situations were reversed, and he was the one trying to piece everything together.

But whatever was causing the awkward silence,

whether it was his discipline or his uncertainty, partway through their first cup of tea, he began to unbend and asked her questions. She filled him in on everything that had happened up until now.

"This is all so strange," he said at last.

"Yep. Yep, it is. But what about our lives *hasn't* been strange?"

"That is true," he agreed and seemed to relax, even chuckling softly before turning serious once more.

"Go on," she urged. "Ask whatever questions you have."

"We were true Rasoren and Kyrsu to each other? The link was formed?"

He was talking about the mental link that had allowed them to think and move as one. A link that forged them into the ultimate fighting unit.

"Yes," she said, seeing no reason not to tell him. "But when we became vessels for the demigod twins' powers, it shattered that bond. Gregory says it will return. However, I have seen little evidence of that yet. It might take months or years."

"Ah." Obsidian's ears flicked to half-mast before snapping upright again when he realized her attention was on them, reading his tells.

"Go on," Anna urged. "Ask another question. Anything you want."

"What was it like?" His tone was very disciplined,

but she could still sense a wellspring of curiosity behind the words.

"Our bond was the strongest Rasoren and Kyrsu link the gargoyle elders had ever seen. Master Maradryn once mentioned she thought it may have been because I was the second female gargoyle ever to exist, and you were the one to have converted me. But we later learned the Divine Ones' plan is for us to grow into a being like the Avatar, our two souls growing into one in some distant future time."

Her last words left Obsidian speechless for long moments, but he eventually overcame his shock. "A second avatar pair?" he asked in a marveling tone.

"So we were told." Anna shrugged, still unable to process that information herself. It all seemed crazy still. "But whatever the reason, our bond was a powerful gift, doubling our magical strength and our physical abilities. We could share power, making us stronger still. And that same bond allowed our two minds to process everything we saw and sensed on the battlefield at twice the speed. It left no room for doubt or fear. We became an unparalleled fighting unit during those times."

"Then it sounds like we grew into the great potential Adept Thayn once told me we would. I am glad that is how it all unfolded." He halted and glanced off into one corner of the room with a faraway look. Then he closed his eyes and sighed a long, almost shaky breath. "I always feared that the Battle Goddess had laid some bit of dark spell work upon my soul, and one day it would awaken, and I would...." He fell silent.

"There is nothing evil in your soul. Never fear that." Anna reached out and placed her hand on his arm.

"That is a relief. But is there more you can tell me?" He made a helpless gesture with his hands. "I feel... so...."

His frustration became apparent, and Anna wanted to hug him, but she held back, uncertain if the eighteen-year-old version of Obsidian would think she thought him weak. She continued with words. Words were usually safer than actions, and she didn't want to fuck this up.

"You feel so hollow? Like something is missing. Cored out and trimmed away like you're somehow less now, even though you're a vessel to a demigod's power?"

He nodded without looking at her, then added in a rush, "How did you know?"

"Because I felt the same upon first waking—still feel the same if I'm honest with myself. We saved the realms but lost some part of ourselves."

He rocked forward slightly and then back, his wings unfurling a fraction before he mastered whatever powerful emotion he was feeling. He cleared his throat and looked her in the eye.

"Thank you for telling me this." He paused and tilted his head to the side. "For you, this must have been a painful reminder of what we've lost."

Anna glanced down at her half-empty teacup, his words hitting the truth. It wasn't just that they'd lost their Rasoren-Kyrsu link.

This new Obsidian?

He seemed different. She couldn't place her finger on it precisely.

More intense, focused, somehow colder. He stirred an uneasy feeling within her, and she wondered if becoming host to Lord Death's power was changing her Rasoren in some way she didn't understand.

But it wasn't like she could ask him. He didn't remember, so he wouldn't be able to confirm or deny her concerns.

And what about her?

Was the Battle Goddess's power changing her?

Anna shuddered at the thought.

He searched their surroundings for a time and then broke the awkward silence. "Tell me more about the bond we shared as Rasoren and Kyrsu."

This time, his tone gave nothing away. But perhaps talking was the answer. Maybe they just needed to get reacquainted, like the first time she'd awakened from a stone nap to find thirteen years had gone by.

"There was so much more to the bond than just making us better fighters," Anna began. "I'm not sure I can explain it, but I'll try."

"Thank you." Warmth entered his voice at last.

She glanced sidelong at him to find him watching her

once again. But when he was caught staring, he swiftly looked away, his spine going ramrod straight once more and his wings held so tensely they quivered with each breath.

Jeez, someone was uptight.

She almost smiled, but she'd never laugh at him, not after once having been in his position and needing him to answer her many questions, a few of which had been somewhat awkward.

"Off the battlefield was when the bond showcased its true gifts—unconditional love and acceptance. We knew each other's every joy, pain, and heartache, every minor flaw and uncharitable thought. And in knowing them, we accepted them for what they were and forgave each other, but most importantly, we forgave ourselves. Our past mistakes. All the stupid things that happen along the road of life, all the pain, all the horrible things that can befall a person—with our bond and the unconditional acceptance it allowed, we learned to forgive ourselves. We learned to let go hurtful things that haunted us."

Anna fell silent, her throat too tight to continue. She hadn't been lying when she said she missed their unique bond. She just hadn't realized how much she'd missed it until now, with this new Obsidian sitting next to her.

A large, warm hand with fingers ending in three-inch-long talons settled over her right hand and gave it a gentle squeeze.

"It sounded beautiful." He was looking at her once again; this time, he didn't look away.

"It was." She inhaled sharply and then let it out slowly, striving for calm but continued to feel uptight.

Anna noticed Obsidian's tail swaying back and forth restlessly. Seeing her notice, he glowered at the betraying limb and coiled it around his waist. The blade-tipped end came to rest between them on the couch. The tip still twitched, but he seemed—not exactly calmer—but more determined.

"You told me to ask any question," he said slowly, then added, "and you would answer truthfully."

"Of course. We've never intentionally kept secrets from each other—or, at least, we always eventually got around to divulging them."

"Good. Because I was wondering... that is..." he paused, and the silence stretched again.

"Go on."

"I mean, were we..." He cleared his throat, then broke her gaze. "Gods. This is more awkward to ask out loud than when it was just a thought in my head."

A tingle of warning raced down Anna's spine. She was sure she knew what he was going to ask, and she didn't want to open that can of worms today. But she had promised him she'd freely answer his questions, so if he screwed up the nerve to ask, she was obliged to answer.

He rumbled out a curse in an ancient tongue and

then met her gaze squarely. "My future self and you. Are we mates? I mean, do we become mates in the future? Uh, the past. I mean—"

Anna took pity on him and answered. "You mean to ask, are we mates, and you just don't remember because those memories haven't been restored yet?"

"Yes," he said, sounding pained. "That."

"I'm glad Gregory could restore as many of your memories as he did, and it's Obsidian and not Shadowlight I'm having this conversation with. Fuck. I feel like a pedophile or a cougar or something just thinking about having to have this conversation with eighteen-year-old you."

"I'm an adult." He grunted, then added, "What's a pedophile?"

"A disgusting subhuman creature. They prey on children. This has nothing to do with that. You're allowed to have questions, and I promised to answer. And the answer to your question is no. We're not mates."

He glanced down at his hands and then away. "You did not find me worthy then?"

"What?" Anna shook her head and then grabbed his hand, threading her much smaller fingers through his. "No. It wasn't anything like that. You grew up to be a wonderful Rasoren and my dear friend. It was just too complicated. That's all. We gave ourselves more time before crossing that bridge. With the bond, we never really knew if what we felt was natural or the product of the link."

"Ah." He said nothing else, but she could still sense his self-doubts. And that was not something he needed right now.

"I..." She cleared her throat and went for it. "I had a lot of emotional baggage to work through, and you were vital in helping me find healing. Before I met you, I had gone through a difficult time. I was even once engaged but broke it off."

"Engaged?"

"A human tradition. It's something two humans do when they intend to wed. A wedding is when two people decide to mate for life, or at least that's the general idea."

Obsidian's intense gaze focused on her, and she thought she'd rendered him speechless a second time today, but he finally responded.

"When I was a cub and converted you, did my actions lead to you breaking this engagement off?"

"What? No. No, of course not," Anna was quick to reassure him. "It was over long before I met you."

"Did you wish to talk about it?"

"I'd rather not. That first telling was painful enough. If you wouldn't mind waiting until the rest of your memories return. It will only be a few days, according to Gregory."

"I understand." His voice was a low rumble, and he

turned their hands over and covered hers with both of his. "And I would never willingly cause my Kyrsu pain."

"I know. And as for the rest, after I woke from my thirteen-year stone nap to find Shadowlight had gone and grown up, it took me a little while to get reacquainted with the older version of you. And since I'd thought of Shadowlight as my little brother, it was... it was just...."

"Painfully awkward?" He supplied for her. At his words, some of the tension in his body eased, his wings relaxing for the first time.

"Yes," she agreed on a soft exhalation, then started laughing. "Our first meeting after I woke up from my thirteen year stone nap was.... memorable."

He didn't press her for more. He was letting her off, she realized. Yet it felt like a cheat, not trying to explain it all better. "There were complications other than just the link's influence. For one, I only had a few short weeks to grow familiar with adult you, and much of our time was taken up by training. But our friendship and our Rasoren-Kyrsu link brought us closer together than many mated couples ever experience. Thayn and Lord Draydrak said our souls were linked." Anna leaned closer and bumped shoulders with him. "You need never fear you were unacceptable to me."

His tail uncoiled from around his waist and dropped to the floor in front of the sofa, relaxing once more.

Anna turned her head, pretending to drink from her tea but was scoping out his tail.

Yep. The blade-tipped end was relaxed, indicating a much more mellow mood.

Good. She didn't want him thinking she'd found him lacking when it had been her hang-ups that caused the tension between them.

They were silent for a time, but it lacked the earlier tension.

Now to keep it that way.

Anna finally decided the night called for a bit of television and snacks.

He'd liked when she'd read Pride and Prejudice to him as a kid, and a quick scroll through the streaming services found an old Pride and Prejudice miniseries her mom used to watch. A little nostalgia was just the thing to make her Rasoren feel more at home here.

CHAPTER FIFTEEN

"Lord help me, she cackles like a hen," Anna muttered, waving her bowl of popcorn at the screen. "Hell, that woman gives chickens a bad name."

"I like the rest of the actors. I think they've done a fine—" Obsidian snapped his teeth together and sat straight.

Anna immediately looked for anything she could use as a weapon even as she asked him, "What do you sense?"

"Magic," he breathed, his eyes drifting closed, and she felt his magic flow across her skin as he worked to pinpoint the source. "It's an incoming portal."

Anna leaped over the back of the couch and ran to the door, which she nearly ripped off its hinges. As she'd expected and hoped, there were still guards outside.

"You," she shouted at the nearest one. "Get on your radio and call in an incoming attack. We've got a portal forming in front of the fucking TV."

With that, she darted back inside, unwilling to leave Obsidian to face whatever was on the other side of the portal by himself. The soldiers were fast on her heels. But once back inside, she cursed she hadn't grabbed a weapon from one of the other soldiers.

"Give me a sidearm!"

A blond-haired Master Corporal tossed his piece to her. She snatched it out of the air and the magazine next. Then she cursed that they didn't have any weapons a gargoyle could use. She didn't want Obsidian using his magic again so soon. It sure as shit hadn't gone so well last time.

She was already back beside Obsidian, and they put the kitchenette at their backs to give the soldiers a direct line of sight to the forming portal.

Casting an eye over the surface of the small kitchen island and not seeing what she was hunting for, she cursed softly.

Who the fuck did not have a block of knives sitting on their counter?

The other soldiers took up positions around the room.

In the seconds she'd been hunting for another weapon, Obsidian had moved, taking up a defensive position between her and the portal.

She was having none of that and stepped up beside him, shoulder to shoulder, with her sidearm trained on the portal.

Even now, Anna could make out the subtle currents of magic coalescing in the air in front of the screen. The portal's power blew outward violently, unstable in appearance for several seconds, but then the tremendous currents of magic were sucked back toward the center of the vortex, dragging papers and pillows and blankets along with it.

"Just me, or is that one hell of an unstable portal?"

"Not unstable," Obsidian murmured, as if he feared to speak louder and possibly draw the power's attention. "Just very powerful and built quickly. I think it's a portal from the Magic Realm."

A moment later, the portal's magic calmed, the fast-moving currents circling the outer edge slowing as she watched. Before she knew what he was doing, Obsidian was leaping forward, effectively fouling any shot the soldiers had at whatever might come through that portal.

"Obsidian, get out of the way!"

But it was too late.

The mirror-like center of the portal vanished, showing the view to another place. Or, more likely, another land.

"It's Lillian," Obsidian called. "Weapons down."

Anna raced up to join him, still wanting to box his

ears for leaping forward before he could have known for sure that it was his older sister on the other side of the portal.

But he was correct. There was a very concerned and agitated-looking Lillian. She was standing with one hand resting against her rounded belly, heavy with child, and the other hand braced against the trunk of a giant tree.

"What's wrong?" Anna barked out before the other woman could.

"I can't feel Gregory!" Lillian shouted and then modulated her voice. "He had been mentally linked with me while hunting this new enemy. He and the Null were on their trail. Then he just vanished. Anna, I cannot sense my other half!"

Lillian's words struck cold dread in Anna's heart.

A trap. It had to be another trap.

But what could trap an Avatar—a being so ancient and powerful, it predated the entire fucking universe?

Anna turned to one soldier behind them, where he stood still at the ready. "You. Get on that radio and find out where Gregory and Corporal Erika Emerson were scouting. They've found something and they need our help."

"There's no time for that," Lillian shouted.

In the next moment, the hamadryad shifted, its branches quaking, and then a bough reached through the portal. Anna jumped back in surprise.

Raw power spiraled up from the tree's roots to spin

around the trunk in a growing energy vortex. Then, with no warning, a lance of pure spirit magic raced down the bough, leaped through the portal, and slammed into the wall behind Anna.

Anna's gaze followed its trajectory, expecting to see an enemy jumping out of the shadows to attack. But there was only a mundane wall. After a moment, Anna realized the power hadn't harmed the wall, instead crawling across it and forming itself into a familiar shape.

A second portal spell?

"That will drop you close to the last place I sensed Gregory. Go," Lillian ordered. "You need to help them. Gregory isn't yet fully recovered from the war. And Erika isn't yet anywhere near a fully mature null. Whatever Gregory was hunting is far more powerful than anyone guessed."

Anna swore in her head. "Gregory told us not to go through a portal. World ending shit could happen."

Lillian's brows scrunched, but then she looked to her hamadryad tree as if communicating with it in some silent fashion, which she likely was. After a moment, the other woman looked up again, directly at Anna and Obsidian.

"The hamadryad Sorceress agrees with my mate's assessment. It's too dangerous for either of you to travel through a portal to the Magic Realm. But Gregory and Erika are still on Earth. For now. Traveling through my portal will not harm you. The Mother's Sorceress has given me her reassurance."

Anna's eyes widened. Unless Lillian was talking about herself in the third person, that meant Lillian's soul, the female half of the Avatar soul, was currently residing in Lillian's hamadryad tree. Another little detail Anna wasn't aware of.

'Really need to read more of those briefing reports,' Anna mused.

But there was no time to worry.

And she trusted the Sorceress.

If the enemy got their hands on the male half of the Avatars or the most potent null ever to have existed, Anna didn't want to hedge a bet on what the enemy would do with all that power, but it wouldn't be anything good for Earth or any of the three realms.

"Anna," Lillian shouted across the distance between worlds, "Use the Battle Goddess's magic to defeat this enemy, but do not let Obsidian call upon Death's. That power is too dangerous to use untrained."

Anna nodded and then clapped a hand on Obsidian's arm. "You hear that. If you use your death magic, we might all die. Got that?"

"Indeed."

Then she glanced back at the soldiers. More came racing in from out in the hall at that moment.

"Boys. On my six if you love Earth." Anna ran toward the Sorceress's second portal.

Obsidian, running on all fours, caught up to her in two strides. They hit the portal at the same time.

Once again, she reflected that fate had her running into battle without proper gear.

'Fucking need to get my game on.'

Unlike the first time she crossed a portal just days ago, this trip didn't land her in the middle of a silent compound devoid of life. This portal dumped her in the middle of a fucking firefight. "For fuck's sake! Obsidian, to me!"

Her gargoyle partner was just as surprised to jump into the middle of a fight, but they'd both been trained in the Gargoyle Legion. They knew how to fight as a team. He galloped back to her side, offering her his back.

Anna leaped upon him, and together she and her gargoyle mount darted across the wide field and toward what looked like an abandoned warehouse. The tall grass hid some of the bodies, but Obsidian leaped and darted around anything in his path, cutting across the field at a ninety-degree angle to get them out of the line of fire as swiftly as possible.

"Remind me to curse out your sister next time I see her!"

"She couldn't have known she was dropping us in the middle of a battle," Obsidian answered as bullets and RPGs whizzed past them. Spears of enemy magic and volleys of fireballs arched through the air, but nothing hit them.

"Are you able to use your shadow magic?"

His large, deer like ears poked out of his thick mane, and he gave her a sharp nod. "I'm recovered enough for that."

"Good. We're going to need it."

Obsidian tore across the meadow, heading for a line of trees halfway to the abandoned warehouse while Anna clung to his back. The tree trunks and underbrush provided cover. But perhaps there was something Anna could do to help.

Closing her eyes, she reached deep, calling to that magic that had been so eager to overpower her before Gregory had repaired her vessel. She hadn't felt it so much as stir since she'd awakened from her healing, but now it awoke and rushed outward just as eagerly as she remembered. It swiftly homed in on the nearest enemy.

"Let's not scramble my brain like what happened to Obsidian's last time," she told the magic. *"Gregory might not have enough power to put us back together. Hell, he might be in such*

awful shape, it will be us trying to fix him. So don't get us killed."

Her new magic seemed to almost nod in agreement.

Too fucking weird.

But there was no time to worry about her peculiar magic. Battle awaited.

Her magic picked out its first target, shaping generous amounts of power into a long, deadly silvery-blue spear. As if under the control of another, Anna's arm launched the javelin at the enemy.

Magic swirled around her body in a way it never had before, and Anna had a sinking feeling that was because the power was leveling up. But it was already so powerful. How could she hope to control it if it continued to grow in strength? And clearly, it had a will of its own.

'Mind on the task at hand,' Anna reminded herself, tightening her legs around Obsidian's sides. *'Win the battle first, rescue the Avatar and the Null, and then worry about the willful magic later.'*

She surrendered to the power. It swiftly created three more spears and sent them to hunt the enemy. Her magical weapons found the hostiles as if outfitted with the magical version of laser guidance systems.

She grinned savagely as she sent another wave of spears rushing toward the enemy line. Anna and the other soldiers—the new arrivals and the teams already hunting with Gregory and the Null—advanced on the building.

Now it became more dangerous. They no longer had a clear view of the enemy—neither knowing their numbers nor location inside the building's dark corridors.

Three team leaders converged on her location. They were strangers, but apparently, she and Obsidian's reputations were already circulating, for one soldier tossed her a radio. "Stay in contact. We'll follow you in."

She nodded. "We need eyes inside that building first. Obsidian, can you get us in there without them sensing us?"

"Doubtful. If they can sense Gregory coming and set a trap for him, they'll be able to track any gargoyle's location."

"Damn."

"I have another idea," he said and then paused, glancing around at the other humans as if uncertain how much he should reveal to them.

"Let's hear it."

He huffed and then spat it out. "I can see souls."

Er... what? Anna adjusted her seat and then shifted forward enough to thump his shoulder. "Say that again."

"I see souls."

And when had he been going to tell her that bit of news?

But that too was a question for another time. "You can see souls even if they are behind cover, like in that building?"

"Yes."

"And are you calling upon your death magic to pull this off?"

Because if he was, then that was a deal-breaker right there.

He hesitated before answering. "I don't think I'm actively calling upon the power to achieve this. It's something I've been able to do since Captain Newman gave us the tour of the living quarters. It was a little disconcerting at first. But it's an advantage we'll need in this battle."

So that's why he'd been upset. "Okay. Fine. We'll use your gift, but if you start to feel any other powers rising, we're getting your butt off this battlefield. Understand?"

"Yes, my Kyrsu."

CHAPTER SEVENTEEN

Together they prowled closer to the building, Anna on his back and shrouded in as much shadow magic as he could muster. The human soldiers followed closely behind. However, they were moving into flanking positions to cover more of the building.

Obsidian's heart pumped with exhilaration. His spirit soared. This was why he and his Kyrsu had been created. To ride into glorious battle together and destroy their enemies.

"Ease up there," Anna hissed in his ear. "There's nothing glorious about battle. Putting your enemies in the ground is just grueling, bloody, backbreaking work."

He huffed but grinned savagely. She *was* correct about war and battle not being glorious, but having Anna riding with him, her new power flowing around him, most certainly was glorious. She might deny it, but he'd felt her emotions as their dormant link stirred to life.

Anna gloried in what they were, delighted in the ability to protect her world and the ones she loved— rejoiced in riding into battle with him. She couldn't help it. While she might not have been born in the Battle Goddess's kingdom as he had been, his blood had reshaped her as surely as if he'd had a hand in her making.

It was the secret dark part of his nature he hid from his gargoyle brethren and the other servants of the Light.

But Anna was a part of him.

Like him.

They were more alike than different. It's why they made such a unified team on the battlefield, a deadly pair that even this new enemy was learning to fear. He halted, hiding in a patch of deep shadow as he studied the rundown building.

"Can you tell what's happening in the building?" Anna asked.

"No. I can only detect their locations," Obsidian narrowed his gaze, and that other power allowed him to behold the dark and tattered souls of the enemy. He didn't share that bit of information. "All the surviving enemies are now within."

"Yeah. About that. These assholes seem to excel at traps, and I'd really like to live through this battle. Even knowing the enemy's location, how will we pull off this rescue without getting ourselves, our men, Gregory, or Erika killed? We need a plan."

She'd said the words more to herself, but he answered her question, anyway.

"We know our two magics are compatible. I can feel your magic as you formed those spears. I think I could even direct them if I tried." He paused, seeing Anna's frown.

"Yeah-no. That's too close to you calling on Lord Death's power."

"But we'd be using your power, not mine. I'd only be using my new gift of seeing souls to guide your magic."

"I don't like it. It's too risky."

"Riskier than letting them escape with an Avatar and the Null?"

"Fuck."

"We're a team," he whispered. "We've got this."

Anna's scowl didn't lessen, but there was something in her gaze—capitulation—and he knew he'd won this argument.

"Fine. We will attempt to join our powers, but we damn well pray to every god we know for this to work."

Obsidian grinned but sent a silent prayer to the Divine Ones that he and his kyrsu had the strength to carry out his plan.

"Ready?" he asked Anna.

"As I'll ever be."

Then she closed her eyes, and her power reached for him. It was like a dam had broken, her power rushing over him, into him. It was so much it was almost painful, but then Anna touched his mind, and he forgot his discomfort as their powers merged.

He sensed the moment Anna could see what he saw, see the souls within the building, see everything about them.

"I can see them all. Even the Avatar's..." Her tone was one of awe, and he could understand that emotion.

When he'd first seen the Avatar's soul, felt its power, saw just a hint of its ancient knowledge, felt how many lives it had lived—its long immortal existence stretching back through time before even time existed....

And that being needed their aid. It was a humbling thought.

"You know each soul?" Anna mumbled in awe. "Or at least can sense what they are, what they have done, how long they've existed?"

"Yes." He turned his attention to the Null's soul next. Hers was almost as ancient, though not as powerful as the Avatars, though still impressive.

But the other souls...

He shivered. Now that his gift was bolstered by Anna's magic, he could see the enemy even more clearly. Shards of tattered souls enrobed in hate, greed, and savagery were all he saw when he looked upon the warlocks.

Anna hissed, telling him she'd just beheld their enemy.

"And I thought their leader was an ugly fuck." Anna paused, and he felt her take in the number of enemies. "There's over a hundred of them in there. Where the fuck are they all coming from? Their leader got a fucking magic 3D printer churning out evil henchmen somewhere?"

He didn't even try to puzzle out the meaning of her words. "Now that you can see them, do you think your magic can hunt them while using my power to track them?"

"I'm game to try," Anna said, her tone saying she would do more than try. "Those ugly bastards need to get the hell off my planet. Let's see if we can send them to the Spirit Realm for a little divine judgment."

Obsidian grinned as she began to do precisely that.

Her first spear of power raced across the distance. When it encountered the outside wall, it passed right through.

"Nifty. Wondered what would happen," Anna muttered as she was shaping the next spear to fling at the enemy. This one also found its mark, dropping the enemy before the beast knew it was dead.

He and his Kyrsu continued to hunt down the invaders; their two powers joined, growing stronger every moment their minds worked as one. Five enemies fell, then ten, then twenty. But as much as he didn't want to admit it, there was a toll.

The Death magic slumbering in his soul began to wake. This wasn't the ability to see souls. This was something else. Something more dangerous. But instead of feeling dread, he felt at peace.

'There was nothing to fear,' the power sleeping in his blood whispered almost seductively.

He narrowed his eyes, and he huffed out a breath.

But there was a reason he wasn't supposed to call upon this power. Anna had said it was dangerous. And Anna was rarely wrong about such things. His muzzle scrunched. Or was it Gregory who had said it was dangerous?

Strange, he didn't remember talking to the male half of the Avatar.

No. Wait. Anna had talked with Gregory, and she'd passed the Avatar's warning on to him.

His memories seemed muddled, his thoughts growing hazy.

He heard Anna curse, but it was muffled, like the sounds in a forest blanketed by thick fog. Distantly, he thought he felt her shake his arm. Then his shoulders.

But he wasn't sure, and then even that didn't matter as his consciousness floated away to some other place.

A sharp pain bloomed along his muzzle and jerked him back to the present. Anna was drawing her arm back to slug him again, but he reared away and rubbed his stinging muzzle.

"You with me?" Anna asked.

"Yes."

"Thank fuck. No more magic use for you."

Around them, the human soldiers had moved upon the large warehouse. Overhead, the thunder of the mechanical flying machines Anna called helicopters drowned out most other sounds of battle. But he knew a fight was going on inside the building, and he could see the flashes of gunfire and other explosions through the shattered windows.

Several of their fae allies had arrived as well. He spotted the black streak of the pooka as the pony galloped straight toward the building. When he was almost upon it, the pony leaped ten feet into the air and sailed through a window. A moment later, there was screaming, followed by an invader's body flying out the window.

Human soldiers with guns at the ready and coven members, their staffs raised high and glowing with power, closed in upon the exposed enemy. Together, the two forces rained down bullets and lethal magic spells until the enemies' shields and defenses were shredded.

Soon, a second body was kicked out of the building, straight through a wall this time. Once again, human and coven forces moved in upon the enemy.

The pooka wasn't the only fae in the battle. Greenborrow had shifted to his giant troll form, a six-foot club in the leshii's hand. One powerful swing of his magic-laced weapon took out a wall, bricks and debris raining down onto the grass. Then the massive leshii entered the building. There were more grunts and screams of pain, but above those, he heard the fae's booming laughs as he crushed his enemies.

More human, fae, and coven members rushed through the breach the leshii had created.

"We should join them!" Obsidian snarled, feeling guilty and angry that their allies were fighting and dying while he stood looking on.

"Big nope to that idea." Anna grabbed him by the shoulder and applied pressure until he understood she wanted him to kneel. "We've thinned the herd. Did our part. Time for you to sit down."

He knelt, and then she planted her hands on either side of his head, turning his face this way and that until she'd satisfied whatever concern had her looking into his eyes, nose, and ears. She even pried his mouth open and peered inside. His other senses, which had been dormant until then and he hadn't even realized it, awakened full force. Aches and pains throbbed throughout his body, and a headache pounded viciously behind his eyes.

Then he discovered his mouth was full of blood. He tasted its metallic tang.

"Sorry. Hit you pretty hard to snap you out of that.

You were bleeding from your eyes and ears and wouldn't release your hold on the death magic. That's why I hit you. The bloody nose was from my punch. Apparently, my right hook has a little more power when I panic-channel a demigoddess's battle magic." She tore a length of fabric from the hem of her shirt and dabbed at the blood. "Your new magic was about to scramble your brain again. I may have freaked out a little."

Anna continued to dab at the blood, and he realized his raging headache was getting worse.

"Don't try to stand," she ordered, as if reading his thoughts. He'd been about to rise and carry them some-where safer in case his body decided he needed to turn to stone to heal. He wouldn't leave his Kyrsu alone to defend them both with danger so close.

"Lie down. Rest," Anna ordered, her tone leaving no room for argument. "Reinforcements are here, and we've got clan and coven healers inbound. Just hold on, and don't call your magic again. Not even your shadow magic."

"I won't."

Then Anna's fingers were combing through his mane, and he closed his eyes, leaning into her warmth. There was something very comforting about his Kyrsu's voice as she whispered what was likely nonsense to him, but he didn't care. It was still lovely. He could hear her concern and love for him in her rough, emotional filled tones.

The sounds of battle diminished, and he worried his senses were growing dull again. But, no, when he raised his head and looked around, it was to see Gregory and Erika emerging from the building. The Avatar looked less than pleased about something, but the humans were securing the building, so they'd won the battle.

That was good.

What could have the Avatar so riled up?

He got the answer to his question moments later.

"Some of them escaped through another portal spell," Gregory snarled, even as he dropped to kneel next to Obsidian. The Avatar's hands were gentle as he took a firm grip on his head. And then, much as Anna had, Gregory examined him. Magic flowed across his skin from the contact points of the older male's fingers.

Soon his headache was in retreat, and he could think a little more clearly. Though he was bone tired once more. Anna hadn't moved from his side, so when Gregory was finished with the healing spell, Obsidian slumped to the ground and found his head resting in Anna's lap.

"Sleep," Gregory said, and there was a command behind the words that Obsidian couldn't refuse.

CHAPTER EIGHTEEN

*M*oments after Gregory had ordered Obsidian to sleep, he scooped up the bigger male and hoisted him over his shoulder with a grunt of effort, then walked away. Anna scrambled to keep up, following close on the Avatar's tail. They walked in silence, and she would have asked him where they were going, but he seemed in a bad mood. She kept her mouth shut and jogged after the big gargoyle carrying the even bigger gargoyle.

Her question of where they were going was answered a moment later as another portal formed in the air twenty feet ahead. The silvery mirror-like surface of the portal vanished when they were within ten feet of the doorway, revealing a view of Anna's new living quarters. Gregory crossed the portal, and Anna hustled after him.

Between one step and the next, Anna left the overgrown field with its long green grass and abandoned buildings and was again back on base, looking at the now familiar couches and the tiny kitchenette area.

Lillian paced on the other side of her portal. She stopped dead as she got her first look at them.

"By the God and Goddess, what the hell happened?" Lillian asked, voice thick with concern.

"The Null and I both stumbled into a powerful trap," Gregory grumbled as he set Obsidian down on the ground directly in front of his mate. Lillian knelt as close as possible to her brother without crossing the portal's threshold.

"It was my fault," Gregory said, without looking away from the healing spells he was weaving over Obsidian.

Anna noticed Lillian gesture wordlessly at her tree. In response, a tiny thread of pale green magic rose from the roots and flowed across the ground, crossed the portal's threshold, and wound its way around one of Gregory's thick calves and up his body. He used the extra magic to shape a second healing spell.

Once that one had sunk below Obsidian's skin, Gregory continued his explanation. "I found the enemy's trail but didn't reckon on them having time to set a trap sophisticated enough to capture either the Null or myself. I certainly hadn't thought they'd have time to construct one for each of us." He grumbled unhappily. "I won't be making that mistake again. And this wasn't just a few newly turned warlocks. There were over a hundred of them of varying ages."

"This is bad." Lillian's words were clipped and harsh.

"You think?" Anna muttered in her head, then knelt next to Obsidian.

"There is one blessing to this mess," Gregory continued. "The warlocks are trapped here on Earth. This mostly magical-less realm is hampering their powers greatly. We would face a more dire situation if they had been created within the Magic Realm."

"Small blessings indeed," Anna muttered with a thick application of sarcasm.

Gregory smacked her hip with the flat of his blade-tipped tail. Anna yelped, more in surprise than pain, but still rubbed where the blow had landed, too shocked to do anything else.

Had he really just fucking swatted her?

Yes, he had. Anna's blood pressure rose, but she clamped her lips together.

"You're welcome," Gregory drawled.

"For what?" The words escaped her mouth before she could stop them.

"For my aid. I always endeavor to aid younglings in learning mastery of all things, their own stray thoughts and runaway mouths included."

'Youngling? Why not rub salt in the wound, oh wise and ancient one, who tripped into the enemies' trap and needed my

help to get free?' Of course, Anna didn't say any of that out loud.

He looked down the length of his muzzle at her, and she had a good view of his slightly flared nostrils and the tips of his fangs as he half smiled.

"I heard that, Cub."

Fuck.

"I heard that as well."

Shit. She needed to relearn the art of mental shields.

"Indeed." Gregory grinned suddenly. "I will mention to Thayn that the Kyrsu of the Gargoyle Legion has forgotten some of her studies while she napped for two years."

Dammit. The last thing she needed was that old trickster having fun at her expense. And he might be the oldest of the gargoyles by thousands upon thousands of years, but he was far from old and crippled. No one willingly crossed swords with him in the practice ring. And he was just as lethal outside the ring.

Maybe if she got Gregory back to talking with his mate, he'd forget about her flippant words and his planned punishment.

"Not likely," he muttered with a grin. "But you have a point, young one. The warlocks are trapped in this realm, which limits their potential. We should be very thankful for that."

"Duly noted. But trapped? Are you sure about that?" Anna risked another tail thumping to ask. "They can create portals, so I'm not sure how long they'll be trapped."

"A valid concern. And, yes, if they were given time to build up their strength by feeding upon the souls of this world, they could create portals strong enough to breach the Veil Between the Realms and travel to the Magic Realm, where they would become a hundred times more powerful."

"Like a freaking army of blood witches."

"Exactly."

When Anna glanced toward Lillian, she noticed the other woman wasn't interrupting, instead listening closely with a frown plastered on her features. Anna was willing to bet that while the other woman had a better understanding of what a warlock was than Anna did, she didn't know everything and was listening attentively to discover what other horrible bits she lacked.

Anna couldn't help feeling that they were also allies. While Lillian had been born the Mother's Sorceress and the female half of the Avatars, she'd also been raised on Earth, knowing nothing of her heritage. And it seemed the soul of the Mother's Sorceress was currently living in the hamadryad tree.

Anna didn't know what had occurred to bring that about. Still, considering Lillian was big times pregnant again, Anna would bet it was willingly done so Lillian and Gregory could raise children together for the first time in their existence. Anna knew having the Avatar soul residing in the hamadryad tree limited what memories Lillian could access easily.

Gregory had taken the moment of silence to give Obsidian another going over with healing magic, but now he was looking at Anna again. "He will be fine. You both will be. The Divine Ones created you and Obsidian for this purpose. I have faith in you," Gregory said, then placed a heavy hand on her shoulder. "However, neither you nor he will go anywhere near a warlock for the foreseeable future. Not until you are recovered and trained to use your new powers."

His words took the wind out of Anna's sails. "Pardon? But you just said this is our purpose, that you have faith in our abilities."

"That may be, but you and he are in no shape to face warlocks again soon." His gaze cut away from Anna to land on Lillian. After a moment, he returned his attention to Anna. "You should not have been asked to come to my rescue. The Null and I would have freed ourselves, eventually."

"You hoped you would!" Lillian barked at her mate. "And mind reading goes two ways. I've already sorted through your memories of the battle. When you were captured, you weren't certain that they couldn't yet create a portal to another world. If they'd escaped with you and Erika...."

"But that didn't happen."

"Because I sent Anna and Obsidian to rescue you," Lillian fired back.

"That's not entirely accurate."

Lillian stood with her hands on her hips, glowering at her mate. "What are you rambling on about, you overprotective caveman?"

Anna didn't want to be in the middle of this married couple's verbal boss fight and cast subtle glances around, looking for a place where she'd be out of the way, but still close enough to monitor Obsidian.

"You didn't send the Rasoren and Kyrsu of the Gargoyle Legions to rescue me," Gregory growled out. "You sent the equivalent of an unarmed human woman and an adolescent journeyman-level gargoyle into battle."

Lillian's brows furled, and then her eyes widened as she turned her gaze to Anna. "Forgive me. If I had known that you couldn't call your armor and weapons to you, I would never have sent you into such danger so poorly armed." Lillian's eyes narrowed as she pinned Gregory with a look. "But if some colossal idiot had taken the time to explain all the little details, then none of this would have happened."

Anna didn't know about that. Shit tended to happen one way or another.

Lillian sighed, her voice calmer when she continued. "Gregory is correct. You and Obsidian cannot go anywhere near the warlocks again until you are ready.

We'll send more fae allies to help with this fight. Until you and my little brother are fully healed, the risk of you losing control of your new powers is too great."

"What if we aren't given a choice?" Anna asked. "It seemed like they were hunting Erika. What if they manage to capture her while Gregory isn't here, and the allied forces might need our powers to save her, like the first attack? He has already explained that he can't stay here much longer. He'll need to return to you in the Magic Realm to ensure your child receives the magic it needs to live."

Lillian and Gregory both frowned unhappily. Anna couldn't blame them. They'd just been forced to face what would likely be the first of many such clashes between duty and family throughout their long lives.

After a long silence that suggested the two Avatars had been speaking at length to each other in mind speech, Lillian cleared her throat and turned to Anna. "If the worst comes to pass, you must use your power. Erika can never remain in the hands of the warlocks. I do not know what purpose they would use her for, but my elemental dragon son would take exception, and he has the potential to be far more deadly than blood witches, warlocks, or whatever our new enemy calls master."

Commander Gryton was a law unto himself. She'd seen the beast he'd kept imprisoned for thousands of years finally let loose on the battlefield. His true nature

—that of an elemental dragon—was epic-level scary shit.

On the other side of the portal, the largest of the hamadryads shifted, the branches moving as if in a strong breeze. Lillian and Gregory both jerked their attention to the tree. The Avatars were creepily silent, as if having a conversation with it.

'What a strange life I lead,' Anna thought as she waited for the Avatars to finish their conversation with a tree.

Gregory tensed, every muscle in his body suddenly taut.

"No." The way he hissed out the one word had Anna's hackles rising.

"It can't be." Lillian's voice echoed his horror.

"That's not possible," Gregory mumbled, more to himself.

Anna's tension grew tenfold at what she saw in their eyes: fear. The freaking Avatars, beings older than the entire universe, feared something.

"You going to tell me what has got you spooked?" Anna asked.

At last, Gregory drew in a deep breath, and then with one more long look at the hamadryad tree, he answered. "The hamadryad says there is another possibility. I must return to the Magic Realm with one of the warlock bodies to prove if what she fears is true. She will examine it and tell me what she finds."

"What the hell?" Anna shouted before she could

school her response. "What can be worse than the Battle Goddess, a blood witch, or these new warlocks? And why aren't you saying what it is?"

"To mention its name out loud is to draw its attention and forewarn it that we know it exists once more and that we are hunting for it."

"Okay. Now you're scaring me."

"You should be scared. Every living creature on your planet should be scared if my Sorceress is correct, and she is rarely wrong." Gregory stood. "I must return now. The sooner I go, the sooner I can return. Tell no one else what I have said. We don't know if the warlocks have infiltrated the human military. And it's not just the military. We don't dare risk enlightening the clan or coven for the same reason."

"I must tell them something. I can't lie."

"Evade the truth if you are asked about my absence. Tell them I'm taking a warlock body to my Sorceress for her to discover its origins. Half-truths are not lies. Once I find the truth, and it is safe to bring our allies in on the secret, I will."

"Fine. I hate this, but I'll do what you ask."

And just like that, Anna was flirting with court martial for the second time in her military career.

CHAPTER NINETEEN

Shortly after the Avatar left to collect a warlock body, Major Resnick entered—no wait, she reminded herself, he'd been promoted while she'd slept as a stone statue and was now Lieutenant-Colonel Resnick. He looked her over and then at Obsidian, the sleeping gargoyle's head still in her lap. Sensing someone else in the room, Obsidian jerked awake. He blinked blurriness from his gaze and then hauled himself upright and moved to the sofa. Anna and Resnick joined him.

"I'm thrilled to see you and your gargoyle partner survived, mostly unharmed. But where did that other great brutish beast of a gargoyle go? Gregory can't keep violating base security and just pop in and out wherever and whenever he feels like it."

"Actually, I think he can. Literally. Goes with being an ancient demigod and all."

"Do you know how many reports I've written and how many times I've had to smooth ruffled feathers because of that particular demigod?"

"Been asleep, so no. But I can imagine," Anna said, doing her best to keep a straight face. Besides being her CO, Lieutenant-Colonel Resnick was like another uncle. He and her father were best friends, even though there was well over a decade of age difference between the men.

Because of that, she knew Resnick better than most did. He wasn't really angry at the Avatar. He just loved to bitch when people were a pain in his ass.

And Gregory was stubborn and set in his ways. She was certain Resnick's complaints were valid.

"Unfortunately, I'm not here just to reminisce," Resnick said. "The command council wants a word with you."

Of course they would. She'd expected as much after how she and Obsidian had raced into battle without being green-lighted for the rescue mission. Anna drew in a deep, calming breath.

But Lieutenant-Colonel Resnick proved what a great CO he was by convincing his superiors to hold the debriefing in Anna's new quarters, telling the other senior officers that nasty shit would happen if they tried to separate Anna and Obsidian. That might very well have been the truth, but Anna was still grateful for his aid at putting her mind at ease. She didn't want to leave Obsidian just now.

Resnick—bless his heart—somehow knew her mind without her having to utter the words aloud. Speaking of blessings, her CO had also convinced his superiors to keep their questions short, making her second debriefing in as many days as easy as possible. Eventually, it was over, and Anna and Obsidian were left alone in their new quarters.

It didn't feel like home. To be honest, nothing felt like home anymore. Not Earth, not the Magic Realm. The one place that had felt like home to her was on Second Legion's training island, surrounded by all her new gargoyle friends, with Obsidian a steady presence at her side.

Haven was the closest place she'd thought of as home since her life had collided with magic and gone south. She glanced over at Obsidian.

"You hungry?"

"I could eat."

"I'll have something brought to us. You're supposed to be resting, so no gallivanting around the base for us."

"But shouldn't we be helping clean up or hunting for the escaped enemies?"

"Resting." She drew the word out long to stress that fact.

Obsidian scrunched his muzzle. "I feel fine now. We could join a search party."

"Yeah-no. You say you feel fine, but I know you aren't. Gregory said you would need to rest for the next twenty-four hours, and I'm not to leave you."

"Just the two of us?" He perked up. Clearly, her eighteen-year-old Rasoren enjoyed her company as much as the twenty-one-year-old version.

"Yep. For now, anyway. I don't know everyone else's schedule, but I'll try not to bore you." She stood and stretched. "Be right back. I'm going to see if our friendly babysitters are outside. If so, what did you want me to tell them to order?"

"I'll have what you're having."

She snorted with humor. "That's cheating."

"How so?"

"Never mind. My choice it is." By the time she opened the door, she'd decided on a good old-fashioned cheeseburger. The Magic Realm didn't have burger joints. Damn, she'd missed fast food. It might not be good for you, but man, nothing could lift the spirits like junk food after a long, bad day.

After leaving one of their guards with her order, she was just turning to return to Obsidian when a voice called out.

"Hey, roomie. Hold up."

Anna peered over her shoulder in the voice's direction.

Jason was strolling toward her, a massive grin on his face.

"I'd heard you were one of my roommates," Anna muttered, her hopes for a peaceful night evaporating.

"Sure am," he said as he glided past.

Anna's shoulders slumped, and she allowed the door to swing closed. It opened a moment later.

"Am I invisible? Pretty sure that's a gargoyle power, not a null one." Erika laughed at Anna's expression.

"Sorry," Anna apologized. "Got distracted by Jason's ego entering the room."

"Happens to the best of us," Erika said and then added, "Hey, you look like shit. You should get some rest."

"Thanks," Anna mumbled and rolled her eyes at the back of the other woman's head. However, she was glad to see Erika. The Texan was a sensible and down-to-earth woman, with the bonus of being able to suck the life out of Jason if he was too much of an ass.

Anna smirked and asked, "Has Jason ever annoyed you enough to knock him on his ass with your null abilities?"

"Once." Erika's one eyebrow arched. "Surely you and Obsidian haven't been here long enough to be on the receiving end of one of Jason's pranks yet. Even the Jester of Not-Normal has his limits."

"I haven't yet hit my limit!" Jason called from next to the bar where he was rooting through the mini-fridge. He pulled out a beer and waved it at them a moment later. "Want one?"

"Sure," Obsidian said, and he prowled closer to Jason.

The witch looked dumbfounded for a moment, and then he laughed. "Why not? You're technically twenty-one now."

Anna walked between them and snatched the beer right out of the air.

"Dick move. In what scenario do you think giving the vessel for Lord Death's power an alcoholic beverage is a good idea? Inquiring minds want to know."

Anna tossed the beer back at him as she walked by.

"Okay. I'll concede that wasn't one of my brightest plans...."

"You think?" Erika muttered on her way to the fridge.

"Why, yes! I do think from time to time." Jason laughed and puffed out his chest. "I'm actually brilliant. Genius level even."

"Evil genius, maybe." Erika snorted and turned her back on him. More interested in the water bottle Anna handed her.

"You'll get used to him eventually," Erika muttered. "And if he gets too out of hand, I can always feed him to a certain elemental dragon I know."

Anna arched a brow again. "Hmm. How does that

work exactly? The last time I saw Commander Gryton, he was busy sacrificing himself to save all of us. But from what you mentioned before, he isn't dead. And did you say he was doing time as a sun?"

"He's still very much alive. But no one wants him anywhere near Earth at the moment, not until he gets his chaotic fire magic under control. But I can track his state of mind with this." Erika grinned and tugged the neck of her t-shirt down, exposing a sizeable glowing symbol that pulsed with power.

"Is that...?"

"The piece of Gryton's soul his Avatar parents grafted onto me to let me help him control his power? Yep."

"Isn't it..."

"Growing? Yep, it is." Erika frowned for a moment. "It'll suck come bikini season."

"And how, exactly, are you all 'this is fine' while having a piece of his evil, fiery little soul growing on you like that?"

"Because it's making me a more powerful null. Being forced to absorb the vast quantities of magic the elemental dragon sends my way when he's having a tantrum has upped my game in what I can handle. That's come in handy with this new super-powered enemy."

"Huh. I always thought they did that so you could help them control him. Didn't realize it would make you more powerful."

Erika shrugged. "Six of one, half a dozen of the other, as my granddad would say."

Before they could debate the finer points of keeping the forbidden offspring of the Avatars from eradicating entire worlds when he was in a bad mood, a knock came, and a moment later, a soldier arrived, carrying two trays piled high with food.

Jason whistled and strolled forward to give the trays a once over. "How the hell do I get room service?"

"You?" the soldier said in a dry tone. "You don't." Then he set the trays, with their load of burgers and fries, down on the coffee table in front of the largest couch and turned on his heels, heading back toward the door.

"Ah," Jason said and grabbed his chest. "My feelings are hurt."

The soldier ignored Jason, apparently having dealt with the male witch enough to know not to respond and feed the beast. A moment later, the door closed, the man having safely escaped Jason. Anna envied the soldier.

Ignoring Jason, she walked over to the food, and after selecting a cheeseburger from one tray, she settled on the sofa next to Obsidian. Erika joined them, sitting in one of the flanking chairs. Jason settled in the one opposite. When Obsidian offered one of the burgers to Erika, Anna sighed and shoved one in Jason's direction.

Watching him pout for the rest of the evening would ruin her appetite.

They ate while having a relaxed conversation, chatting about some of the hunts Erika and Jason had been on. Anna learned that many bases worldwide were taking part in the top-secret project to eradicate all the enemy soldiers who had escaped to Earth at the end of the last battle. From their conversation, Anna learned there were two types of hostiles, with some hiding in the wilds while others attempted to blend in with the human populations, depending on their shapeshifting abilities.

They'd also been quick to learn that the enemies hiding in the human populations were the more dangerous variety, for they hunted humans, using their victim's life force to sustain themselves on Earth, with its lower concentrations of magic.

Mostly, the various black ops teams were focused on hunting down the enemies that posed the greatest threat to humans, leaving the ones hiding in the wilds for now. As the enemy warriors were tracked down, they were captured or killed. If they surrendered, they were escorted back to the Magic Realm, where the Legion gargoyles were waiting to deal with them. Erika eluded that more than a few of the prisoners were allowed to live.

"A few get to live?" Anna wasn't sure how she felt about that.

"Yep," Erika said. "The gargoyles can sense if they are evil beyond redemption or if there's hope for them.

Surprisingly, there is hope for a few of them. Though they certainly don't get off scot-free. The gargoyles make them do the Magic Realm's version of community service. They are tasked with protecting the kingdoms they once helped conquer, as well as helping them with agriculture and infrastructure projects—all under the watchful eyes of the gargoyle legion. The punishment is a term of five hundred years to start. If they have redeemed themselves and proven trustworthy enough to become upstanding citizens of the realm, they will be allowed to strike out on their own."

Having been an unwilling guest in the Battle Goddess's kingdom for a few months, Anna could attest that some members of that demigoddess's army were far eviler than others. A few had even conducted themselves with honor and had they been given a chance to take another life-path, they likely would have.

But others deserved only a swift death.

Eventually, the conversation wound down. Even Jason's motor mouth slowed, and he yawned several times, saying he was off to bed. Erika stood and stretched as well. Then she headed to the kitchenette to grab a glass of water.

Anna followed Erika to the kitchen, with Obsidian padding silently behind them both. She noticed Obsidian was still wide awake and knew he should head off to bed, needing the sleep, but she sensed he was resisting so that he could sit up with her. They'd been through enough that she knew the root of his fear.

She pretended to place a hand on his back for balance as she stepped around him to reach the fridge. But really, she was hoping to catch a thread of his thoughts. Because of all the crap that had happened to him as a kid, he'd developed abandonment issues and secretly feared Anna would one day vanish from his life as so many others had. He'd still possessed that fear as a battle-hardened adult to some degree.

She couldn't blame him for being a little clingy. But she knew the perfect activity to put him to sleep.

"Hey, Erika," she called to the other woman.

Erika finished her water and put the cup in the sink. "Yeah?"

"Does anyone read paperbacks around here?"

Erika grinned. "You mean like actual dead-tree books?"

"Yep."

"Lucky for you, Greenborrow is a big reader. He's got an enormous collection. I've raided his library on more than one occasion."

"Perfect. He's one of our roomies, right?"

"Yes, but he's still out on patrol, hunting for signs of the warlocks. His team isn't due back until morning." Erika paused and then grinned. "His is the fourth door down on the boys' side. Though he has powerful wards."

Anna's answering grin faltered. Dammit. If she still

had her gargoyle shadow magic, she could probably dismantle Greenborrow's spell in no time. Usually, she wouldn't just go barging into someone else's room like a... well, like Jason, but now that she'd thought about it, she really wanted to read to Obsidian, to help reestablish that easy affection they'd once shared.

Besides, while he was getting stronger by the hour and Rasoren Obsidian, war leader of the Gargoyle Legion, would soon be back to his old self, it couldn't hurt to ease the transition a little. Eighteen-year-old Journeyman Obsidian was doing his best to adapt, but he had to be out of his element. Anna reasoned the best place to start reestablishing that bond of trust and affection was to go back to things she and Shadowlight used to enjoy. And reading had been number one on the kid's list of favorite activities.

Well, besides eating. And the two activities usually went hand in hand, with Anna reading as they enjoyed some of Gran's baking.

"Now, now," Erika said, drawing Anna from her thoughts. "There's no need to get all sad. I might know a null who can walk through shields."

"A raid behind enemy lines!" Obsidian said, his tone a low rumble full of realistic-sounding menace. As he prowled closer, he grinned, showing off his very white and very sharp teeth to full advantage. "A leshii's magic is no match for me."

"Wow. Gear down, big trucker," Erika said with a

laugh. "Wasn't planning on slaying any innocent books today. Besides, you will not be using your magic again anytime soon. Doctor Avatar's orders."

Obsidian practically deflated, his ears and tail drooping. Erika arched a brow at the dejected gargoyle and then turned a questioning look at Anna.

"Gargoyles are naturally competitive," Anna explained. "The harder the challenge, the more fun they'll have winning it. You just dangled a treat in front of him and then snatched it away."

Obsidian made a huffing sound and leveled a glower at her. "Traitor. You're my Kyrsu. Aren't you supposed to be on my side?"

Laughing, Anna patted his chest. "I'm always on your side, but Erika is correct. Neither of us should use magic for the next little while."

CHAPTER TWENTY

*T*he book hunting trip had been successful, and Anna now had three items of stolen property laid out on the coffee table—a classic, an adventure novel, and a sci-fi title. She'd also discovered something about the leshii she hadn't known. He liked to read romances, and going by some covers and blurbs, the racier, the better. Anna felt more than a smidgin of guilt for invading his privacy and raiding his shelves. But Erika had soothed that guilt by saying he used to leave his quarters unlocked so anyone could borrow a book. But he had started putting up shields after Jason had played some kind of prank on the ancient leshii while he'd been sleeping.

Of the three books she and Obsidian had selected, she was only familiar with the classic Jane Eyre. She'd had to read it in school but didn't remember it. But as a cub, Shadowlight had loved Pride and Prejudice, so they started with the one most like an Austen, as far as Anna could guess.

If it sucked, they'd find some more Austen books tomorrow.

Once again, they settled on the couch as they had earlier, the gargoyle sprawling and taking up most of the room, leaving Anna to squeeze herself into a one-foot area. It reminded her of watching TV with her dogs back home in her parent's house as a teen years ago.

And with that memory, Anna was reminded of her family. She was both looking forward to and dreading that reunion. As for her dogs, Britney and Tanner, they'd been well into their senior years long before magic had crashed into Anna's life. She wasn't even sure if they were still alive.

A lump formed in her throat, and she quickly picked up their chosen book, focusing on it instead of her family.

"Why are you sad?" Obsidian asked.

Dammit. Did he miss anything?

"It's nothing. I was just thinking about my family. I guess I miss them more than I knew." Then she remembered that Obsidian had lost his mother in the final battle, the dryad having sought to redeem herself after serving the Battle Goddess for hundreds of years.

Anna had never been a fan of the cold-hearted bitch, but River had been Obsidian's mother, and the woman had turned her back on everything she'd ever known to escape with her son, bringing him to Earth to hide him here. Had River not betrayed her goddess, Anna would never have met Obsidian. She owed that dryad a life debt.

Realization struck. Shit! Obsidian wouldn't even remember his mother was dead—since he had no memory of the final battle. He'd also lost two of his best friends. But so much had happened. He hadn't yet had time to ask about any of them.

And chicken that she was, Anna patted Obsidian's tail and then began reading the book's first chapter.

If it were in her power to keep sorrow away from him for a bit longer, she would. She could deal with the guilt of keeping secrets later. She'd give Obsidian this one evening of peace.

Eventually, Obsidian shifted and stretched.

"This is a nice enough arrangement," Obsidian commented. "But I must admit to missing Haven."

"I miss Haven, too. There wasn't time between leaving Second Legion's home and preparing for the final battle to miss it at the time. But I miss our mentors and all our gargoyle and dryad friends."

When Obsidian looked at her sharply, she could have kicked herself for the mention of friends.

"The final battle... my friends." His jaw flexed as he fought to master himself. "We won, but what was the cost? How many of our friends never made it off that battlefield?"

Shit. Shit. Shit.

Anna opened her mouth and then closed it again. Lillian had ordered her and Obsidian not to get into any stressful situations.

Telling him whom all had died in the final battle was going to be stressful. No way it couldn't be. But better it came from her than someone else, surely?

"After we absorbed the power of the demigods, we didn't have long before our bodies forced us into the stone sleep, certainly not long enough to learn the total casualties. I only know the names of the people we encountered during the battle and immediately before we turned to stone. And after I woke and discovered what was going on here, it hadn't occurred to me until just now that you wouldn't know."

Obsidian nodded, but his expression was cold, devoid of any emotion. "You can tell me now."

"I..." Anna sighed and steeled herself for the pain she was about to cause. "It was chaos on the battlefield, more death and magic than I'd ever witnessed. After one skirmish, we discovered Meadow and Truth wounded." She paused and then added softly, "Mortally. They... they died in each other's arms, but you were able to say goodbye."

He turned away, his shoulders hunching forward like he'd taken a blow to the gut. In a way, he likely had. "I'm so sorry, Obsidian."

The gargoyle, Truth, and the dryad, Meadow, had both been two of his closest friends while Anna had been in the embrace of the healing stone sleep. Of the two, Anna suspected he felt Truth's death more sharply, the two gargoyles having been friends longer and having trained together for years. Obsidian had also admitted to confiding many things to Truth that he would typically have only shared with his Kyrsu. Truth had stepped up to take Anna's place while she could not carry out her duties.

Truth had been a good and caring person and one of the toughest gargoyles of Second Legion. Anna had been thankful Obsidian had such a loyal friend.

"I'm sorry we could not save them," Anna murmured while gazing at the ground, giving him a moment of privacy with his pain.

After the silence became too long, Anna looked at him and reached up to rest a hand on his shoulder. As he stared off to some unseen distance, he was so still that he might as well have been stone.

"How?" he asked, turning back to her. Even so, he wouldn't look her in the eye.

"It was a trap—a spell created by the blood witch. Many of our allies were caught in it and didn't survive. I'm sorry."

"As am I." He was silent for a time, and Anna thought she might be spared having to cause him more pain today, but he speared her with a look. "Who else?"

"At the end of the battle, we came upon the unicorn. He'd sacrificed himself for his friends."

Obsidian nodded. "He was a noble beast. I was honored to have known him."

"As was I."

They were silent for a time, and he tilted his head and studied her. "I sense you are holding back."

She didn't miss the weight of his gaze, but she didn't speak. A moment later, his tail bumped her gently.

"Holding back the truth will not make it hurt less later," he said in that deep, rumbling voice of his. "Tell me what you know."

Anna nodded. "I'm sorry. Your mother did not survive."

A grunt of surprise escaped him. "Which one?"

She hadn't even been thinking about his adopted mother, the dryad healer, Maradryn, who'd taken him in when he'd arrived at Haven.

"Your biological mother," Anna clarified. "River died protecting Lillian's body while she was fighting in spirit form. Your mother saved your sister's life."

"So, my mother redeemed herself at last."

His words, so cold and harsh, surprised Anna. It was such a contrast to how he'd reacted on the battlefield that it was jarring. At the time, kneeling next to his mother as his father held her, Obsidian had sobbed as River told him how much she loved him, how proud he'd made her. She'd died shortly after he'd reached her side, but he'd been in time.

But it made sense, Anna supposed. This new Obsidian hadn't lived those memories, hadn't seen how his mother had fought alongside the allied forces to aid her son and daughter and make them proud. He'd never seen his mother redeemed. He'd only ever known her as the dryad confidant of the Battle Goddess, who'd only turned traitor to her goddess because her love for her children only slightly outweighed her loyalty to her goddess.

"Obsidian, there's something you need to see in my memories," she said, reaching out and gripping his arm. "You are doing your mother's memory a disservice if you don't. She had changed a lot while we were away in Haven. She had attempted to serve the Light to make amends for all she'd done in the past. And while it's up to the gods to judge if her efforts were worthy, I think they were. Look into my memories for that time after the battle."

Obsidian drew back. "No. We are supposed to rest, not call upon our magic."

"It's important and shouldn't take much magic. I think it will help you heal. And the Divine Ones need us healed and whole for what's coming with these warlocks. Besides, it's not a great weaving of magic, and we won't be calling on the twin's deadly powers. It will just be your gargoyle magic accessing what remains of our Rasoren-Kyrsu link. If it feels like it's too taxing, we'll stop."

The slant of his ears told her he was conflicted, but after a few moments, he took a deep breath and exhaled, the tension flowing out of his wings and body. Obsidian took a step toward her. And then another until they were standing toe to toe, which put her at about eye-level with his pecs. His large hands came to rest upon her shoulders for a moment and then moved up to cup her head, his thumbs resting at her temples.

Anna closed her eyes and attempted to reach for his mind. It wasn't nearly as strong as when they shared the Rasoren-Kyrsu bond, but she still felt him. Soon his essence was moving back along the link, and he was in her head. It was a familiar sensation. One she'd missed more than she'd admitted until that moment. With a sigh, she pushed away the longing and summoned up her memories of the battle, swiftly focusing on the one when they'd found his mother.

It would be from Anna's perspective of the event, but she hoped she and Obsidian were close enough that he'd be able to ignore her presence and watch the memory like he was reliving it himself.

It seemed to be working, for, after several moments, he rumbled out a pained sound and then was silent for a time as the memory unfolded. Anna wasn't sure how much time had gone by, but one minute he was silent and stoic, and then next, her big Rasoren was gasping out great gut-wrenching sobs.

Stepping into him, she wrapped him in her arms and hugged him as if she would lose him if she let go. He was speaking, but Anna didn't know what he was attempting to say, his words too broken and stilted, so she just rubbed his back and held him harder.

"She found her way," he finally murmured between sobs.

He sucked in several deep breaths and then wiped at his eyes. Before long, he had himself back under control. Though Anna was glad to see Obsidian wasn't as cold or untouchable as before. There was warmth and life back in his gaze.

In a calmer voice, he added, "River found her way to the Light in the end."

"Yes, she did." Anna squeezed him. "That's what I wanted you to see."

"Thank you, my Kyrsu." She didn't miss that he sounded much like the old Obsidian. And when he bowed down, pressing their foreheads together and simply stood, breathing in her scent, she knew she'd done the right thing.

"If there are other memories you want to see, just let me know," Anna added. "We can attempt this again."

"I would like that."

Obsidian released another ragged breath. "Thank you for showing me that. I would never have known...." His voice broke and then drifted into silence.

"You would have remembered in a few days. But some things are too important to wait." Anna squeezed him and then stepped back to peer into his face, but he'd already mastered his brief emotional outburst. "This is a lot for anyone to process. Did you still want me to find out what I can about the other casualties? Or would you prefer to wait a few days?"

"I don't want this hanging over me. Please inquire about that information."

"I'll do that first thing in the morning." Anna paused again. Not wanting to leave him when he was hurting, she grabbed a blanket and gave him a little shove toward the sofa.

When he understood what she wanted, he settled on the end he'd claimed earlier.

She curled up against his side, sliding her arm around his waist and taking a moment to simply enjoy his warm scent. It reminded her of sandalwood and hints of patchouli incense. The urge to rub her cheek against his shoulder and run her fingers along his abdomen took her by surprise. Then, realizing her fingers had released the blanket to do just that, she aborted the move and jerked forward, snatching the book off the coffee table instead.

'*Yeah, Mackenzie, better grab that book and start reading before sniffing at your barely-fucking-legal Rasoren's delectable scent turns all awkward,*' Anna scolded herself ruefully, realizing that cuddling had been awkward enough when he was twenty-one to her twenty-four, but now...

Now she felt like a cougar just because she noticed his scent and remembered how much she enjoyed it.

Fuck my life.

But, thank the gods, Obsidian didn't seem to notice anything odd about her behavior. With a happy rumble, he wrapped a wing around her shoulders, dragging her closer so they could both take turns reading from the book.

Eventually, Obsidian fell asleep on the sofa. Moving carefully, she extracted herself from under his wing, grabbed a couple more blankets, and tucked them around him. It took a moment to locate the light switches, but after finding them next to the outside door, she turned off all but the small one over the kitchen sink.

While gargoyles had excellent night vision, this part of the compound was windowless, and she was just plain old human again, with shit-poor human night vision.

Besides, she never knew when things would decide to go south. Better to be prepared.

Glancing around at the darkened area, she debated going to the room she'd picked, but in the end, she just grabbed the last blanket and claimed the other couch as her own.

CHAPTER TWENTY-ONE

"*D*on't forget my fireball shelving system," a gruff voice said. "One fireball has some kissing and a little heat and adult situations. This level is only slightly above my smaller 'clean' romance reads section. But with either section, if you're looking for something with more details, you'll be disappointed and needlessly suffer Bang Anxiety all the way to the end. You following?" The voice was Greenborrow's.

"I'm following," Obsidian agreed, sounding far too keen.

"Good. Two fireballs have kissing and heavy petting but fade to black. Three fireballs have on-page sexy times, no closed doors, but tame vanilla. Four fireballs—that's where the different flavors of kink kicks in. Five fireballs are so hot you'll get sunburn. Six fireballs—the book just caught fire. Seven fireballs—the house is on fire. Eight fireballs—the atmosphere just ignited. And then we have nine fireballs, also known as nuclear fission," Greenborrow said with a chuckle. "Those are the ones that are so hot even Commander Gryton would get such a boner he'd bang Erika."

Anna knew she shouldn't be listening. But her other choice was to 'wake up' in the middle of their smut book talk—big nope on that one. If she could have melted through the floor and escaped unseen, she would have.

"The steamier, the more fireballs. The shelves are all marked. And since you're inexperienced and Anna is human, you likely need all the help you can get to figure things out with a human. But I know Adept Thayn and Gran are physically intimate with gargoyle on human action. Or maybe that's human on gargoyle action. Gran is one adventurous lady."

'What... the... Fuck!' Anna shouted silently in her mind. *'What the actual fuck!'*

"Remember what I said. My shelves are always open for avid readers. And I'm very good at matching the perfect book for any reading mood."

"I will come to you for your... expertise should I need advice, Ancient One," Obsidian said in a hushed voice.

"By the way, good morning, beautiful," Greenborrow said.

There was a long pause. "I'm not talking to the gargoyle, Anna. You might as well get up since you're awake."

Anna grunted and opened her eyes to study Greenborrow. The ancient leshii was dressed in overalls with no shirt or shoes today, looking like a redneck farmer. Not unusual for him.

He also had a huge grin plastered on his face. "Don't mind me. I'm just corrupting another young mind."

Anna coughed and muttered a hoarse greeting as she stretched her legs.

What had they been talking about before Anna woke?

And Obsidian? She snuck a glance in his direction. He didn't even look the slightest bit embarrassed. How long had he been talking with the leshii? What other topics of a... sensitive nature had they been talking about?

Wait. Never mind. She didn't want to know.

"Just a friendly warning," Greenborrow offered. "You two may not want to fall asleep watching TV or reading. Jason can't be trusted. I once woke up to find I was wearing different... clothing."

"Noted. But thanks for the warning." Anna yawned, stretched, and pretended she hadn't heard a word from their earlier conversation. "Have you heard if we're expected anywhere today?"

"No. You two are on R&R for the foreseeable future," Greenborrow said and stood, coming over to Anna and patting her shoulder. "You have my condolences since Jason is also still on R&R. He's concussed from the hit to the head he took in battle. And as a result, he's bored out of his mind."

Anna grunted, and Greenborrow laughed.

"Might I suggest the courtyard garden? It's lovely and large enough for getting some exercise. Plus, I rounded up some juice and Danishes for breakfast."

Anna's lips twitched, but she held back a smile. "Danishes are hardly breakfast food."

"They are 'anytime' food when you're as old as I am, dear."

She couldn't fight him on that and conceded the point.

CHAPTER TWENTY-TWO

*A*nna and Obsidian were stretching their legs on the manicured paths of the large courtyard garden they'd found with some help from their current babysitter, Erika. The courtyard garden took up a good amount of real estate, and Anna knew there was no way this extravagance would be part of any standard military base. When she'd enquired, she'd been told by Erika that this was one of the requirements their clan and coven allies had stipulated. It was a hardline that no amount of negotiations had been able to downsize.

Not really a surprise, Anna had admitted, with the likes of Greenborrow and the pooka as part of the team. The fae clans were naturally more comfortable in a forest than in a building. And Anna had to admit, gargoyles were much the same.

Anna glanced over her shoulder at Erika, where the

other woman was following along behind at a leisurely pace. She directed her question at the Null. "Can just anyone come here whenever they have a free moment, or is there some kind of schedule?"

It wouldn't surprise her if there were. Many of the fae and the coven required peace and privacy to work some of their more complex spells. And they needed to draw their energy from the natural world for some of it.

"No schedule. Any of the magic users can come here whenever they want. That includes you and Obsidian. A few human members from the black-ops teams are regulars as well. It builds trust and comradery and all that."

Ahead of them, Obsidian started down another side path.

"Don't think we're moving fast enough for the gargoyle," Erika said, a slanted smile on her lips as she watched him. "He seems different from the Rasoren Obsidian I met two years ago."

"Yeah." That reminded Anna that the Null had never met him until he was Rasoren Obsidian.

She frowned. "He seems more formal and intense than Rasoren Obsidian, but maybe that was just because I didn't know him."

Anna lowered her voice. "I think he's struggling, trying to prove that he's a worthy Rasoren even though he doesn't remember completing his training. And now he's overcompensating."

"You okay with all this?" Erika asked suddenly.

Anna frowned down at the gravel of the path. "Have to be, don't I?"

"Dealing with the shit as it happens and being *okay* with it are two different things, you know?"

Anna had never thought of the Null as being astute, but then again, she hadn't really had time to get to know her. They'd both been busy dealing with their own responsibilities before the war.

Ahead, a snort of surprise and a grunt issued from the direction they'd seen Obsidian last. Anna and Erika glanced at each other and then broke into a run. They raced around the corner and nearly collided with Obsidian's broad back. He stood upright with his wings spread.

Anna ducked under one and came up on the other side, facing another portal being birthed into the world.

"That better be Gregory," Anna muttered.

"Better safe than sorry," Erika said as she reached for her radio and called it in. "That said, it probably is the Avatar. He said he'd be back this morning. And he never clears it ahead of time through proper channels like he's supposed to."

Anna wondered why 'proper channels' thought they'd be able to control the behavior of a being older than the universe. She trained her sidearm on the portal. The soft blue spell running along the length of the gun, the one designed to protect the firearm from tampering by foreign magic, flared in the cross currents of the forming portal.

"And for the record," Anna muttered, "I'm not paranoid for wanting a weapon while strolling the gardens."

"Didn't say you were," Erika answered, her weapon aimed at the portal, just in case. However, her ability as a null would likely be much more helpful if whatever was coming for a visit wasn't Gregory.

The portal's magic heaved and shifted, vibrating slightly. Though it quickly turned into more of a tremor.

"That's new," Erika muttered. "Think that's the signal to move our sweet, god-fearing asses."

Anna backed up until she bumped into Obsidian. He wouldn't move his big, stubborn ass.

He chuckled at them. "It's only Gregory. I can see him on the other side of the portal."

Anna stared harder at the portal, but the mirror-like surface hid anything on the other side. "How the hell can you see him?"

Obsidian huffed another sound of humor, as if the humans were entertaining him again. "I can see his soul. It's hard to mistake."

"Right. Your freaky new power."

A moment later, the portal's mirror-like surface vanished, confirming Obsidian was correct. On the level of weird shit she'd encountered since discovering magic was real, Obsidian's ability really wasn't all that odd. At least, that's what she told herself.

"I carry dire news," Gregory said as he joined them.

The gargoyle looked around, scanning the garden and

the windows lining the courtyard's walls. He huffed unhappily and then glanced at each of them. "We need to talk, but not here. Come with me."

With that, he turned from them and strode to the center of the courtyard, where there was a large open area of grass for sitting or picnics, but Anna doubted the Avatar had anything so mundane planned for the area today. They joined him, standing in a semicircle, each of them looking on questioningly. He motioned them onto the nearby benches.

"I'll explain what I've learned in a moment. However, I need to complete a bit of spell work before a team of your brethren come tromping over and asking a bunch of questions I dare not reveal the answers to just yet."

Anna and Erika shared identical looks that said, 'what have I gotten myself into this time' before turning their attention back to the Avatar, watching to see what he'd do next. They didn't have long to wait.

Standing in the center of the grassy area, his head tilted down and his eyes closed, he didn't look like he was doing any kind of fancy magic spell, but then between one breath and the next, the air temperature dropped by a good thirty degrees and Anna's breath was suddenly fogging the air.

Beside her, she heard Erika mutter something uncomplimentary and rubbed her arms, trying to keep warm. The cold continued to build around the unmoving gargoyle, and Anna knew he was drawing on magic from the Spirit Realm. This was big time magic, epic advanced level shit, something only the Avatars, djinns, and maybe a certain pair of demigod twins could pull off.

Whatever the hamadryad Sorceress had found out after examining the body of the warlock, it couldn't have been good news for any of the realms if this was Gregory's response.

The temperature dropped several more degrees when Gregory snapped his wings open. Rings of power blazed to life on the ground in a circle around him. With bright silvery magic bleeding from his talons, he began drawing symbols in the air, the lines and runes pulsing with energy. One by one, he sent the floating symbols to halt at specific points along the rings of power, aligning in some fashion that made sense to the Avatar but was meaningless to Anna.

"You can join me now," he said, gesturing for Anna to take up a position on one of the symbols to his right and for Erika to take another to his left. Then he indicated Obsidian should stand opposite him. "You've all traveled through portals before, but never one so hastily made here in this magic-poor realm. What is the human phrase? It will be a rough ride, yes?"

"So, you're just abducting us?" Anna asked.

"Yes."

"And portal travel is now suddenly safe for us?"

"No," he paused and then huffed. "But you are with me, and this is not that long of trip. You'll be fine."

"Well, at least you're honest," she said, adding, "Any chance you'll tell us where we're going? And for how long? By the way, you're breaking a shitload of rules. Gonna have brass so far up your ass over this, we'll be able to see them when you yawn."

Gregory's lips pulled back from his fangs in a gargoyle grimace. "Besides that being the most vulgar thing anyone has said to me in at least three lifetimes," he paused and leveled Anna with a much put-upon expression, "we serve a higher power and are needed elsewhere at the moment. Your souls were created for this purpose. Rules conceived in the Mortal Realm by short-lived men with even shorter sight and less understanding have no bearing on your duty."

'Right. I'll just quote the demigod at my court martial,' Anna thought darkly.

"Ready?" he asked in warning.

Anna and the others nodded.

"I doubt any of you are," Gregory said, his tone full of dark amusement.

CHAPTER TWENTY-THREE

Portal spells always felt a little like having the ground fall out from underneath you and then seconds later, getting launched on a rocket. Then the spell activated. Within seconds, Anna decided she wanted off this ride. She was sure her skin went north, skeleton east, guts south, and soul went into the fucking west. There was a spinning sensation and then a painful jolt. After a brief mental image of all her parts merging back together, she gasped air into her starved lungs.

Moaning reached her ears. It took her longer than she wanted to admit that some of those pitiful sounds were coming from her mouth. At least she wasn't crying like a baby.

However, judging by the grass tickling her nose, she was on the ground curled in a fetal position.

She was jolted out of her misery by a warm, sloppy gargoyle tongue washing her face. Loosing a string of swear words, Anna batted away Obsidian's muzzle before he could attempt a round two. Blinking her vision clear, she found herself facing her Rasoren. At least he was spread-eagled and looking more than a little dazed, too.

Lifting her head, she spat grass from her mouth and spotted Erika picking herself up off the ground. Anna supposed she should do the same. She swiftly discovered that forming the thought was easier than actually willing her body into carrying out her brain's orders.

"Come on. Up we get," Anna muttered, giving her uncoordinated limbs a pep talk. Her vision swam as she came to her feet. She would have fallen back on her ass, but a large hand connected with her rear and gave her a little shove until she was mostly vertical again and had recovered her center of gravity. Obsidian rose to his feet behind her.

She didn't mention the hand on her ass, since in his defense, if she'd fallen, she would have landed on him.

"You call that a portal?" She directed her question at Gregory when the world stopped spinning, and she could find him. "Did you forget some important part of the spell?"

"No. And you'll be fine." He barked out a sharp laugh. "Though you *do* have an awe-inspiring imagination. But I assure you that at no point in the trip did your skin and skeleton part company."

"What about my guts?" She rubbed at her middle. "I'm pretty sure something got left behind."

He snorted again. "Stop complaining. You've suffered worse in the past and will probably suffer worse in the future."

"Thanks for that inspirational talk." Anna rolled her eyes at him. "Much appreciated."

Gregory shook his head, looking bemused. "Humans are an odd species."

"Thanks," Erika muttered, joining the conversation. "Always nice to know exactly what you think of us."

"I did not say it as an insult. Just a statement of fact." Gregory rubbed the side of his muzzle. It was a tell all gargoyles seemed to share when they were baffled by something. In this case, humans.

She glanced at the other woman and then turned and took in Obsidian's appearance. He looked almost fully recovered already. Erika, on the other hand, looked worse than Anna felt. Her pale skin was even paler than normal, freckles practically blazing against her skin. Her short red hair stuck out in all directions and had collected leaves and various bits of other debris.

Anna clapped the Null on the shoulder. "You going to survive?"

"Unfortunately, but I think I'm starting to miss the afterlife."

Anna laughed and thumped Erika on the shoulder a second time. "Sounds like you'll live."

Turning in a circle, Anna found they were surrounded by dense underbrush and towering trees. There wasn't a single sign or sound of civilization. Once she finished taking in the sights, she turned back to Gregory. "So, what's so dire that you had to drag us all the way up to Fuckwhere Ontario?"

She could see him mouthing the words 'fuckwhere' before he growled. "Gah! You mortals and your swearing and your sarcasm and your disrespect." Gregory just shook his head. "If Gran were here, you'd be black and blue with bruises."

Er... right. She'd caught enough blows from Gran's quarterstaff to feel the truth in Gregory's words. One swiftly learned not to swear in front of the formidable older witch simply known as Gran. "Yes, but she's not here. So, I and my potty mouth are safe. Now get to the world-ending news you obviously need to share but couldn't back at the base."

"We shall be free to discuss what my Sorceress suspects shortly."

Anna and Erika again cast each other silent, questioning looks. Erika mouthed, 'how should I know?'

They were kept in the dark for the next twenty minutes while Gregory created another powerful weaving. But with this spell, he was taking his time. Eventually, a shimmering impenetrable shield blocked her view of the forest and sky. Though no natural light could penetrate the twelve-foot dome surrounding them, they weren't in complete darkness. The shield walls gave off a subtle blue-green glow, providing enough light for Anna to see her three companions.

"It is safe for us to speak now," Gregory said. "No power can penetrate this shield. It is a much smaller spell of the type used to create the Veil Between the Realms."

No wonder no light or sound could reach her ears. It probably even blocked oxygen and smaller particles.

"Anna, you were correct from the very start. The creature you singled out as the leader of the warlocks is no warlock himself. He is something else. Only something very powerful can hide its presence from me, even here in this realm. My Sorceress thinks it is a true demon. An ancient creature that is evil given physical form. Lacking a better name, they have always been called void demons, named after the void that is their prison." Gregory paused and gestured at his body. "Being born into a flesh and blood body is somewhat limiting, in that my awareness and my magic are limited to what stresses flesh can tolerate."

"A void demon. That's what we're facing? I don't even know what that is," Anna muttered.

"There are a few creatures capable of hiding what they are from me in my current form. And the leader of the warlocks might not be a void demon. Pray to the

Divine Ones that my Sorceress is wrong. But we must find out the truth, and there is only one way to do that. We need to summon a djinn to aid us. However, the summoning of a djinn can be felt across the three realms if a person is skilled enough in magic to sense and read the meaning of the disturbances in the flows of magic."

"And our new enemy, whatever it is, is something powerful enough to do that?" Anna guessed.

"Unfortunately."

"That's going to be a problem if you're trying to hide the fact we're onto him."

"Exactly. It's a good thing there is already a djinn in this world."

"There is?"

"Yes. Toward the end of the final battle, when it became apparent that there would be no winner and both sides would lose, three of the Battle Goddess's most powerful captains banded together, stole the djinn's bottle, and ordered him off the field of battle. Then they all escaped to Earth."

"Wait. Hold up. Are you talking about Captains Sorac, Vaspara, and Bervicta? Are they still here on Earth? And the djinn—that thing we saw fighting Gryton's elemental dragon when they were tossing entire mountain ranges at each other—that djinn, he's here on Earth?"

"Yes. But the humans don't know that. I alluded that

he and the captains escaped back into the Magic Realm and have since been evading me."

Anna's stomach hit her toes. Why the hell was that unstable, ticking time bomb with a payload greater than all the nuclear ordnance on Earth still on the planet? She'd assumed the captains and the djinn would have been top-level targets, some of the first to be taken out by the joint task force and their Avatar allies.

But that hadn't happened. The unstable djinn was still here on Earth.

The hell?

"Naharnin is his name," Gregory bit out the words, a bitterness in them. "He is the most ancient of the djinn and the Avatar soul's oldest companion."

And Gregory sounded protective of his buddy. That there was another big ole surprise. Anna hated surprises.

"After the final battle, when I returned to Earth to assess the damages caused by Naharnin and the captains' escape to this world, I reached out to my friend. I found a being I barely recognized, so scarred by what the blood witch had done to him that he was holding onto his sanity by little threads. Only one thing calmed and restored him to his former self for short periods."

Gregory paused, and Anna almost felt his emotional turbulence swirling behind the words.

"Since being with Sorac, Vaspara, and their draklings soothed him, I allowed him to stay in hiding with them. He does not trust the humans of this world not to retaliate against the captains, and so he, not-so-nicely, warned me off from coming for him or sending anyone after him. He is determined to stay with the captains until they have raised their clutch of young firedrakes."

"Sorac and Vaspara and their offspring are here on Earth?" Anna asked. "I trained with them for months as a captive in the Battle Goddess's kingdom. But they weren't without honor. I'm glad they were able to escape with their draklings."

Gregory nodded. "Naharnin told me he, Vaspara, and Sorac took the firedrake's eggs and made their escape together weeks before the final battle. They thought themselves finally free of the Battle Goddess and their dark destiny. Vaspara and Sorac had known of the blood witch's madness and just how dangerous a captive djinn was. They had planned to find a way to get Naharnin to us so that we might be able to free him before he destroyed their world. But their plans were foiled." Gregory's fingers slowly closed into fists. "The blood witch was able to track them across half the distance of their planet using the blood magic spells she'd used to capture and entrap the djinn. My understanding is that they were forced to fight in the last battle or watch the infant firedrakes be enslaved by the witch."

Anna felt pity for the two captains. "And they have been hiding here peacefully ever since the final battle?"

"Yes. And the harpy-hybrid, Bervicta, is with them. I gave Naharnin my word that I would not hunt him and would keep his location a secret from the humans if he did nothing to harm this world."

"So, you were just going to trust his unstable ass about that?"

Gregory snorted. "I am keeping a close eye on him and his new family. But rest assured, I do not plan to leave them here. My Sorceress has cloned Lillian once more and is growing the body in the hamadryad. Once the new body is mature, the Sorceress will return to this world and provide safe passage back to the Magic Realm for him and his family. If he is still unwilling to trust, she will stay with them, ensuring that neither the draklings, the captains, Naharnin nor the humans of this world come to harm."

"You're making my head hurt," Erika muttered. "And by telling us this, you're putting me on the spot. I must report all of what you just said to my superiors."

Gregory grunted. "And have you told your superiors what my son is currently doing?"

Erika snapped her teeth together and exhaled sharply through her nose but didn't utter another word.

"I thought as much," Gregory said, and chuckled. "It's likely wise you haven't mentioned by son's activities. Your human superiors don't need to worry about that. And if they learned the truth, they'd likely try to exile you to the Magic Realm, but you are needed here."

Erika still didn't comment, but her expression spoke volumes. She was keeping a secret from their superiors.

"I don't like any of this. I don't want to know any of this. It's not just Erika you're putting on the spot here, Gregory!" Anna bit out, wondering what secrets the Null and the Avatar were keeping from the allied forces' other members. It absolutely had something to do with Commander Gryton, the elemental dragon demigod currently doing time as a star somewhere else in the universe, far from Earth.

"None of us have to like this," Gregory said with a deep sigh. "But it is the best option when I cannot leave Lillian for long while she is still pregnant with our djinn child. And I fear it will take a lot to change Naharnin's mind. And to attempt to capture an unstable djinn—the most powerful of his kind—wouldn't end well for anyone. That is why the Sorceress's plan is the safest."

"And it wouldn't just be the djinn," Anna said in sudden understanding. "We'd be fighting the three surviving captains. If cornered, they'd fight, and I can attest to just how very deadly opponents they'd make."

"You understand the dilemma?"

"Yes. Still don't like it. But I understand."

Erika jumped into the conversation. "Y'all might understand the dilemma, but I can guarantee that Earth's leaders and our militaries will not get all cool about any of this."

"Erika is right," Anna agreed. "This isn't going to go over well with our superiors."

"That's why I'm asking you both to keep this secret

for me. It is for the greater good. Your planet, and your human families, will be in much more danger if your leaders decide to make a move against the djinn. But if they don't know he's still here, they won't hunt him, and he will not act to defend his new family."

Anna fisted her hands, fighting the urge to punch something.

Why?

Why did everything have to be so freaking complicated?

"Fine," Anna muttered. "I'll keep your secret. But if all this shit backfires, I'll have words with you in the afterlife."

Gregory coughed and then grimaced. "There will probably be a lineup. You might have to wait somewhere behind the Divine Ones, Gryton, Lord Death, and an assortment of others."

"I'd wait," Anna muttered. "What else would I have to do, being dead and all?"

"Same!" Erika huffed out.

"I, too, would wait in line," Obsidian muttered, finally joining the conversation. And his tone suggested Gregory's plan wasn't sitting well with him either.

But the Avatar merely laughed at them. "You three, have a little faith. I am confident in my Sorceress's plan. All will turn out well in the end." He paused, then added, "There may just be a few rough patches to get through first."

"Since I assume you didn't drag us out here just to confide in us about your djinn secret, why are we really here?" Anna asked.

"Because if there is a void demon loose on Earth, I will need a djinn to confirm that for me."

Right. Anna felt her brows descending and tried to smooth her resting bitch face into something more pleasant.

"Are you going to summon your djinn friend right here, right now?" Anna asked, already knowing his answer, but hoping she was wrong. "Like now, now?"

"Yes. I have no choice. Every moment we wait is time the enemy has to strengthen their numbers and mobilize another attack against us. So far, we have been lucky. These warlocks are newly created, none older than a year or two. They haven't yet had the eons to gain the knowledge of the first warlocks. But they are cunning and ambitious and learn quickly. They will become more formidable by the day."

"You're just a bucket of cheer," Erika mumbled.

Gregory sniffed, drawing himself up to his full height. "Knowing that I'm about to annoy a powerful djinn, one that will have more natural power than me here in this realm, puts me in a serious mood."

"You know what?" Erika huffed out. "You suck at pep talks."

"Then it's good I'm old and powerful and can do useful things," he deadpanned. "Like knowing the intricate spells required to summon a possibly hostile djinn into an impenetrable shield, isn't it?" Then, to prove his point, he began summoning power from the Spirit Realm once more.

Erika raised her hands in surrender and Anna grabbed the Null's arm, tugging sharply.

"We'll just all stand...." Anna gestured to one spot along the wall of the dome that looked just like the rest of it. There really was no place out of the way. "Over here. All nice and out of the way while you summon a djinn."

And if they all huddled together, they might not be frozen popsicles by the time the Avatar was finished with his spell work.

Power from the Spirit Realm was fucking cold.

CHAPTER TWENTY-FOUR

S itting with Anna and Erika huddled against him for warmth, Obsidian watched as Gregory created another elaborate spell to summon a djinn. To create one powerful weaving inside another was no easy task. Such powerful spells in close proximity tended to destabilize and destroy each other. He attempted to memorize the patterns and runes and the order in which the Avatar utilized them, but after Gregory had burned the fiftieth rune mark into the grass, Obsidian gave up.

Perhaps Rasoren Obsidian could have memorized each rune perfectly, but Journeyman Obsidian failed. He cast a quick sidelong glance at Anna. She arched an eyebrow at his scrutiny.

"Don't expect me to memorize that. You were always better at the magic stuff than me. I got a headache after the first five minutes of watching him work." Anna bumped shoulders with him. "So, if you were hoping I'd be able to help you remember all the bits of that spell, you're shit out of luck."

Then they both glanced over at the Null. She looked bored, but when she noticed the direction of their gazes, she laughed and said, "Don't look at me. I just eat magic."

"Your control is quite good," Obsidian commented, realizing he didn't feel her feeding upon his magic, even with her tucked close. He'd read a little about nulls in his training, but his mentors had only touched on them because they were so rare. He hadn't thought he'd ever meet one, or he would have done a little more digging. But he remembered that most nulls never learned to control their ability entirely and would always feed upon the nearest magic source.

"I'm linked to an elemental dragon through a tiny piece of his soul grafted onto mine. It was learn swiftly on the job or die. And Gryton is only a slightly less lethal teacher than his dragon." She snorted with humor once more. "Though the dragon has a more pleasant personality."

"Wouldn't take much," Anna muttered from his other side.

He agreed; he still hadn't liked Commander Gryton even after learning the Avatar's son had protected them in the Battle Goddess's Kingdom. At least as much as he could without betraying that he had switched sides and served the Avatars.

But before Obsidian could dwell on all the reasons he disliked the fire elemental, Gregory completed his spell and turned back to them.

"I am ready to summon Naharnin. However, I will be essentially kidnapping him from his bottle. It will be… unpleasant for him." Gregory frowned. "He may be a touch hostile. Do nothing to gain his attention. I will keep him focused on me. Once he calms, I will explain why we are here."

"Wait. Why are we even here?" Anna piped up.

Gregory flashed her a gargoyle grin, one more full of teeth than reassurance. "Because I want Naharnin to meet his allies, to know that I trust you three and that he can, too."

Obsidian and the two women nodded in unison.

"But remember to stay quiet until I've ascertained Naharnin's mood," Gregory cautioned, and then when they nodded again, he turned his attention back to the glowing spell in front of him. It was no wider than the distance of Obsidian's outstretched arms, but the power being given off by the relatively small spell was tremendous.

Gregory closed his eyes and began to chant softly.

Obsidian recognized the tone and cadence. It was an activation spell-key.

A small knot of burning power formed between

Gregory's spread hands. The spell spun and twisted in the air, possessing an elegance to the craftsmanship that even Obsidian recognized and envied. Perhaps he'd be skilled enough one day to create such a spell.

But then Gregory released the tiny key spell from between his hands. It fell slowly, as if unaffected by the gravity of this world. When it touched down, nothing happened at first. But then there was a little spark, and seconds later, the larger spell absorbed the key spell.

The individual rings comprising the spell began slowly spinning in the opposite direction of the two on either side. The spell's glow grew brighter until it was hard to see clearly, but he was confident the runes were each now spinning as well.

A sudden tingling rush of magic swept over him. He felt the two women twitch in reaction on either side, and he tightened his wings around them instinctively, though he doubted there was anything he could do to protect them from what was coming if it wished them harm.

But he trusted the Avatar, so he simply watched the spell with a touch of awe.

The spell expanded upward swiftly until it was a column of bright burning power. It wasn't until after a deep droning tone issued from the spell and it dimmed that he realized something was within the fading column of magic.

The temperature inside the dome warmed in a

matter of heartbeats. The humans no longer shivered, but he kept his wings around them anyway.

At first, he couldn't see anything other than the burning power of its soul. Unlike the Avatar's soul, which was beautiful in a fierce but comforting way, this djinn's soul possessed a terrible burning beauty that threatened to consume anyone or anything foolish enough to cross it. He couldn't help but think he was looking at a Spirit Realm assassin.

"An adept description," whispered a rich baritone voice, mesmerizing in its tone.

Remembering he was not supposed to draw the djinn's attention, Obsidian looked away, studying the spell burned into the ground instead. Or at least he tried to keep his gaze fixed on the grass but couldn't. There was something about the djinn that stole his will. Anna grabbed his hand, and he was certain she felt the same irresistible pull.

Against his will, he found his gaze drawn toward the djinn's burning stare. The world receded until nothing existed except that ancient being.

CHAPTER TWENTY-FIVE

*A*nna blinked, trying to make out a shape within the shadows. She blinked again, but all she saw was darkness inside the column of power. But she felt something. Straining her eyes and other senses, she attempted to pierce the darkness and see inside. But in the end, she didn't have to.

A rippling stirred the air and unexpected color and light spilled from inside the column to bathe the sides of the dome. What could only be described as a fissure split the air and darkness. A being of pure power stepped out of the billowing magic. Energy shimmered around him and then dimmed enough that she could see the being a little more clearly.

Tendrils of magic coiled and danced around his shape for a few moments before being absorbed back into the mass of power that was even now taking on a more solid appearance of a male body. After a moment, those tendrils of burning energy shifted into tattoos decorating swathes of his bronze-toned skin.

His body may now have looked more mortal in appearance, but his eyes...

Anna shivered. Those intense eyes of his still glowed like two pools of molten lava.

Much like the rest of his form, she found his tattoos mesmerizing. They brightened and dimmed as if someone blew across hot coals, making them glow brighter by turns. At least his gaze maintained a steady burn, unlike his tattoos, which reminded her of the tattoo Commander Gryton had sported on his chest. And Anna suddenly understood the two beings were kin insomuch as demigods could be.

This male was beautiful in a terrifying sort of way. His shape and form were designed to appeal to anything with a heartbeat—gender, age, sexual orientation, and religious beliefs be damned. Then she remembered he'd been spending time with a succubus and a firedrake sired by a fertility god. So maybe she shouldn't be surprised by his sexual appeal.

Something shifted within her and a moment later her foreign magic woke, but not to attack a threat. Instead, it seemed simply to want her to witness something. She exhaled a sigh of relief. The last thing they needed was for the power of the Battle Goddess to pick a fight with an ancient djinn.

Her new magic planted knowledge in her mind, telling her that everything about his appearance was a lie, a carefully constructed deception to stun and ensnare the unwary.

It shouldn't have come as a surprise.

After all, a captured djinn must blind his masters to free himself. A task she'd been told a djinn embraced with everything they were. And if they destroyed entire kingdoms to regain that freedom, that was something they were willing to do in order to return to the Spirit Realm.

Anna had seen him on the field of battle, but never so close. And not like this—humanoid seeming. She may not have had to face him, but Gryton and Erika had fought this thing on the battlefield.

But this wasn't a battlefield. It was a much more confined space, and they had the djinn's full attention. Anna, Obsidian, and Erika stood in a huddle, forced to move away from the wall as the djinn circled them.

The hell?

Hadn't Gregory said he would keep the djinn focused on him?

Great job, Gregory!

The djinn walked a circle around them, but he did not attack.

Anna relaxed a bit, enough to draw air into her starving lungs. She noticed the glowing power that obscured his lower body rippled and danced like the light from a candle caught in a draft when he walked.

Finishing his circle, he halted, and so did the swirling power hiding his lower body. Now it reminded her more of a skirt than a swirling bank of fog.

Now that he'd stopped moving, she noticed something else. His body had grown more solid seeming, somehow more substantial. She could pick out more details.

After scanning him for weapons, she didn't see any. But really, he didn't need weapons. He *was* a weapon.

Every inch of him screamed lethal.

He was naked from the waist up. From the waist down, his only items of clothing were a wide belt and the skirt-like power shimmering around his legs. And even those were probably manifestations of his making. She had a sinking feeling he could make her see whatever he wanted.

Her magic said that if he were in a cruel mood, he could toy with his prey for centuries.

"It is good that I am not cruel, isn't it?" the djinn said, his voice as deep and beguiling as anything she'd ever heard before.

Obsidian huffed in surprise beside her, and Anna knew she wasn't the only one made uneasy by the ancient djinn's proximity.

Gregory stepped in close to the djinn.

"Leave the cubs be," the Avatar said and fearlessly

cupped the djinn's shoulder and turned Naharnin to look at him. "Your business is with me."

All the djinn's intense focus turned to the Avatar, and Anna released a shuddering breath.

Glancing down, she noticed she still had hold of Obsidian's hand. Or maybe it was him with a death grip on her fingers. Whichever it was, she had no plans to release him anytime soon. She also noticed him holding one of Erika's hands on his other side.

No one wanted to be in this trap with a possibly insane djinn.

CHAPTER TWENTY-SIX

"I am always pleased when our duties draw us together, my friend." The djinn's voice had softened slightly, a hint of something else coming into it, something almost possessive, but there was also a tenderness that stole much of the djinn's earlier harshness. The sharpness of his features also softened, as if his appearance shifted to fit his mood. "Though, I must say, meeting half of the Avatar soul while it is housed in a flesh and blood body is always a rare treat. One I'd like to explore more later...."

"Enough with your innuendos." Gregory chuckled and grabbed the djinn, dragging him close for a hug. "I have missed you, my friend."

The djinn froze, his body still with an unnatural tension, but after a moment, Naharnin relaxed and allowed himself to be held. The two remained wrapped in the gargoyle's wings for some moments.

Obsidian might be young and still naïve about many things. But he was experienced enough to know the signs of a deep and ancient love when he witnessed it, and he was certain the djinn loved the Avatar soul no matter that it was currently split in two and this half housed in a male body. Such love was not taboo among the gargoyles or most of the other fae races, so Obsidian watched, happy to see two such ancient beings reunited.

Beside him, both Erika and Anna seemed to have been surprised by the revelation but accepting of it.

"Had I known I would receive such a warm and enthusiastic," Naharnin's voice dipped low, stressing the word and making it sound anything but innocent, "greeting, I would have visited much sooner."

Gregory barked out a sharp laugh, folded his wings, and pushed the djinn to arm's length, but didn't release him. "We do not have time for your mischief. I've summoned you here because I have dire news."

The Avatar launched into all that had happened in the last few days, concluding with what the hamadryad Sorceress suspected regarding their enemies. At last, the Avatar asked the djinn, "Will you help us?"

"Without question," the djinn agreed. There was a long pause, and then he added, "But I have a request of my own."

Gregory's look turned guarded. "Very well."

"May I examine the two younglings?"

Obsidian knew the djinn had to be referring to him and Anna. Erika, well young in years, was a null, and Gregory had said she was one of the first batch of souls created. So that would make her ancient, possibly nearly as old as the djinn. Or maybe older.

"That is up to them," Gregory rumbled. Though when Naharnin turned to look at them, Obsidian noticed the Avatar nodded his head to indicate it was safe.

"Do I have your permission to approach?" Naharnin asked politely.

Obsidian nodded, already sensing the djinn didn't need to ask. He was powerful enough to do whatever he wanted.

The djinn turned to Anna next.

"Sure. Have at it," she said.

Naharnin laughed, and Obsidian got the impression that the ancient djinn was entertained by them. Perhaps it was how he viewed all young creatures? Obsidian relaxed, since there was suddenly nothing hostile in the djinn's demeanor.

After walking over to them and studying them for a few moments in silence, Naharnin tilted his head, a new light coming into his gaze, softening its harshness a touch, like when he'd looked upon the Avatar earlier.

"Obsidian, did you know that the Divine Ones tasked me to aid them in creating your soul? They needed new beings that would grow in power to one day rival their Avatars. Yours is the first soul I have ever helped shape. They usually create all new souls, but they wished for my input because of my longtime friendship with the Avatar. I was honored to aid them in creating the souls that would eventually grow into their second Avatar."

He reached out one hand, and before Obsidian could react, those long, elegant fingers slid into his chest. There was no pain, just a strange caressing sort of tingle along his internal organs, but it was still one of the strangest sensations he'd ever felt. And he did not like it.

"Holy fuck!" Anna shouted, advancing on the djinn. "Your, 'do I have your permission to approach' and our agreement that you may approach is absolutely not the same as 'can I shove my hand in your chest' just for the record."

Obsidian tightened his hold on Anna's fingers, though he wasn't sure if it was to caution her to moderate her words or if it was simply because he desperately wanted the comfort of their connection.

"Be at peace, younglings. I have no wish to harm you. I simply dislike seeing something I had a hand in creating so damaged." The djinn regarded Anna with a steady look. "Do I have both your permissions to help the young male better control his power?"

"Uh, yeah. Sure," Anna murmured. Though this time, her tone was appropriately subdued and polite. As for Obsidian, he was too shocked to speak or react as the djinn continued whatever he was doing.

Naharnin closed his eyes and bowed his head, and Obsidian felt a small surge of magic tingle deep inside. He was relatively certain the djinn was healing some damage to his soul. It did not hurt and was over more swiftly than he'd thought.

When the strange tingling subsided, Obsidian gulped down a large lungful of air.

It struck him then that this being truly was his creator, in a sense.

"No," the djinn said as he slid his hand free. "The Divine Ones are your creators, like all the souls of the universe. I only had a small part in your making. They allowed me to plant the spark of what type of personality you would develop."

"May I ask you something?" When the djinn gave a very slight bend of his head, Obsidian continued. "If you had a hand in my making, does that mean you had a hand in Anna's creation?"

"I did not. That honor was granted to another." The djinn laughed and tilted his chin in Erika's direction.

Both Anna and Erika stared at each other in disbelief.

"No way," Anna muttered.

Erika just blinked in surprise.

Gregory bellowed in laughter. "Indeed, fruit never falls far from the tree. How did I not figure that out sooner?"

"You have been busy," the djinn told Gregory. "You would have figured it out sooner or later.

Erika and Anna were both still in denial or shock, Obsidian wasn't sure which.

The djinn glanced at Erika. "Surely you already knew you're the most ancient celestial warrior, even as I'm the most ancient djinn."

Erika made a gasping noise before answering. "There was mention of celestial warriors. But... nothing... detailed was discussed."

"Your education is lacking, my ancient friend. We're siblings, of a sort. It only made sense that you would shape the personality of the female half of the new Avatar pair, as I did the male half."

Erika's mouth opened and then closed, her face going blank. "I... I've got nothing."

"You are saying Erika created my Kyrsu's personality?" Obsidian ventured to ask when neither of his two companions seemed able to form complete sentences.

"Isn't it obvious?" Gregory gasped out between chuckles. "They are so similar, so much so, that I think a certain celestial warrior may have just cloned her own personality. Anna may swear more, but they share very similar character traits. Even my son was drawn to Anna at first, when it is really—" Gregory dissolved into another bout of belly laughs before he finished his sentence.

Anna and Erika stared at each other and then shook their heads in denial again.

"Does that answer your questions?" the djinn asked Obsidian.

"Yes." Obsidian bobbed his head, not knowing what else to do. "Thank you."

The djinn smiled then. "You are most welcome."

"They both have made the Divine Ones proud," Gregory agreed. "However, our time is limited. Will you go on the hunt and discover for us if our Sorceress is correct in her concerns?"

"I shall." The djinn bowed to Gregory and then vanished so suddenly Obsidian jerked and leaned forward, trying to get some sense of what kind of spell the djinn had used to travel to another location.

Gregory chuckled, probably at his expression. Obsidian attempted to school his features.

"Do not be ashamed. No youngling is born knowing all there is to know. Djinns are not hindered by flesh and blood. They are magic—they are the energy that drives the universe. They need no spells to harness that power."

"Now what?" Anna asked, beating Obsidian to it.

"Now we wait," Gregory said. "In the meantime,

perhaps we can do a little training to strengthen you both. I believe you are recovered enough."

All three moaned and groaned at the Avatar's suggestions.

CHAPTER TWENTY-SEVEN

*I*n the end, Anna and her two fellow students were too nervous and distracted by whatever news the djinn might discover to focus on the Avatar's lessons. After what was likely less than twenty minutes of trying and failing to teach Anna to summon her power at will, Gregory hissed, "Enough!"

"Sorry," Anna muttered in apology, but wasn't sorry at all. A mentor couldn't just drop a bombshell like earlier and then expect an apprentice to be able to focus on a lesson like any normal day.

Had Erika really helped create her soul?

Nah. No way. But then again, Erika wouldn't have been Erika at that point. She would have been a—a celestial warrior. Anna didn't really know what that was, but after seeing and feeling the djinn up close, she had a better idea.

Anna gave herself another mental head shake.

"Fine." Gregory dragged the word out. "I see you three are all useless at the moment. Besides, Naharnin says he's returning. We will continue with our lessons another time. But we *will* continue them."

True to Gregory's word, the djinn returned, appearing in their midst as swiftly as he'd left. One moment the ring of magic that Gregory had used to summon him was empty, and the next, the djinn was back in all his bronze-skinned and molten-tattooed glory.

"Sorry to be the bearer of unpleasant news," the djinn said, his expression harsher and colder than before. "Our Sorceress was correct. There is a void demon here on this planet, free to endanger the three realms once more. I can only assume it has somehow survived in the void all these millennia, and the blood witch created a spell powerful enough to breach the Veil Between the Realms and dragged one of those monsters from its endless torment."

Gregory cursed in what sounded like more than one language. When he was calmer again, he nodded to the djinn. "Thank you for finding what I could not, dulled as my senses are trapped in this flesh and blood body."

"It was my honor to help. And it was good to feel the power and essence of the Avatar once again. I have missed the taste of your power." The djinn reached out and touched the soft membrane on Gregory's closest wing. For a moment, a hint of vulnerability and sadness bled across the djinn's expression.

"Then stay," Gregory said in a rush, sounding like he was having a conversation they'd had more than once already. "Let me send you back to the Magic Realm. Our Sorceress will heal the damage the blood witch's enslavement has caused."

"No. I will not go back. Not yet. I have given my word to the firedrake and his mate that I will help raise the little draklings. Without me, they would starve in this realm. There isn't enough magic to raise all fourteen of them."

"I shall see that the drake and his family are given safe passage. The humans need not even know."

"It is not the humans that concern me," the djinn said and paced. "The legion gargoyles and their fae allies may not see it as you or I do. The captains have spilled enough innocent blood that the legion will judge them accordingly. I will not risk a fight or go back on my word. The firedrake and the succubus tried to save me from the blood witch. They later removed my bottle from the field of battle, saving me from having to fight you. The forces of light would have lost many more warriors had I been forced to stay and fight for the witch."

"My gargoyle brethren are reasonable. They would allow the drake to raise his family."

"I said no. If you and the Sorceress were both fully

recovered, I would bring the drake and his family to live with you and the Sorceress. But neither of you is whole. And there is no time for a fight with the legion over this, not with a void demon on the loose. I will stay on Earth to aid you should he need me. Now free me to return to my bottle."

"Naharnin, be reasonable!"

"No!" The djinn spun away from Gregory, giving Anna a good look at Naharnin's expression.

She was reminded that this being, powerful and immortal though he was, had been in the possession of the darkest of blood witches. He'd nearly been broken. And while Anna had no doubt the djinn would heal himself in time, his expression reminded her this djinn was not particularly stable.

After a moment, the djinn's expression cleared. That earlier hint of desperation, that look of a panicked and cornered animal, vanished as fast as it had come. When he spoke again, he sounded almost tired. "I will come to your call should you need me, but if you care for me at all, allow me to return to the draklings so that I may know the peace of their unconditional love for a time."

Anna riveted her gaze upon the Avatar and didn't miss the look of pain that crossed his face. And at that moment, she wanted to be anywhere else but in this dome trapped with an Avatar and a djinn, two beings who cared for each other, but both were too proud to bend or compromise their own beliefs in what was the best course of action.

But to Anna's surprise, Gregory made a liar out of her in the next moment.

"Fine. I release you from my summons." Gregory reached out and pulled the djinn into a firm embrace, pressing their foreheads together. "But my Sorceress and I will come for you one day when we have defeated this present danger, and it is safe to expose your existence. You have my word that the firedrake and his mate can raise their young alongside mine. The younglings can all grow up together, and you will have a hand in the raising of both."

Naharnin went utterly still for a moment and then exhaled soft, whispered words. "I would like that, my beloved friend."

"As would I."

Anna didn't think that vision of the future seemed too bad either. She'd love a bit of peaceful downtime. Now, if Fate and evil would just take a nap for a few centuries, that would be nice.

"You know how to track the void demon and its nest of warlocks using a portal now?" Naharnin asked.

"I do. Thank you for your suggestion."

Naharnin stepped away from Gregory. "Now we must part. Send me back to my bottle."

"I swear, I'll see you free of that enslavement spell one day very soon, my friend," Gregory nearly growled out the words, not trying to hide his rage that his oldest friend was still imprisoned.

"I'd expect nothing less." The djinn laughed, then turned serious again, his gaze seeking Anna and Obsidian, though his words were for Gregory. "Don't coddle the younglings. Trust in their skills and their new powers. This is what they were created to battle. Let them fight."

Anna glanced at Obsidian to find him watching her in return, and he gave her a slight nod, as if to say he was ready.

She raised her chin slightly and returned his subtle nod.

Bring it.

Without further words, the djinn stepped into the spell circle, and Gregory activated it.

The djinn vanished, released from the summons.

While Anna didn't like the idea of that being lurking somewhere on Earth, she trusted the Avatars. If Gregory were willing to allow the djinn this much freedom, then Anna wouldn't betray his existence to her fellow soldiers either, not when others might make shit-poor decisions and start a war they couldn't win with a djinn.

And fuck if she didn't feel just a touch indebted to the djinn. As scary as he was, that creature had a hand in creating Obsidian's personality. Like Erika had hers? She was still trying to wrap her mind around that—she'd been doing a lot of that lately. But one thing she knew with certainty—Obsidian was the best partner she could ever have asked for. And the djinn had helped create that personality.

But dammit all to hell. How many more secrets would she have to keep from her commanding officers?

But as Gregory and the djinn had made abundantly clear, there was a greater threat.

A void demon.

Now that sounded nasty. And going by the amount of caution the two ancient and powerful beings were exercising to make sure the demon didn't know they suspected its existence, Anna was going to follow their lead.

"When do we start the hunt?" Obsidian voiced the question into the heavy silence, making her smile.

Leave it to her Rasoren to get to the meat of the matter.

"Now. As soon as we can prepare." Gregory paused and then added, "We dare not allow this to escalate into a prolonged fight. Or worse, a war. Too many innocent souls would be at risk."

He was right. This couldn't drag out into a bloody war. They needed to hunt down the void demon immediately. Otherwise, it would just keep making more warlocks and possibly things even worse than a warlock. Her mind blanked at trying to conjure up something worse. Surely, she'd already seen the worse the universe had to offer?

Then she realized what she had been thinking. She might as well just shout a challenge to the heavens, taunting Fate to do worse.

But unaware of Anna's thoughts and worries, Gregory turned his attention to the dome and began weaving another spell. Once he was finished, he sent it floating toward the nearest surface of the shield. It collided with the other magic, and as if the dome had suddenly turned to water, the silvery grey substance surrounding them shuddered once and then fell to the ground where it sank into the earth.

"Come," Gregory ordered, already calling his earlier portal spell back into being. "It's time we return to base. I will tell the Gargoyle Legion and my clan and coven allies what I have learned. Then I'll inform our human allies. In the meantime, Anna and Obsidian, you will use this time to rest before we go on the hunt."

Anna narrowed her eyes. "I thought you weren't going to tell anyone about the djinn."

Gregory chuckled. "Did I say I was going to mention the djinn?"

Erika cleared her throat and injected, "Gargoyles lie now?"

"How is it a lie if others assume the wrong thing?"

Anna was actually relieved and let him off the hook. Because if she or Erika had to bring up the topic of how they found out about the nest of warlocks...

Yeah, that would lead to a lot more questions. And if

brass got suspicious, Anna might truly face a court-martial or worse.

Worse, being caged in a lab somewhere.

Obsidian growled softly, almost in her ear. "I'd never let the humans of this world cage my Kyrsu."

Right. Still holding hands. Mind reading.

"Still," Anna said to Obsidian, "let's avoid that complication and let the Avatar take the heat on this one."

Obsidian grinned hugely. "Fine by me. Besides, I'm hungry again."

She side-eyed him. "You know you aren't still growing, right? You don't need to eat your weight in food daily."

Huffing dejectedly, Obsidian leveled her with an accusing gaze.

"Oh, fine. I'll go hunt us up something else to eat."

CHAPTER TWENTY-EIGHT

*I*t was long past dark by the time they'd returned to base. Anna watched as Gregory and Erika set off to inform the allied forces about what the Avatar had discovered about their warlock enemies. However, he'd said he wouldn't yet mention the fact that a void demon was on the loose—not until he had scrutinized all the base personnel and could ascertain if any of them had been compromised.

If he detected no deception or magic spy spells implanted in any of the humans or fae, he would reveal what he'd learned about the leader of the warlocks to a small trusted inner circle. But as he'd said, he'd keep that knowledge tight. The fewer people that knew, the fewer leaks they needed to worry about.

As promised, Anna detoured to the mess. A little snooping in the kitchen uncovered plastic wrapped sandwiches, chocolate pudding and bottled water. Backtracking to the nearest table with their stolen prizes, they sat and ate in silence. The empty and dimly lit room soon had Anna fighting back yawns. Obsidian's ears drooped, betraying his exhaustion, too.

"Come on," Anna managed between yawns. "Think our bodies are trying to tell us something. It has been a stressful few days."

"Sleep is probably wise," he said. "More of my memories return each night compared to the few that return during the day."

Anna glanced sidelong at him. "More of your memories have returned?"

"Some. It's so subtle, I barely notice, honestly." He made a vague gesture with one hand. "It's like I don't even realize I can remember more until I think back to how old I thought I was when I first woke up and then realize I now know more than eighteen-year-old me did."

"How much more?" Anna asked, growing excited at the thought of having Rasoren Obsidian, War Leader of the Gargoyle Legion, restored to her.

"My memories tell me I'm now a little past my nineteenth year." Obsidian's hands rose to gesture vaguely at the air a second time. "But there seem to be a few holes or blurry memories."

"That's excellent news." She came around the table

to give him a hug. "About the returning memories. Not the holes."

Tactile creature that he was, he took the opportunity to press his muzzle along the sensitive skin under her jaw. Warm puffs of his breath raised the tiny hairs along her skin. His nose dipped down, very slightly pushing aside the neckline of her shirt. It may even have been accidentally done.

But his innocent touch still made her nipples stand at attention under her shirt and generated a distant, needy echo down south. It had been so long since she'd felt lust, she barely recognized it.

'Jeez, Anna, get your hormones under control,' she scolded herself. *'It was just an innocent touch and a little warm breath.'*

Anna cleared her throat. Aloud, she said, "We should go to bed. To our rooms. To sleep, I mean."

When she was finished stumbling over her tongue, she snapped her teeth together. Gods. She'd sounded like a fool.

Her gargoyle partner nodded and gestured for her to lead the way.

Obsidian remained a quiet shadow at her side all the way to their quarters, not even saying anything when they entered to find it still empty of their new roommates.

When the silence became awkward, Anna glanced sidelong up at her Rasoren. "I guess we should get some sleep. Though I'm not sure I'll be able to sleep after what Gregory revealed. Still..." She shrugged. "Goodnight, Obsidian."

"Sleep well," he murmured, then turned and padded toward his room.

Anna retreated to her own, where she swiftly stripped off her uniform and chose a sports bra and boy shorts for sleep. After crawling in bed and tossing and turning for ten minutes straight, she got up again.

Maybe an herbal tea would help her relax.

When she exited her bedroom, she found Obsidian out in the hall, prowling toward her room. He froze at being discovered.

"Hey," Anna said in greeting.

"Hello," he murmured and then glanced down at his feet, looking embarrassed to have been caught.

"Can't sleep?" She asked.

"No."

But Anna understood why neither of them could sleep, even if this now nineteen-year-old version of Obsidian didn't.

They'd slept together every night for thirteen years while she was a stone statue. The healers had instructed him to share power with her each night to speed her recovery. And even after Anna woke, she and Obsidian had kept up that little tradition. It had been somewhat awkward the first couple of times, but legion gargoyles lived in glorified tree houses, high up in hamadryad trees. His home only had one room for sleeping, and since he still needed to share magic with her to strengthen their Rasoren-Kyrsu bond, they'd shared his nest.

They had both become addicted to the closeness. Though she'd been truthful when she'd said they weren't mates. The intimacy of sharing a nest wasn't sexual. At the time, she'd had far too much emotional baggage for a relationship.

Looking upon Obsidian's obvious embarrassment and awkwardness, Anna decided it was time for another movie night to break the tension.

"Come on. Let's find something to watch." Grabbing his hand, she tugged him toward the entertainment center.

After twenty minutes of random scrolling, because she was more than two years behind on shows and didn't recognize most of them, they finally settled on what looked like some kind of historical-based miniseries, but it seemed to have some representation. And the main male character was hot.

"This one looks good," Anna muttered with a grin.

CHAPTER TWENTY-NINE

A few hours later, Anna's cheeks were burning, and she regretted not checking the show's rating. She wasn't a prude by any means but sitting watching the show with Obsidian was something else entirely. That awkwardness was only made worse by knowing he was a big old virgin.

Because of what the Battle Goddess had done to him while he was still developing in his mother's hamadryad tree, he could convert other species to gargoyles through any of his bodily fluids. But since the legion healers didn't know how potent he was or if those gargoyles would be enslaved to his and Anna's wills, the elders asked that he not get into a physical relationship until after they knew the full ramifications of the changes the Battle Goddess had worked upon him.

Somehow that had morphed into the big dork 'saving' himself for her instead.

Yeah.

Awkward.

But they'd worked through that to become great partners on the battlefield and friends everywhere else. They'd both concluded that neither of them was ready to take their relationship in a more physically intimate direction. Though there had been desire on Obsidian's part and Anna wasn't immune to her gargoyle partner's impressive body. After all, gargoyles were communal bathers, and he'd given Anna lots of opportunities to satisfy her curiosity. She'd always been proud when she'd managed not to openly ogle him.

Then there had been the time Anna's gargoyle nature had once put her into heat. And the only male she'd been interested in was her Rasoren. Thankfully, he had been swift to figure out what was going on and had been an absolute gentleman, never giving into her gargoyle's demands.

But her heat cycle had only happened once, so she hoped it was only a yearly occurrence.

Obsidian gestured toward the TV, drawing Anna's attention back to the show, where two of the characters were getting intimate on screen.

"I will admit," he said with humor thick in his voice, "to having been curious about human mating. This is answering a few of my questions."

Anna groaned, grabbed a pillow, and shoved it in front of his face. "I've decided you're not old enough to see this."

Obsidian laughed and shoved the pillow out of his field of view so he could continue his 'education' without obstruction. When Anna made to grab the remote, he wrestled her for it, and they both dissolved into laughter until tears ran down their faces.

In the end, they continued to watch the series, laughing and groaning at the heated moments, with Anna again trying to shove pillows at Obsidian during the sexy times. At some point, their banter had morphed into an easy-going teasing, very similar to what they'd once shared while linked by the Rasoren-Kyrsu bond.

Eventually, they fell asleep on the sofa with Anna tucked up against his side and one of his wings wrapped around them for warmth.

CHAPTER THIRTY

The sound of laughter woke Anna. Lifting her head, her blurry eyes focused on Jason in time to see him taking another picture. She noted a few other details, like how she was sleeping spread-eagled on Obsidian.

How the hell had she gotten here?

Right. Movie night. Falling asleep tucked up against his side, a wing keeping her warm.

And now Jason was in her face. It was too early to deal with Jason. She turned her head, burying her nose between the side of one of Obsidian's large pecs and the sofa's pillow.

"It's too early. It can't be dawn. Make Jason go away," she muttered to her Rasoren.

To her delight, she felt Obsidian's tail uncoil from where it was snuggled against her lower legs, followed by the sound of flesh hitting flesh. A pained grunt issued from Jason.

"I told you messing with them would be a bad idea," Erika said, her words half dissolving into laughter.

"But it's going to make such a great picture for the team wall of glory," Jason responded with far too much glee in his voice.

Oh lord.

Anna jerked her head up a second time and peered around until she focused on Jason's grinning face. Next, she spotted the camera.

This was no cellphone camera. This beast was for high-end photography and possessed the biggest damn lens she'd ever seen. Was that even for indoor use?

"Do you have trouble getting that thing through doors, Jason?" Anna growled out.

"Not at all."

"Whatever. But you do realize it looks like you're overcompensating for something?"

"Rib me all you want about my manhood. I'm not the one drooling on Obsidian's pecs while he cuddles me like an oversized teddy bear." Jason grinned suddenly. "That's what I'm going to call this work of art. Obsidian and his teddy bear. It has such a nice ring to it."

"That's it. When I catch you, I'm going to shove that camera so far up your ass, it will be able to take pictures of your tonsils." Her words came out in a good approximation of a gargoyle's growling tones.

"I shall aid you, my Kyrsu," Obsidian said in an equally grumpy tone.

"Good, it's a date," Anna growled.

Jason's actions had made the newly re-establishing bond between her and Obsidian awkward. She could feel it in the way he's stiffened up under her. Or maybe that was because she was spread-eagled on him, her lady bits snug against his impressive schlong. Only the fabric of her boy shorts and his loincloth prevented an even more intimate contact.

And that warm, heavy weight on her ass...

Was that?

Obsidian shifted, carefully lifting his hand from where it had been cupping her ass. Then she reminded herself he was always a gentleman. The sofa was narrower than a bed, and he'd likely just been instinctively securing her so she didn't fall off. He hadn't been groping her ass at all.

Right.

Anna didn't believe her own lies.

She raised her head, carefully not meeting Obsidian's eyes. She sighed when she glanced down and spotted a bit of dampness on his chest. Yes, that was her drool on Obsidian's heavenly pectoral muscles. Just like Jason had said. For fuck's sake.

Why did she have to go and fall asleep on the sofa with her big gargoyle partner?

She glanced back toward where Jason had been, only

to find he'd run off, leaving the door to the hall hanging open.

"Fucking coward," Anna muttered and then sat up, swinging herself off Obsidian without meeting his gaze. She rubbed her eyes and stretched to give herself something else to focus on.

When she glanced at the clock in the kitchen and saw it was four in the morning, she groaned again. "Having to tolerate Jason at this time of night should be a criminal offense."

"Yep," Erika said and then yawned and stretched. "Sorry. If I'd known you two had fallen asleep on the couch, I would have had Jason on a tighter leash. Anyway. It's late. I'm going to bed but will help you hunt Jason down tomorrow if you want."

Anna laughed. "Thanks. Might take you up on that. Goodnight."

With another yawn, Erika saw herself off to bed.

Obsidian sat on the sofa. He hadn't said a word during the entire exchange and now there was a tension between them that hadn't been there earlier. Anna didn't like it. Her face screwed up in anger that Jason's thoughtless action had damaged the budding Rasoren-Kyrsu link. Well, fuck it. She would not let Jason screw this up for her.

She reached for Obsidian's larger hand and laced her fingers with his.

"Let's move to your nest." Then she paused and

glanced up at him. "As long as you're okay with that. We used to share your nest back in Haven."

"I would like that." His voice came out in a deep, rumbling purr. "Very much."

"Just to sleep," she added hastily.

"That's what I meant, too," his lips twitched in humor, and then one of his wings curled around her body and tucked her against his side.

Once in his rooms, they crawled into the nest built into the floor and arranged the pillows until they were perfect. Anna burrowed closer to Obsidian until her back was tucked to his front and sighed happily. Then she urged one of his arms around her waist and she used the bicep of the other as her pillow.

"Just for the record," Anna drawled in a sleepy tone. "No wandering hands, Mr. Barely-legal."

"I may not know what barely legal means, but I thank you for this trust, my Kyrsu," Obsidian said, his deep voice rolling over her senses. "I will not betray it."

"I know." Anna patted his arm. "I've always trusted you."

"And I, you."

Wrapped in the rich, masculine scent of her Rasoren, Anna's eyes drifted closed, a happy grin on her face, and soon she was asleep.

CHAPTER THIRTY-ONE

The following day Anna had awakened relaxed and rejuvenated, but they'd only just finished breakfast when they were summoned to a situation briefing. Now Anna and Obsidian waited in briefing room B and watched as a mix of high-ranking clan, coven, and human military members filed in. After terse greetings, they grabbed chairs and settled around the large central table.

"Apparently, when an immortal demigod older than the entire fucking universe hits the panic button, it lands butts in chairs lightning-fast," Anna muttered softly to Obsidian, where they stood in one corner, shoulder to shoulder.

Jason wandered over and joined them in their out-of-the-way spot. "Yeah. I've never seen this much efficiency in my life," he murmured low. "Usually someone would already be bickering about one thing or another. And the humans aren't usually the instigators."

She eyed the clan and coven members and then the humans. It was like Jason said. For once, the fae council members were silent.

"Humans are normally less argumentative?" Obsidian asked, his expression showing his obvious doubt.

"Depends how many politicians are involved," Jason muttered.

Before Obsidian could respond, Gregory herded in the last of the stragglers, both he and his victims looking harried. He all but shoved the stragglers into the available chairs.

As soon as the last butt was in its chair, Gregory raised his arms and with a flick of his wrists, unleashed a powerful ward spell that raced along the walls, floor, and ceiling, making both the humans and the fae jump in surprise. Only Elder Thayn didn't react, but there was a gleam of amusement in his gaze. Leave it to the old reprobate to find humor at a time like this.

"There is a threat to your world," Gregory's booming voice snapped everyone's attention back to him. "An ancient evil, one which the three realms haven't seen in thousands upon thousands of years. An enemy so fearsome, even uttering its name is to draw its attention."

The room was so quiet that Anna would have been able to hear an ant take a piss.

"When I learned of the location of the warlocks'

nest, I also learned that a void demon was the blood witch's ultimate revenge upon the living," Gregory said, his hands gesturing as if to further declare the importance of his words. "At her death, the demon was released from its summoning circle to do as it pleased in the magic and Mortal Realms. From my past experiences hunting these creatures, I can promise it has plans for this world and its people. Dark plans it will already have set into motion. And since we know it tried to capture the Null, it doesn't take much imagination to figure out what it might use her for."

Gregory fell silent for a moment, allowing everyone to chew on his words.

"The only possible use a void demon would have for a magic-devouring null would be to use her to breach a section of the Veil Between the Realms that guards the void, cutting it off from the other realms, acting as both border-wall and prison. Since the demon failed to abduct the Null, its next logical action will be to create a portal to breach the Veil instead. A much more difficult and time-consuming task here in this realm, but that won't stop the void demon."

The room remained hushed, waiting for Gregory to reveal the rest.

"While this realm is naturally low in magic, there is one huge fuel source the void demon can use to power such a spell." Gregory looked at each human sitting at the table. "You. Your families. Your friends and loved ones. If we don't stop it, the beast will use the lives of humans to power its blood magic spell and open the void to release others of its kind."

Gregory paced slowly down the length of the table. "But that won't be the worst it will do. Once the rest of this void demon's brethren escape their prison, they will feed upon the remaining members of humanity and grow strong, breed until their numbers can spread to another world, and another after that, and so forth until they are an army large enough to challenge the Light's warriors."

Gregory took a deep breath but rushed on before the wave of panicked questions Anna could feel building broke across the room.

"It will be the end times should that happen," his voice dropped lower, an edge of haunting darkness entering his voice. "The Divine Ones would destroy entire worlds to prevent such a catastrophe. They've done so before."

This time, even a demigod's intensity wasn't enough to hold back the deluge of questions as everyone around the table all started shouting at once. Soon everyone was on their feet, the Avatar fending off questions coming at him from all sides.

"Come on," Anna said, urging Obsidian farther from the besieged Avatar, "Let's get out of the way before they turn to us with questions."

CHAPTER THIRTY-TWO

*E*ventually, Gregory calmed everyone without needing to resort to the threat of violence, which was an impressive showing of restraint on the ancient Avatar's part. "Is it just me, or is Gregory mellower than he used to be?"

"Lillian and Gran are rubbing off on my old friend." Thayn's laughter boomed in her ears, scaring a good ten years off her life.

Scowling at him, she ordered her heart to calm. "Didn't anyone tell you it's rude to read people's minds?"

Thayn shrugged. "It's much more efficient than waiting for someone to cough up their true feelings."

Anna was just drawing her breath to retort when Thayn cut her off. "Oh, look. The meeting is about to reconvene. We'll have to talk more later."

With that, he was off to terrorize the humans and fae

clustered around Gregory with harrowing tales of what void demons were capable of.

While his words and manner were specifically designed to get the others onboard with Gregory's plan, Anna thought he took a touch too much pleasure in his task.

"Is it just me, or does he seem like he's entering his second childhood?"

Obsidian tilted his head. "A demon's childhood, maybe?"

"If this menace is impossible to track and can travel anywhere by creating these portal gates, how are we ever going to find it in a world with over seven billion people?" General Trembley leveled the question at Gregory, but Anna thought it was aimed at all the magic wielders.

"I did not say there was no way to track it," Gregory countered. "Only that void demons are difficult to track."

Gregory turned from the assembled clan, coven, and military members to stare at Anna.

She tensed.

"The Battle Goddess's magic can track them. It was why the Battle Goddess was first created. Her magic's need to hunt them is why Corporal Anna Mackenzie woke early from her healing stone sleep. Even in the Magic Realm, that power sensed the void demon here on Earth because Anna's resting place was in proximity to the Earth-bound portal. That magic forced Anna here to hunt the void demon." Gregory paused and bowed his head ever so slightly in Anna's direction before continuing. "Had I ever deemed that the blood witch possessed the knowledge and power and level of insanity required to summon a void demon, or that one could even survive within the void for this long without an energy source.... I would have guessed the reason for Anna's early awakening much, much sooner."

"See," Anna muttered under her breath. "Wasn't my fault I woke early. Damn willful magic."

"However, from what I've learned, we know this void demon must have an unknown number of its brethren trapped back in the void that it's trying to free, and it is working to breach the Veil to free them." Gregory's gaze had drifted away from Anna to study each person at the table but soon circled back to her.

"With Anna's help, we will track this void demon to its den, destroy it, and eradicate the last of the warlocks, so there is no more immediate threat to this world or others. Later, once Anna and Obsidian are fully trained in using their new powers, they, along with I and my Sorceress, in the company of a wing of celestial warriors, will journey into the void to destroy any surviving void demons. We will discover the secret why they've been able to survive when the last void demon should have been dead thousands of years ago. But that is a concern for later. To neutralize the immediate threat, we'll use Anna's magic to sniff out the void demon's lair. Then we will attack it, and I will create a spell to open the void."

Seeing everyone's shocked and horrified expressions, Gregory raised a hand for calm. "Easy. The portal I'll create will only allow matter to travel in one direction—into the Void. Then, with our allies' help, we will herd the void demon toward the portal and drive it through."

The murmur of conversations grew louder as strategic planning got underway.

Gregory cleared his throat, gaining everyone's attention again. "This will need to be what you humans call a surgical strike. We'll need a small but lethal unit. The smaller, the easier it will be to hide our arrival from the void demon. We only have one chance at this. We can't allow him to escape a second time. Once we reveal that we know it's here, the void demon will unleash the maximum damage it can do to this world. Even if it doesn't have the time to prepare spells of the magnitude necessary to breach the Veil, it will still kill millions of innocents to fuel a spell to carry it to another world in this realm."

'That is some doomsday scenario,' Anna muttered in her mind. *'If I fuck this up and die without taking Ugly Fucker down, all the humans of Earth and their fae allies might suffer.'*

No fucking pressure.

"Since these recent revelations have forced me to accelerate my original training plans for Anna and Obsidian, we'll have to adapt." Gregory gestured to the shadows, and Anna watched as Rook and Thayn came forward, weighed down by armor and weapons.

The armor was in the style favored by the gargoyle Legion, functional but with a beautiful artistry to the design. Even from her position across the room, she could see the flowing knotwork etched into the polished metal. The emblem of the Gargoyle Legion, a hamadryad tree flanked by two gargoyles, was emblazoned on each breastplate. The emblem was echoed again on a pair of shields.

Anna noted that one shield was gargoyle-sized, but the other was smaller.

"The Sorceress Hamadryad has created armor for the Rasoren and Kyrsu of the Gargoyle Legions," Elder Thayn said, striding up to them with his arms burdened. "As your mage sight has likely already told you, this is no regular armor. The Sorceress summoned the essence of this material from the Spirit Realm and shaped it into armor. It once belonged to the helm of another celestial warrior."

Anna's eyes widened, looking at the material required to make the two sets of armor. Having seen the twin demigods, she'd always assumed that celestial warriors were also titan-sized, but she just increased that estimation by forty percent.

"The Sorceress also used the same spell work that allows our beaded loincloths and warded wrist, ankle, and armbands to shapeshift with the wearer," Thayn continued, holding out a breastplate for Anna to examine. "So, you'll be able to fight in either human or gargoyle form, and it will shift with you."

Next, Thayn nodded to the breastplate in Master Rook's arms. It was the larger, gargoyle-sized piece. "Obsidian, yours too can shapeshift with you, should you need to appear human at any time while battling our enemies here on Earth."

Anna didn't bother to point out that a big dude in fancy armor and wielding a sword and shield would catch a lot of attention, regardless. Still, that would be more explainable than a winged gargoyle running through the streets.

While the gargoyles surrounded Anna, she noticed top brass with their heads together, shuffling through personnel files and discussing which special forces unit would accompany them.

Once again, the gears of war were turning. Anna only hoped she could toss a big enough wrench into those gears to force them to grind to a halt. She'd seen enough bloodshed in this life already. She didn't want to see more.

CHAPTER THIRTY-THREE

Obsidian watched as Master Rook made a final adjustment to Anna's armor. They'd stayed together and allowed their gargoyle brothers to dress them for battle. Perhaps he shouldn't enjoy this moment as much as he did, not when failure would cost others a price too great to pay. But he had no intention of losing. Not with Anna at his side.

Together, they were strong. They'd defeat this new enemy as they had all others before.

And he could take this moment to witness how beautiful his Kyrsu looked in her celestial armor.

He ran a finger along one bracer, the tingle of power a strange mix of living warmth and the bite of the Spirit Realm's magic.

Anna spotted him petting her armor and chuckled. "It's something, isn't it?"

"Yes."

"The glow is a bit strange and will take some getting used to," Anna said while looking down at herself. "But it's pretty in an elfish sort of way. Never thought I'd find myself wearing elf armor."

Obsidian's gaze landed on his Kyrsu, and he thought the armor wasn't the only pretty thing in the room. Her skin shone a rich, warm brown in the soft light cast by the armor. And the armor hugged her form gloriously, as only perfectly designed and fitted armor could. Even with its superior protection adding bulk to her form, it still accented her curves better than the ugly 'combat gear' of the human military.

Behind him, Thayn gave the armor segments covering Obsidian's tail a sharp tug, as if adjusting them.

"Yes, a very pretty sight." Thayn's chuckle was full of innuendo.

He groaned mentally. Of course, Thayn would pick up on that thought.

CHAPTER THIRTY-FOUR

*N*ot going to screw this up. Not going to screw this up. Not going to screw this up. Anna had been reciting those words like a chant for the last hour as Gregory prepared his spell. Typically, Anna wasn't the nervous type. Hell, she'd gone into battle against the Lady of Battles and her army of immortal and highly trained killers and hadn't been nervous like this. But then again, that time, the battle's outcome hadn't sat solely upon her shoulders, and she didn't have a fractious magic she'd inherited from a demigoddess bucking and kicking for freedom inside her.

If she fucked this up, millions of deaths would all be on her. So, there was no way she was letting the magic off its leash until a particular avatar gave the order.

A large, warm hand engulfed hers, Obsidian's strong

fingers with their deadly talons curling gently around hers. "We've got this."

She turned her head and glanced at him, giving him a weak smile. When he rolled his eyes at her and bumped their shoulders, their armor clicking together softly, her smile grew into something genuine.

"We've got this," she murmured back to him.

Arrayed behind them were the other members of the sixteen-man team, consisting of seven gargoyle mounts and one pooka, and their riders, a mix of fae and human soldiers. Gregory had informed everyone that no coven member would be part of the units, as witches and warlocks were too similar to how their magic worked.

That was a weakness that the warlocks could utilize and infect the witches, creating even more warlocks to fight. The coven personnel hadn't been happy to be excluded from the fight but understood. In their place, Gregory had suggested a pack of dire wolves, as their bites were venomous to warlocks, temporarily neutralizing the warlocks' powers.

Once Anna's magic found the location of the void demon, magical talismans carried by the team members would alert the hamadryad Sorceress of the location and she'd used the talismans as drop points for five other portals. Then sweeper teams comprised of more military, fae, and gargoyles would descend on the area and cleanup the warlocks, allowing Gregory's team to focus on the void demon.

Turning her attention to Gregory, she was in time to see him draw another glowing rune in the air. Each of the other nineteen runes he'd already created hovered in the air ten feet apart, forming a rough circle around the special forces unit. The night breeze caused the magic of the runes to flicker and flare like it would true fire, but the Avatar's spells didn't shift from where he'd placed each one.

She was mildly envious of his magic weaving skill, but then again, a fourteen-billion-year-old being had lots of time to perfect the craft. Her lips twisted in a smile as she dwelled on how odd her life had become, but also realized void demons, non-withstanding, she wouldn't change a thing.

And she damned well would not screw this up.

"Anna, Obsidian," Gregory called them even as he put the last touches on the softly glowing blue rune in front of him. "Come forward."

She and her Rasoren paced forward and stood to Gregory's left where he indicated.

"Anna, once I trigger the spell runes, they will activate and begin opening a portal, but unlike normal, this one doesn't yet have a destination woven into its structure. I've created the spell so that your battle magic can use the portal and direct it to the location of the enemy. Once your magic has a lock on the enemy's location, the portal will target another location far enough away from the demon to create an anchor without betraying our arrival. You must simply embrace the Battle Goddess's power and allow it to merge with the portal spell."

"Understood."

"Good. That will be the simple part," Gregory whispered so that only she and Obsidian could hear. "Once your power has the creature in its sights, you will have a battle on your hands to hold that power back until the special forces units move into place and can herd the beast toward me." His voice had drifted off as it did when he was thinking something but didn't wish to speak it out loud.

"What is it? If you're holding something back," Anna prodded, "it might jeopardize the entire mission."

"We only have one chance at this, and we won't know the location ahead of time. Thus, we can't plan for what kind of terrain we might find ourselves in."

Yeah, that was a tactical disadvantage. But unless the portal spell dropped them in the middle of a volcano, the team was ready for just about anything else.

"We'll handle the terrain," Anna said and drew herself straighter. "And as for my magic, now that I've had a few days to get used to it, I will handle it better this time."

"As will I with mine," Obsidian said.

Gregory gave a little huff, followed by a savage gargoyle grin. "Then let us hunt."

Anna closed her eyes and relaxed her mental hold on

the power. It rose within her, a great wave racing outward from her core—vessel Gregory had called it—where the magic had been trapped. Now that it was free, it wasted no time beginning the hunt.

The silvery-colored magic flowed over her skin and raced down her body, pooling on the ground for a moment before leaping across the distance to the portal like lightning through the clouds.

Fierce and powerful and feeling unstoppable at this moment, Anna allowed the power to run. The energy merged with the portal. Anna's perception shifted from her physical body to the quickly expanding range of land the magic was scanning. As Gregory had said, her power was using the portal's ability to travel to search vast distances quickly.

"South," Anna muttered, only half aware of her body, but she felt one of Obsidian's muscular arms close around her waist to hold her steady as the magic dragged more and more of her awareness away from her physical body.

Leaving her body so vulnerable didn't sit well with her.

"Be at ease, my Kyrsu," Obsidian whispered into her thoughts. *"I will guard your body while you hunt."*

"Thank you," she whispered before her consciousness sped away again, continuing its hunt for the void demon. Her mind expanded outward at incredible speeds,

covering more and more ground. Impossibly fast, she raced south.

Ah! There!

Her magic had the trail. Even as her power felt like a runaway horse, Anna sensed the intelligence behind her magic's actions. It wasn't being unduly reckless, but understood time was of the essence. If the void demon detected her before the rest of her team was in place...

The magic slowed its race across the land but continued arrowing its way south and east, dragging Gregory's portal spell with it.

Then, as suddenly as the mad race began, it ended. The sense of traveling halting so swiftly, Anna took a physical step forward even though she wasn't falling over.

She blinked rapidly and then glanced up at the Avatar. "The magic has stopped hunting."

"Good," he nearly purred. "You've found our target. Come."

And she realized the sides of the portal spell—that earlier had been flickering unstably—were now calm, the portal anchored securely on the other side.

Gregory crossed the portal's threshold, and Anna and Obsidian swiftly followed. The other thirteen members of the sixteen-man team were close on her Rasoren's armor-covered tail.

The violent whirling sense of distortion and extreme

vertigo churned her stomach and her brain in that now familiar way of portal travel. Though this time, it lasted only a moment, the distance far, far shorter than traveling between the realms.

CHAPTER THIRTY-FIVE

nna stepped from the portal and found herself in a night-shrouded forested ravine, a narrow river flowing slowly southward. The moon was high in the sky, but the stars weren't visible. There was too much other light-noise to see those faint pinpricks of light against the velvety darkness.

If that hadn't been enough to tell her they were near some urban center, the not-to-distance sound of traffic was a chilling reminder they were somewhere gargoyles didn't want to be seen. Sirens screamed into the night as an ambulance and firetruck made their way to some location northwest of Anna's current location.

The rest of the team fanned out to secure the immediate area, the pack of twelve dire wolves spreading out to ghost along close to the gargoyles. Anna turned her attention from the distant sounds of the traffic and the nearer river wildlife to what her new magic was doing. It was still hunting, urging Anna back into motion, wanting her to move toward an unknown destination north of her current location.

"It's dropped us a little farther south than the target's location," Anna said, and she came to stand between Gregory and Resnick. "It's urging me to follow the river north."

Gregory merely nodded, but he dragged in a deep breath. "Be on the alert. I smell canines. The scent is fresh, and it smells like there have been many nearby. We don't want them to give our arrival or location away. Tread softly, my kin."

Lieutenant-Colonel Resnick joined them.

"That rough portal ride scrambled our tech, but this section of the river looks uncomfortably familiar. And your mention of dogs. I have an idea where we might be. If there's a parking lot and boat launch about five hundred meters that way," Resnick said, pointing south. "Then I know exactly where we are. Hold on a second while we confirm."

He nodded to Sergeant Maribel, and the sniper turned on his heels and bolted off into the shadows. He wasn't gone for more than two minutes, and then he was back, giving Resnick a grim nod.

"Shit," Resnick cursed softly and then ordered in a whisper. "All gargoyles, use your shadow magic and disappear. Shield the rest of us as well. I want teams of one gargoyle and one human or fae. You know your assigned partners. We're in the middle of freaking Toronto. That's the Humber River." He pointed at the smooth glassy surface of the calm water. "And we're currently in a branch of the Toronto Ravines. We could stumble across a bystander at any moment, and the last thing we need is a hysterical human screaming their lungs out and warning the enemy. Everyone stay frosty and steer clear of civilians. Radio silent. I want us in and out with no one the wiser."

"Agreed," Gregory rumbled, and then dropped to all fours and held a wing away from his side. Resnick muttered something under his breath but didn't hesitate and gingerly mounted, settling on the gargoyle's back.

Erika joined them, already mounted on Master Rook, and looking absolutely like a natural, Anna mused darkly. It had taken Anna weeks to become proficient.

Turning her attention back to Obsidian, Anna grinned. "Your turn."

He shifted and dropped to all fours. Anna mounted swiftly, much more comfortable riding a gargoyle than poor Resnick, who looked like a city-slicker on a trail horse.

Or maybe it was more the fact that he was riding an ancient being.

"Obsidian, you know I've never mentioned this, but I'm glad you're young like me and not some million-year-old celestial

whatever," she whispered into his mind. *"It made all this less stressful than it might have been."*

He twisted and rubbed his muzzle along her calve in affection, and then he was moving off, heading in the direction her magic had indicated.

The unit went silent after that until Gregory slowed, allowing the rest of them to cluster up together. The fae, humans, and dire wolves were close enough, they brushed against each other. As Anna marveled at how much the various species had come to trust each other over the last two years, the gargoyles' individual shadow magic shields merged into one larger dome that allowed everyone inside to see each other.

Gargoyles were attuned enough with the others of their kind that they could sense each other's location and movements without needing to see their partners, but the humans and the other fae didn't have that advantage. And that currently included Anna herself.

"This area smells heavily of marshlands," Gregory said, his muzzle scrunching as he inhaled another deep breath. "Resnick, is the terrain passable on foot, or will we need to fly?"

"It's maintained parkland along much of the river," Resnick said, keeping his voice low. "One benefit of dropping into the middle of a highly developed urban area like Toronto is that there will be clear paths to our target. And at least this time of night, gargoyle shadow magic shouldn't have difficulty hiding us from mundane eyes."

"I sense humans," the banshee said in a husky voice. Her strangely bright eyes seeming to miss nothing from her perch on the back of the pooka. "Perhaps homeless, but I can't sense their exact whereabouts or intent. There is too much iron in the surrounding city. It's distorting my magic."

Resnick nodded sharply. "Understood."

Gregory huffed. "The city will mess with all the land's energy and our tracking magics. We'll be blinded to some degree as well."

Resnick nodded a second time.

While Anna's gargoyle senses may be dormant, her new magic definitely wasn't. She could still feel its pull, its desire to hunt now that the trail was as clear and bright to her as a white marble path in the moonlight.

"My tracking ability is unaffected," Anna told the others.

"As I had hoped," Gregory said and started north along the river, the rest of the company falling in behind him.

Obsidian touched Anna's thoughts. *"I can sense every soul in this city."*

His words hinted at his unease, but mounted on his back, one hand braced between his shoulder blades, she could feel what he felt. The Lord of the Underworld's power was far more overwhelming than what Anna fought.

It was beautiful and terrible. He could feel the souls like bright sparks of light in the vast darkness of the universe. He could feel when it was their time to return to the Spirit Realm. He knew the times of their death, felt their deaths. All of them, everywhere. Not just this planet. Not just this realm. All of them. All over the vastness of the universe.

He could reach out and touch any of those souls to give them comfort or guidance. Or he could carve out any corruption or send the wicked to the Divine Ones for judgment.

It was too much for one mortal mind to truly comprehend.

"Obsidian, that's enough," Anna said sharply to him in mind speech, so their conversation would remain private. *"We'll use my power to hunt them. I don't think any mortal mind should have felt what we just did."*

He nodded jerkily and exhaled a shaky breath. "I did not mean for that to happen. Sometimes the power overwhelms my defenses, and I find myself carried away by the vastness of it all."

"Save your power until we're engaged in the battle. No one minces warlocks like you do." Her attempt at humor earned a chuckle from him, and Anna patted his shoulder again.

Ahead, the silence of the night shattered in a raucous

sound of angry honking, hissing, and flapping of wings. Obsidian tensed, ready to leap forward, but Anna squeezed his shoulder.

"Hold up. Pretty sure that's a Canada Goose attacking a fourteen-billion-year-old avatar."

CHAPTER THIRTY-SIX

*A*head, Gregory was swiftly sidestepping to avoid the charging goose. He was silent as he used his wings to block the enraged bird from attacking Resnick. Watching it all unfold, Anna would have been laughing her ass off if there wasn't the possibility that the goose had just betrayed their presence to the enemy. Anna gritted her teeth and waited. Eventually, the gargoyle had moved far enough inland that the goose deemed the threat driven off and returned to its nest along the shoreline.

Gregory just gave himself a shake and watched after the bird with bemusement, like he didn't understand why something so small would be so foolish as to attack a gargoyle, but the Avatar had taken the higher road and allowed the nesting bird to live.

When the Avatar motioned for the unit to move,

Obsidian and the other gargoyles moved forward but steered clear of the nest. Even the dire wolves gave the bird a wide berth. Though Anna noted everyone kept an eye on the large goose, where it glowered at each of them with her neck lowered and beak opened threateningly at them.

Once they bypassed the goose, Obsidian overtook several other gargoyles to pace beside Gregory and Resnick. No words, either aloud or in mind speech, were exchanged, the group relying on hand signals now that they were closing in on their targets.

So far, so good. And luckily, the goose hadn't seemed to alert the enemy to their presence.

Anna's magic still guided them, but after a ten-minute gargoyle run from where the portal had deposited them, the gargoyles were able to pick up the scents of warlocks. Soon after, the banshee could differentiate the tracks of humans from the land-tainting trail left by a warlock, the land's magic seeming to recoil from the beasts.

When they came to an enormous expanse of parkland, her magic urged them east. Even shrouded by their shadow magic, the gargoyles stayed close to the areas where denser tree cover offered the best concealment from the bright moon overhead and the scattered streetlights over the walking trail. At this hour, the park was primarily empty of humans, though she heard music as one nighthawk was out for a run, and a few other civilians were milling about in the park. She suspected one or more of the smaller groups were drug dealers or teens out for some mischief.

And the humans weren't the only users of the park. The gargoyles kept coming across deer in the area. But luckily, none of the park's human or wildlife visitors were aware of the company of gargoyles and their riders ghosting through the trees.

Soon her magic was urging her north again. This time, a fence blocked their path. Beyond was a silent cemetery decorated with artful landscaping, rows of elegant memorial stones, and thick with shadows cast by the mature trees.

The only movement she saw within the cemetery was more of the tame-ass deer, but her roiling magic shouted that this was where the void demon was this night. She signaled to the team that they'd arrived.

Gregory bobbed his head, and Resnick slid off his back, giving silent orders to the company even as the Avatar headed back to the river with Erika, where they'd bait the trap. Everyone already knew the plan and their places and made their way into position.

Meanwhile, Erika would use her powers as a null to hide Gregory's magic as he opened the Veil Between the Realms, creating a gateway into the Void. Between Erika's nullifying powers and Gregory's powerful shadow magic, they would effectively hide the gateway's existence.

The team of gargoyles and highly trained operators would move in on the nest of warlocks, selecting drop points for the Sorceress's portals. Once the battle was engaged, the allied forces would kill or distract as many of the warlocks as possible in the first volley. Then it was Anna and Obsidian's job to maintain a target lock on the sole void demon and cut him off from the rest of the warlocks.

From there, Anna and Obsidian would drive the void demon toward the hidden Null and gateway, while Gregory, once he'd activated his spell work, would flank the demon from the right. Thayn would take the left, and Anna, Obsidian and any gargoyle not battling warlocks would keep the monster moving forward.

Gregory assured everyone that the void demon would seek to avoid Anna and Obsidian at all costs once they embraced their magic and allowed it to rule them. Together, their magics could land a killing blow.

But Gregory didn't want them to use their magic and over-extend themselves. Hence the hidden gateway. He just wanted them to posture and make the void demon run away from them, straight into the hidden gate. Once the demon was close, the Veil would sense it and aid them in recapturing it.

That was the plan.

The plan could go sideways in a thousand different ways and directions.

But it couldn't be allowed to do that.

She wouldn't allow something with barely a shard of a soul to destroy her whole damned planet. It wasn't going to happen on her watch.

But while the rest of the team spread out to flank the cemetery and approach from the other three sides, Anna and Obsidian could only hold their positions and wait.

Then she heard the first muffled shots from the snipers, followed by shouts of warning from the warlocks. Moments later, five portals were flashing into existence. The first of the sweeper teams hadn't even made it through the portals before magic was blasting across the cemetery, spells being tossed back and forth between warlocks, fae, and gargoyles. The first bodies hadn't even hit the ground, and Obsidian was already vaulting over the fence, Anna clinging to his back.

She hunched low, a rifle in one hand, ready if she needed it, but she already knew bullets would not win this battle.

Closing her eyes, she surrendered to the Battle Goddess's power. Below her, she could feel when Obsidian did the same, his death magic rising upward, almost to caress her power in greeting.

Then together, moving as one body and mind, they raced across the cemetery, between the rows marking the dead, to stop an enemy before he could destroy an entire city, or worse.

CHAPTER THIRTY-SEVEN

Now that her magic had her fully in its grip, she could see the void demon with her magic-enhanced sight. But it wasn't so much that she could see his form, as she could see as he devoured all the land's magic and the unprotected souls near his location. She sensed through her link with Obsidian when several of the deer and other wildlife dropped even as they tried to flee. Dead. Their souls and spirit energy consumed to fuel a spell.

As Anna and Obsidian drew closer, her Rasoren understood what was going on a moment before she did.

"He's already built a portal!" Obsidian shouted over the sounds of battle. "Don't kill the warlocks! He's using their deaths to help fuel the spell."

Anna heard Resnick cursing close at hand, but then Obsidian bolted past the human and a group of gargoyles where they were battling a dozen warlocks. She could only hope the others could injure the warlocks enough to neutralize them without resorting to killing them.

The fastest way now to end this was to end the void demon. Once he was dead, he wouldn't be able to channel the souls into fuel for his portal spell.

Anna and Obsidian used the chaos of the battle to cover their approach. Ahead, the demon's portal spell had begun to glow with a chilling reddish, unholy light. A wave of the power raced over her skin, and she shivered, feeling unclean. Inside, her magic roiled harder, rising, coating her skin, and then expanding out, forming a protective shield around her and her Rasoren.

But before the shield could fully form, an explosion rocked the ground. Below Obsidian's feet, the earth shook harder.

No, she realized, not an explosion. An Earthquake triggered by a spell deep within the ground. Dirt, grass, and stone monuments flew upward as the ground ruptured. Only Obsidian's fast reflexes and mighty wings got them into the air in time to prevent them from getting caught in the main spell.

Still, a magical shock wave hit them, and they both went tumbling sideways. Obsidian twisted in the air and beat his wings hard enough to slow them a moment before they hit the ground. She bailed from his back and went into a roll. When she came to her feet, she was standing in front of a stunned warlock, also struggling to regain his footing now that the ground had stopped shaking.

She dived behind a monument.

Of course, battles didn't always go as planned, and she hadn't expected this one to be straightforward given what she'd seen the warlocks and void demon do up until now. But Anna decided Ugly Fucker had just been toying with everyone last time. Either that or he'd grown more powerful from feeding off souls here in the city. Anna wondered if there'd been a sudden rash of unexplained deaths or missing persons. She hoped not, but didn't have time to think about that now.

"This sucks balls," Anna muttered as the monument she was hiding behind took a hit, the stone shattering and forcing her to scurry to the next bit of shelter. While she knew she could kill the warlock, she needed to save her strength for the void demon. Just when she thought she was going to have to waste power on the evil henchman, Obsidian leaped over a monument and landed next to her.

With a whoop of delight at his timing, Anna vaulted up on Obsidian's back and squeezed his shoulder. Then, once they were moving away from the others, she whispered to him, "Let's hurt this bastard."

Obsidian's mighty hindquarters bunched and flexed, and then he sprinted out from behind their cover, pelting toward the enemy. Anna clung to his back, her magic already racing out before them, seeking the void demon even as Obsidian's death magic hunted the nearest enemy.

Even before they'd covered half the distance, the demon's portal began to shimmer more brilliantly with its reddish-brown light, beginning its opening sequences. Anna's magic was having none of that and sent a harpooned of raw magic, not toward the void demon, but the complex spell.

Obsidian's death magic shredded the warlocks standing in the way, and Anna had an unobstructed view of her spear as it struck one of the portal spell's runes. At the contact of the two powers, a retina-searing detonation occurred. For the second time that night, Anna was knocked from Obsidian's back by a blast wave, but her celestial armor absorbed the hit, and Anna swiftly rolled to her feet with only a few more bruises. It could have been much worse, and she knew it.

Obsidian was righting himself a few feet away. She noted he seemed unharmed.

Swiftly scanning the area, she spotted the demon's fiery portal spell unraveling, the lines of power connecting the runes destabilizing as one rune after another ruptured, vaporizing into puffs of crimson-colored mist. The stink of blood magic was still heavy in the air, but the breeze kicked up, helping to freshen the air. The crimson fog dissipated as she watched.

Anna's gaze raked over the area, searching for the

void demon, but her battle magic was already urging her back toward the river, telling her exactly where the beast was.

"He's running!" Anna shouted, and she sprinted to Obsidian's side and leaped onto his back. Together, they gave chase. Obsidian raced full out, flying over obstacles in his path, though he was careful to stay low enough to avoid making an easy target of them. But Obsidian was also careful not to close the distance too quickly. They needed him running toward Gregory's hidden gate in the Veil, not stopping to make any kind of last stand. They had to let the demon stay ahead of them to do that.

Something neither Anna nor her magic liked, but it was necessary to keep the void demon running in the direction they wanted him. On either side, she could feel the other gargoyles racing along with them, like bloody big border collies herding sheep.

They were almost back to the river when Anna swore, seeing a part of their plan crumpling.

Just ahead, Erika slumped on her side, unconscious or just unmoving. Well, that wasn't entirely accurate. Something was moving.

CHAPTER THIRTY-EIGHT

Magic fire raged around Erika, but she didn't seem to burn. As they neared, Anna still didn't see any apparent wounds. And she would have seen them if there were any to see. The Null was naked, the fire having burned everything away but leaving her skin unharmed.

Was this some new defensive ability she'd mastered over the last two years?

Or was this something else?

Something far less benign.

Like the fiery power of an elemental dragon?

"I think things just got more complicated," Obsidian shouted to be heard over the roar of the fire. It howled like a forest fire, though it didn't move away from the fallen null.

"That's Gryton or the dragon protecting her, isn't it? Didn't think he could do something like that."

"I didn't either, but it feels like his magic. It can only be him." Obsidian paused. "He's not hurting her. Her vital signs are normal, from what I can sense. And it's not her soul's time to return to the Spirit Realm."

Anna did a double take, but then nodded. "Okay. She's in no danger. At least not from Gryton. Not currently. The void demon is another matter altogether. Let's go. We can't leave the Avatar to fight the demon on his own. He'll be nearly tapped out from creating and holding open the gate."

Obsidian bolted into motion, his long-legged strides eating up the distance between them and the void demon. As they drew closer, she could see the flickering of powerful magic. It could only be Gregory's spell work.

As they raced closer, she saw two beings fighting directly in front of the portal. Gregory, the larger of the two, was trying to physically force the demon closer to the Veil, where tendrils of power were reaching out from the gate, lashing and twisting as they tried to snatch the demon.

But Anna could sense how depleted Gregory was and how much power the void demon still possessed. Then, in a last burst of power and speed, Gregory launched at the demon, tackling him and trapping him in his powerful arms. The demon twisted and fought, unleashing raw magic in all directions, but the Avatar did not let go and backed one step at a time toward the Veil.

"Fuck! He's going to sacrifice himself!" Anna shouted. "Not on my watch!"

A bright flash of crimson erupted between Gregory and the demon, tossing them both into the air. Gregory hit the ground and slid to a halt in the gate's threshold. The demon crashed to the ground between Anna and the grasping tendrils of the Veil, where they thrashed in the air.

"Rook! Thayn!" She bellowed the gargoyles' names. "Help Gregory. The demon is ours."

The pointy-eared bastard rose to his feet, but whatever spell he'd hit Gregory with had depleted the demon.

Her power raged within her, urging her to go on the attack once more, to exterminate this creature once and for all. Below her, Obsidian's magic reached up, caressing her as if asking to be invited in.

But if their powers merged...

It would be like giving War and Death free rein.

And wasn't that precisely what the void demons would rain down upon Earth and her allies if the demons weren't stopped?

"Yes," Obsidian growled in her mind. "That is exactly what they will do. And while we may hold sway over the powers that we perceive as War and Death, this power comes from the Divine Ones. It was not entrusted to us so that we would harm, but so that we would help protect all of creation from the likes of the void demons."

Her Rasoren was correct.

Their powers were intended to be gifts, not a curse. Anna exhaled slowly, allowing her eyes to drift closed. With her magic coiling around her, she did not need eyes to see this enemy. Reaching down with an ethereal hand, the fingers splayed wide, she reached into Obsidian, drawing his power up into her where it merged with her battle magic.

Yes. She knew how to kill this demon now.

As if they were one mind, Obsidian leaped into motion as her thoughts delivered her plan.

Within her, the twin powers of War and Death forged a weapon powerful enough to kill a void demon. As they closed the distance, she called forth the weapon from her own body, birthing it into being with a scream of rage, pain, and determination.

She shaped all that magic and emotion into a three-pronged trident. Then, with her battle magic enhancing her strength, she lobbed it at the retreating enemy. The spell trident continued to solidify as it flew. It grew in power, and she realized it was feeding on the now collapsing portal spell and all the stray magic left from the battle.

Perhaps sensing his death approaching, the void

demon turned toward her at the last moment, tossing a shield up.

But it wasn't enough.

Her aim was true, and the trident-like energy weapon dug deep into Ugly Fucker's chest. The force knocked him off his feet. Even so, he struggled to stand.

"You should have stayed out of this." He coughed up some black substance that may once have been blood, and he grimaced but still managed enough breath to speak. "The Void's quest did not involve you. Yet now you will die for your foolish loyalty. You should have let us have the Null. Now the elemental dragon will win her, and the three realms will burn to quench his hunger and desire."

Anna patted Obsidian's shoulder. "I've heard enough of this bastard's words, my Rasoren."

"As have I." Obsidian broke into a run, his strides growing in length. Anna's body flowed with his as if it was the most natural thing in the world, linked by their twin powers.

She smiled when Obsidian's thoughts flowed into her mind, showing her what he planned a moment before he lowered his head like a charging bull and plowed into the void demon at full speed. With a mighty heave of his neck and shoulders, he launched the void demon toward the waiting Veil.

Like an octopus snapping a tendril around its prey, the Veil Between the Realms grabbed the void demon and shoved it through the gate, the rest of the tendrils giving chase. The gate collapsed, taking a chunk of the trees, grass, and dirt with it. But the void demon was now back where it belonged.

Greenborrow hooted in delight, and she hadn't realized he and the other fae were so close behind her. "Ha! Never thought I'd see a void demon in my lifetime or wanted to, for that matter, but seeing that one's ending was the highlight of my existence!"

He started toward them and then halted. "I was going to give you both congratulatory thumps, but as that would likely be the last thing I did in this life, I think I'll hold off."

The leshii gestured at them, indicating the magic still flowing between and around her and Obsidian's bodies.

She blinked once, then a second time, slowly coming back to herself.

Right.

The danger was over.

She focused on her power but didn't fight it. "Thank you," she whispered to it. "You have saved my planet and likely others. You have my eternal gratitude and can live within me for however long you need, but the danger is over now. Return to your slumber until you are needed again."

She wasn't sure if the power was sentient enough to

understand all her words, but her intent must have reached it, for the flow of power welling up inside her slowed from a raging river to a fast-flowing stream, then a slowly trickling spring, until even that dwindled to nothing.

Anna dismounted from Obsidian. Her body felt exhausted now that she didn't have the magic buoying her up, but it was the best kind of tired.

Victory.

Beside her, Obsidian gave himself a shake, coming out of the magic-induced berserker mode he'd been in.

"You okay?" she asked him.

He lunged up and shifted to stand on two legs. Reaching for her, he dragged her closer, and she rested her head on his chest and allowed him to wrap them both in his wings.

"I am now," he rumbled over her head. "I did not know how this battle would end. I do not fear death or even sacrifice if it serves the Light, but I feared the possibility of either losing you or dying and leaving you behind."

His arms tightened around her.

"I feared the same," she whispered into his breast-plate, wishing there was nothing between them at that moment, that she could rest her ear directly on his chest and hear the powerful beat of his heart unobstructed by the armor.

She drew another calming breath and then patted his

breastplate. "Come on. I think it's time to go home before an army of police descends upon this park."

The sound of many sirens drew closer even as they stood there.

Resnick came trotting over to them. "Nice job. But it's time we were elsewhere. Anyone who's mobile, help the ones that aren't to the portal."

Anna glanced over her shoulder and noticed a new portal already glowing softly in invitation.

"Gods, I love my Sorceress," Gregory said as he limped past them, being half supported by Master Rook.

Anna noticed the pooka carrying a stunned-looking Erika, the Null now clothed in a blanket and no longer on fire. She took both to be good signs.

The other injured were carried through the portal first, and then the dead were gathered and transported. Anna and Obsidian were the second to the last through, even now making sure the others were protected. Though this time, it was just in case the local police force arrived before everyone was through the portal. Resnick brought up the rear.

When the last batch of personnel crossed over, leaving only Anna in the company of Resnick and Obsidian, she turned to her Rasoren and bumped shoulders with him. "Let's go home. I could use a long, hot shower, clean clothes, and a soft nest."

"Sounds perfect," Obsidian rumbled as they crossed through the portal.

"Separate showers and separate soft nests, right?" Resnick asked from behind Anna. "In case your dad pumps me for information when he gets back."

Anna rolled her eyes and snorted. "You can tell him that what his grown-ass daughter does in her free time is none of his business."

Resnick was still making strangled choking sounds as he followed them through the portal.

CHAPTER THIRTY-NINE

After a long night of debriefings, Anna and Obsidian had returned to their quarters and collapsed into his nest, where they slept until midafternoon. Hunger had eventually driven them from sleep. Now cleaned and showered and dressed in a t-shirt and fatigue bottoms, Anna relaxed on one end of the sofa while Obsidian hogged most of the length. But it worked since she presently had her feet in his lap, getting the best foot massage in her life, his strong fingers working honest-to-god magic. It was damn near orgasmic. And by the grace of whatever divine being had decided to bless them, they were alone, their roomies off somewhere else in the complex.

Obsidian's fingers pressed harder into one sensitive spot, and Anna nearly melted into the sofa.

"That's perfect. Right there," she purred. "Fucking perfect. Don't stop."

"Wow," Erika's voice drifted through the room, coming from the direction of the door. "We'll come back later."

"You mean *you* can come back later," Greenborrow said. "I live here, and I'm sure nothing is going on that a ten-thousand-year-old leshii hasn't seen and enjoyed many, many, many times."

"You're terrible," Erika muttered.

"Hey," came Jason's cheerful voice. "If they didn't want an audience, they should have gone somewhere private."

"It's okay," Anna called to Erika. "Nothing scandalous is going on. The guys are going to be disappointed."

Just then, Jason came around the couch and glanced down, his devilish expression turning into a pout when he saw Anna was fully clothed and just getting a foot massage. She leaned back and grinned at Greenborrow. Only his eyes were visible above the stack of board game boxes he was carrying.

"By the way," his voice came to her, muffled slightly by the boxes, "I knew nothing was going on. But even if something had been," his bushy gray brows wiggled suggestively, "I have more class than to interrupt young love."

"Sure." Anna snorted, noticing that Jason and Erika

were loaded with snacks, enough to feed a small army. She nodded at Greenborrow's boxes. "What's with all that and the food?"

"It's game night," he said, placing boxes on the floor every four feet apart.

It turned out game night was a weekly tradition, come rain or shine or battling void demons. Resnick and the rest of the team arrived with beer and other cold drinks. The banshee came with three trays of homemade salsa dip and several bags of corn chips. The pooka trotted in, bringing nothing but his savage self, and settled down between Erika and the banshee, his glowing yellow eyes missing nothing.

That's when Anna realized Erika was on the fae's menu. When Anna raised an eyebrow, Erika just laughed. "I know. The fae are about as subtle as gargoyles. Thanks to Gryton's little show, I think I've got enough stored energy to power a city for a week."

"Yeah. I meant to ask. What happened back there? I didn't think you'd absorbed enough magic to put you out of the fight."

"I hadn't." The other woman looked embarrassed. "But apparently, my powers as a null don't protect me from tripping over my feet and smacking my head on a rock."

"Your helmet should have protected you."

"Oh, it did. I wasn't even hurt," Erika said, lowering her voice so the other humans in the room wouldn't hear. "But I think a certain dragon may have panicked or was just pissed off that a void demon was stalking his pet Null again...." She cleared her throat. "Anyway. He pushed so much magic at me to keep the void demon at bay that it overtaxed my systems. And you saw the result."

"Glad you weren't hurt."

Erika laughed ruefully. "Just my pride as everyone got blinded by my freckled, lily-white ass."

Anna tried not to laugh. She really did and thankfully was saved by Gregory arriving. Only seconds after he arrived, another portal began forming in front of the TV. No one was concerned, so Anna assumed it was Lillian or the hamadryad Sorceress's doing.

And sure enough, the portal opened onto a view of a grassy meadow full of wildflowers and dominated by three large hamadryad trees. Anna knew two of the large trees belonged to Lillian, and the third tree had belonged to her and Obsidian's dryad mother, slain in the final battle two years ago. In the shadow of the hamadryad trees, Anna spotted a stone gargoyle. Even over the distance, she recognized it was Obsidian's sire.

He must have noticed Stalks the Darkness at the same time, for he approached the portal and bowed his head in a show of respect. Anna had been told the older gargoyle was healing well and should awake in as little as three more weeks.

She hoped that was true. Obsidian and Darkness hadn't been given a chance to be just father and son yet, since Darkness had missed most of Obsidian's childhood through no fault of his own.

Anna came to stand beside Obsidian and bumped her hip against his. "Did you want a few moments alone? I can do my scary bitch routine and chase off all the riffraff."

He snorted. "No. I'm fine. I can feel him. It is as the reports said. He's healing well."

At the moment, there was still no sign of Lillian, so Anna and her Rasoren went and sat on the couch and watched the others set up.

They didn't have to wait long. Soon Lillian appeared and walked up to the portal. Well, it was more of a waddle. Being that heavily pregnant had to suck, Anna reflected. Deciding she was glad she didn't want kids.

"Sorry," Lillian called as she crossed the last of the distance to the portal, stopping just on the other side. "Had to pee."

Gregory crossed the portal, scooped his mate into his arms, and then settled her in a pile of thick pillows and blankets on the ground a few feet in front of the portal.

"Since I can't be in the Mortal Realm at the moment," Lillian said, "this is the next best thing. And

Gregory told me Gran, Oath, and Major-General Mackenzie have just arrived on base. Anna, I'm sure you and your dad will have lots to catch up on."

"My dad's here?" Anna grinned and bounced forward on her toes before composing herself once again.

Obsidian nuzzled her hair with affection. "Go on. I'll be fine. Besides, it's been a long time. I'd love to talk with my sister."

Anna hugged him and then headed for the door.

—————

CHAPTER FORTY

—————

*A*nna sat on the couch and watched, having bowed out of the play, wanting to spend time with her father. As soon as he'd seen her, he'd scolded her for finding more trouble while he'd been away and then given her a bearhug nearly strong enough to crack ribs. Then he dressed her down again but broke off, laughing and hugging her with tears brightening his eyes.

Now they just sat and talked, catching up on so many things. Like how he'd lost a bet to Resnick and that was why her dad was now clean-shaven. She'd never seen him without a beard in her life. It made him look younger, even with the laugh lines and crow's feet. Apparently the year-long bet was almost over, and he'd be allowed to regrow his beard during this summer's family reunion. And that was only one tiny thing she'd missed in the two years she'd been asleep. It would take days to learn all she'd missed.

"I'm so proud of you for helping to save the entire goddamn planet again, but I won't lie and say I didn't wish it was someone else's daughter." His expression softened, his voice turning gruff again. "Not knowing how long you'd be out was bad enough, but then I had to keep lying to your mother and brothers."

"So, my brothers are still in the dark about all this?"

"Yes. And not by their choice. But if your brothers were granted clearance, they'd get dragged into this shit-show. And let me tell you, the higher-ups wanted that, saying since you and I and your uncle worked so well with the magic users, there wasn't any reason to think your brothers or cousins couldn't handle it. But I refused, and a certain Avatar had my back on this topic, to my great surprise. Handy having him in my pocket. Still, the whining I got from the higher-ups was nothing compared to the harassment your brothers put me through. I haven't had a moment's peace, and I know keeping them in the dark harms our relationship, but it's better than having them learn the truth and get drawn into this mess."

Anna opened her mouth to speak, but her dad cut her off.

His expression darkened. "Bad enough, one of my family is neck deep. The Magic Realm doesn't get to sink its claws any deeper into my family."

Her father paused and then glanced in Obsidian's direction, where he was facing off against the pooka. Anna's Rasoren had glanced over his shoulder to watch her father.

Someone had clearly been listening.

"Present company excluded," her dad pitched his voice to carry. "You saved my baby girl and earned my eternal gratitude."

That seemed to soothe Obsidian, and he returned his attention to the board game, and Anna returned to her conversation with her dad.

There was a downside to coming from a highly competitive military family, Anna mused, compressing her lips in thought. And her father was absolutely correct. If her brothers learned about this, they wouldn't let their little sister deal with this situation alone. "Sam knows about all this?"

"Your uncle has known about all this almost as long as I have."

That didn't come as a surprise. Many soldiers from various earth militaries had taken part in the final battle against the Battle Goddess.

Then something else occurred to her.

"The cousins, do they know?"

"Nope. He and I agree about keeping magic away from the rest of the family. He thinks one gargoyle in the family is plenty of magic."

Obsidian made a soft, huffing growl.

Someone was still listening to their conversation.

"No offense intended," her dad explained. "But I can't just stand by and let magic create more chaos for my family."

Obsidian excused himself from the game and joined them. His expression morphed into something a touch sheepish. "I understand your concern, and while I thank the Divine Ones daily for placing Anna in my path, I can also see your viewpoint."

"Smart boy," her dad said with a grin before directing his next words at Anna. "Now that you're awake and recovering, your uncle and I will do everything in our power to make sure you can visit your mother and brothers soon. The Avatars said a vacation surrounded by your family would be the best thing for you."

That was likely true, and she very much wanted to see her family again. She missed them. Missed normal. But that would mean leaving Obsidian behind. She wasn't ready for that yet. Instead, she redirected the conversation. "What bullshit cover story did you and Resnick come up with to tell our family?"

Her father made a pained sound. "The official unofficial story is that you've been on a deep cover mission for the last two years."

"Official unofficial story?" she said with a grin. "And absolutely no one would believe that."

"I told your mother and brothers that it was highly

classified, that they don't have the clearance, and I couldn't get it for them."

Anna's smirk grew broader.

"Yeah. They still didn't buy you being on a two-year secret assignment either." Her father sighed. "They've been trying to find out what really happened to you. They've now tapped just about every backwater channel and still haven't given up."

"I wouldn't either if it was one of my brothers in my place."

Her father's grin turned into a smirk. "I'm secretly proud they haven't given up. Even though it's a pain in my ass every time I see one of them. Hell, every visit is like I've been dropped in the middle of hostile territory."

They had a chuckle at her brothers' stubborn determination, and then her father turned serious once more. "All jesting aside. I promise I will do everything in my power to make sure you can visit your mother and see your brothers soon. Hell, I'm already planning to move heaven and earth to ensure the entire family will be at Mackenzie Pac this summer."

"Mackenzie Pac?" Obsidian asked in a deep, rumbling tone.

"The mother of all family reunions," Anna and her father said in unison.

Obsidian looked even more confused, his ears drooping down, one corner of his muzzle curling up over a tooth, though it wasn't a snarl, more the gargoyle version of resting bitch face. Even his tail had ceased all motion as he tried to work out what Anna and her father were talking about.

Anna took pity on him and explained about summer camping and family reunions and how they'd had one every summer, with as many family members participating each year as possible.

Afterward, Obsidian looked troubled.

Likely concerned for the same reason Anna was.

"God," her father said and started to laugh. "You two look like kicked puppies. I'm working on getting Obsidian clearance to come, too. It's a paperwork nightmare like you wouldn't believe, but I promise you that your uncle and I will make this happen. And we've got a certain pair of Avatars in our corner. It just hinges on if Obsidian can still shapeshift into a human, but Gregory thinks that won't be a problem."

Anna leaped up from the couch and grabbed Obsidian, giving him a big hug. "You're going to get to meet my family."

"The world will never be the same again," her dad muttered, but humor laced his dark tones.

Anna knew he wasn't really displeased.

"Come on, you three," Lillian called from her side of the portal. "It's game night. No slackers allowed!"

"Wait!" Jason called, drawing everyone's gaze.

"Before we get all competitive over board games, there's something I want to show everyone."

Anna stared, her face lax with shock as she looked upon the epic-sized photograph that took up most of the wall space in the back hall. How had Jason found time to do this? Wait! The how didn't matter.

Unless she was thinking of *how* she was going to kill him.

"Jason!" she bellowed. "You're dead, you spineless ballsack!"

She and Obsidian had followed Jason to the back hallway, trailed by a few other guests. Now Anna was glad her dad hadn't made it this far yet. Resnick had gotten one look at the picture and spun on his heels to intercept her dad.

As Resnick had gone one way to stop her dad, Jason had dashed away in the opposite direction, laughing as he ran, knowing she would hand him his ass.

Beside her, Erika looked at the photo and whistled. "I'm not sure if that falls under sexual harassment. But it's something along those lines. This is low, even for Jason."

"He fucking doctored the picture to make it even worse," Anna snarled, nearly seeing red. "I was wearing a fucking sports bra and boy shorts. My ass was not hanging out of a red teddy."

She could hear Jason's laughter from somewhere in the front room, and then he shouted at her. "As promised, I titled it Obsidian and his Teddy Bear."

Anna turned away from the photo and found Obsidian still staring at it.

"You," she barked at Obsidian, and then waved at the massive picture on the wall. "Make that disappear. I'll be back after I've finished beating the crap out of Jason."

Anna left Obsidian and Erika and shoved her way past the others. Jason must have seen her coming because he took off out the door and bolted down the hall.

CHAPTER FORTY-ONE

After his Kyrsu had gone, Gregory and Thayn and come to see what all the fuss was about. They took one look at the picture and then each other, and they broke into a run to chase down Anna and Jason. However, Obsidian didn't know if it was to save Jason or to help Anna bury the body.

With a grunt, Obsidian cast a shadow magic weaving over the image. No one else was going to gawk at his mostly naked Kyrsu. And while gargoyles and many other fae races thought nothing of being naked, he knew most humans were more guarded and did not like to show more flesh than necessary.

Which had always mystified him, but looking at this picture, doctored as Anna called it, he knew it was nothing like what had happened. The actual scene had been innocent.

This...

This was... not innocent.

And he hated it because it upset his Kyrsu.

But he also... liked it?

He liked it because he'd never seen a picture depicting him and Anna together, and he liked that part. It also made him uncomfortable because it stirred a heat in his loins. With a shake of his head and a huff, he removed it from the wall and noticed the paper was made from magic, which explained how Jason had pulled this off so quickly.

Obsidian removed the glass covering and carefully rolled the material before tucking it under his arm and carrying it to his room.

Obsidian finished hanging the image in his room, a little smile curling his lips as he began weaving a shadow magic shroud over it. Anna hadn't liked it being seen by other eyes. Actually, he was sure she'd wanted no one to see Jason's 'gift.' Still, Obsidian hadn't been able to bring himself to destroy it because it was an image of his Kyrsu in a rare moment of vulnerable innocence. He cherished that moment in time the picture had tried to capture.

He frowned at the bit of red silky fabric and lace, which was entirely fictional. Even so, the picture triggered the moment of waking with Anna sleeping peacefully in his arms. It was that moment of absolute trust he'd never forget.

Jason's arrival had cut it short, but now Obsidian had the picture to remember.

Footsteps out in the hall announced Anna's return. But even if he hadn't been able to recognize the sound of her stride, his new power tracked souls, so he'd still know it was his Kyrsu. A moment later, there was a soft knock on his door. Then it cracked open a little. Anna stuck her head inside.

"Want company?"

"Of course." He gestured her over to the padded bench, where he also settled, since it was the only comfortable spot beside their nest in the center of the room. "Did you get Jason?"

She laughed; her earlier anger gone. "No. He scrambled his ass out of here so fast that even a gargoyle wouldn't have been able to keep up. But don't worry, he's not escaping punishment that easily. Poor bastard should have known better than to run scared in front of a bunch of dark fae. Triggered their baser instincts, and now they've decided to have a Wild Hunt. And Jason is the prey."

Obsidian's ears flicked forward with undisguised eagerness. "And do you wish to take part and need a gargoyle steed?"

She chuckled again. "Nah. I'm just going to kick

back and relax the rest of tonight. Need to be up early tomorrow and down in the mess hall by zero eight hundred sharp. That's when Jason will show up to apologize, or dad will hunt his ass down and drag him to a disciplinary hearing about his conduct. I'm hoping for an apology. Lillian and Greenborrow came up with a great punishment."

His ears flicked again, betraying his eagerness to hear more.

She flashed her teeth at him. "Just before the fae organized the Wild Hunt, Greenborrow came out with a large red teddy. Don't ask me where he got it from or why he had it. But he promised that Jason would either be coming back to the base wearing it, or he'd be walking back naked."

He felt his eyes widen. "Isn't that just as bad as what Jason did?"

Anna nodded, but her grin only grew bigger. "Gregory promised to oversee proceedings to ensure no one gets hurt, and he made a few changes, so it doesn't turn into hazing. Jason will be given a choice to don a gargoyle-style loincloth and return to base and apologize, or he can go straight to the disciplinary hearing."

Obsidian narrowed his eyes. "Jason will take the loincloth. Gets him off easy. Hardly seems like a punishment."

Anna's smile turned into a full-blown grin. "Oh, Gregory created the loincloth on the spot. It's bright red with sequins. Did I mention it's a teeny-tiny loincloth?" Anna held her thumb and forefinger apart and then brought them together for emphasis.

Now it was Obsidian's turn to laugh, but it was swiftly cut short when Anna's gaze landed on the shadow magic covered wall.

"Wait one minute." She pointed an accusing finger at the concealing magic. "You didn't destroy the damned picture, did you?"

Feeling suddenly guilty, he looked anywhere that wasn't Anna or the shadow-shrouded picture, finally settling on the nest. Anna huffed softly and then settled on the bench next to him.

"I didn't realize you'd want to keep it." She laughed dryly. "I should have probably thought to ask what you wanted to do with it. It's not just about me. It caught you at a vulnerable time too."

"I would like to keep it if you'll allow. It's the first picture I've ever had of you."

"Huh," she said, sounding thoughtful, not angry. "We will rectify that error and get some pictures with us, the team, and the other fae. If that's not against regulations. As for 'Obsidian and his Teddy Bear,' we'll keep it. Hidden in here. Behind a shield of shadow magic. No one else sees my big booty hanging out of a bit of satin. And Jason will delete any other copies he has."

"Deal." Obsidian shifted closer and nuzzled her hair. "Thank you for understanding, my Kyrsu."

"You're welcome." She grinned suddenly. "But after chasing Jason out of the building, I'm wide awake. Want to raid Greenborrow's library? He said it's always open to book lovers."

He grinned sidelong at Anna. She took in his look of mischief, and her eyes widened. They both leaped up from the bench and raced for the door. He made it there first, gently shoving his Kyrsu to the side, though he made sure his tail steadied her until she regained her balance, before he took off at full speed.

"Cheater!"

"How's it my fault if you tripped?" he bellowed back at her.

"I didn't trip!" she shouted as she thundered after him. "A Classic! Not something from the Greenborrow Library of Smut!"

"First person there gets to pick the book. Loser reads it out loud."

"You're just making up rules as you run!" Anna's words were broken by laughter and panting, but she still raced after him, and Obsidian didn't care what they read as long as they were together.

It was these moments with his Kyrsu that he loved best. The love and joy of being in each other's company. He prayed to the Divine Ones that they would have many more such moments over a long lifetime.

And if it could be a peaceful lifetime, that would be nice too.

The grimoire's cover snapped open as she angrily flipped through her pages, seeking the spell that would trigger her traveling. She needed to leave this place now that the hunters had left. She'd remained in her hiding spot inside a dying tree while a group of humans in uniforms had finished investigating what had gone on in this boneyard surrounded by the vast city. Now, at last, it was safe to call upon magic and begin her work anew.

She'd watched all that had gone on and cursed the foolishness of the void demon and the warlocks. They'd been too bold and brazen in their actions. Their impatience, that very rashness that made them aggressive and deadly on the battlefield, was their downfall in this game of deception.

But she was older.

The Grimoire of Blood and Lost Souls had witnessed entire civilizations rise and fall. With age came patience and wisdom. She'd waited this long to resurrect her sisterhood. Her patience would pay off in the end. But at least the warlocks and the void demon had fed her enough power that she'd been able to continue to build her new coven.

The new blood witches were young and weak still, but they showed the promise of great potential.

And under her guidance, they would rise to rule the three realms once more.

THE END

THANK YOU

I hope you enjoyed reading Sworn to Shadows.

ACKNOWLEDGMENTS

I just want to take a quick moment to thank Kickstarter and my loyal readers for making my Gargoyle & Sorceress series such a success.

Thank you from the bottom of my heart.

You're awesome.

Bye for now,

Lisa Blackwood.

BONUS SCENE

Thank you for reading Sworn to Shadows.

I've also written a scene about Jason's return and apology to Anna. It will be available for free to my newsletter subscribers come the middle of September.

If you'd like to read it as part of my weekly newsletter, just signup below.

https://landing.mailerlite.com/webforms/landing/c6a7h9

BOOKS BY LISA BLACKWOOD

Gargoyle & Sorceress

Dawn of the Sorceress

Sorceress Awakening

Sorceress Rising

Sorceress Hunting

Sorceress at War

Sorceress Enraged

Legacy of the Sorceress

Sorcery & Firedrakes

Scion of the Sorceress

Sorceress Eternal

In Deception's Shadow Series (Epic Fantasy Romance)

Betrayal's Price

Herd Mistress

Maiden's Wolf

Death's Queen

The Prince's Gryphon (forthcoming)

Ishtar's Legacy Series (Epic Fantasy Romance)

Ishtar's Blade

The Blade's Beginning (short story)

Blade's Honor

Blade's Destiny

The Blade's Shadow

First Queen of the Gryphons

The King of the Anunnaki (forthcoming)

The Anunnaki's Blade (forthcoming)

Huntress vs Huntsman (Epic Fantasy Romance)

Master of the Hunt

Night Huntress

Dragon Archer

Soul Mage (forthcoming)